Dorothea Ruggles-Brise, John Glen

The Minstrelsy of England

a collection of 200 English songs with their melodies, popular from the 16th

century to the middle of the 18th century

Dorothea Ruggles-Brise, John Glen

The Minstrelsy of England
a collection of 200 English songs with their melodies, popular from the 16th century to the middle of the 18th century

ISBN/EAN: 9783337265601

Printed in Europe, USA, Canada, Australia, Japan

Cover: Foto ©Andreas Hilbeck / pixelio.de

More available books at **www.hansebooks.com**

THE

Minstrelsy of England.

A COLLECTION OF 200 ENGLISH SONGS WITH THEIR MELODIES,

POPULAR FROM THE 16TH CENTURY TO THE MIDDLE OF THE 18TH CENTURY.

EDITED AND ARRANGED WITH PIANOFORTE ACCOMPANIMENTS

BY

ALFRED MOFFAT.

SUPPLEMENTED WITH HISTORICAL NOTES

BY

FRANK KIDSON.

BAYLEY & FERGUSON,

LONDON: 14 PATERNOSTER ROW.   GLASGOW: 54 QUEEN STREET.

PREFACE.

THE present volume is the outcome of an attempt to produce a representative Selection of the Songs of the English People, from the sixteenth century to the beginning of the reign of George III., some of an earlier, and some of a later, date being also included. In stopping short at the last-named period it has been necessary to exclude many other English songs equally interesting, but as the change in lyric music was then so greatly marked, it was felt desirable to draw a distinct line separating the music of the subsequent from that of the preceding age. Our scheme, therefore, does not admit the compositions of James Hook, Charles Dibdin, and William Shield, composers worthy to rank with the honoured musicians of an earlier age and different temperament. Should a demand for a further instalment become manifested, there still remains a wealth of untouched material.

The selection of the melodies has been no light task, and many hundreds of volumes of early music (contained in the musical library of the compiler of the historical notes) have been ransacked for suitable material. No pains have been spared to obtain, by the careful comparison of different versions of an air, the most singable and musically correct copy.

In the matter of the words it has been necessary to exercise the greatest care. To the singer there is nothing more annoying than the presentation of the words otherwise than under their respective musical notes, whilst, on the other hand, there is nothing more fatal to effect than the fact that in a song of several verses the words of all the verses are not equally adapted to suit the rhythm of the melody. It must be pointed out that the songs of the period were frequently very loosely fitted to the music, but the alteration of a syllable here and there has sufficed to render them rhythmically correct.

Another and far graver difficulty presented itself in that many very excellent specimens of English music were set to words which could not possibly be tolerated by modern society. In such cases, rather than reject so much that was good, we have not deemed it vandalism to purify the lyrics, and so make them presentable to the public of to-day. In some cases where this was impossible the words have been entirely rewritten.

All important changes have been fully indicated, but it has not always been thought desirable to cumber the notes by drawing attention to the omission of verses or to the slight alterations above referred to, especially as the fullest information is given as to where the originals may be consulted.

In the compilation of the notes great care has been taken to make them as accurate as could be. In all cases where original sources of information have been available recourse has been had thereto. In regard to songs which have been already dealt with by the late Mr. William Chappell and other writers, the statements of those authors have been independently verified, while in many cases their facts have been supplemented.

It may be fairly claimed that considerably more than half the number of the pieces comprised in the present work are resuscitated for the first time, and are therefore fresh material for modern singers; whilst, with the exception of about a dozen old favourites, the remaining songs are not very commonly known.

FRANK KIDSON.
ALFRED MOFFAT.

God save the King:

A New Suggestion as to the Origin of the Melody.

ALTHOUGH the discussion as to the composer of "God save the King" has not attained the same magnitude as the questions relating to the identity of the Man in the Iron Mask and to that of the author of the *Letters of Junius*, the subject is still involved in the same degree of obscurity as when the matter first became the subject of inquiry more than a hundred years ago. While nothing very definite is claimed to be set forth in this note, yet attention is directed to an overlooked channel wherein the secret may still be waiting discovery.

We shall in the present inquiry pass over all similarities which are known to exist in several early melodies, such as "Remember, O thou Man," in *Melismata*, 1611; Forbes' *Cantus*, 1662, 1666, 1682; "Franklin is Fled Away," 1669; "A Lesson," by Purcell, 1696; and the "Ayre," in a MS. formerly belonging to Dr. John Bull, 1619. For particulars of all these the reader is referred to Chappell's *Popular Music*; Dr. Cumming's articles in the *Musical Times*, 1878; Groves' *Dictionary of Music and Musicians*; and to Richard Clark's *Account of the National Anthem*, 1822. Although the present note is concerned mainly with the consideration of the National Anthem as we now know it, a brief comment on the above melodies may usefully be made.

"Remember, O thou Man" is a religious carol first printed in *Melismata*, 1611, and from thence copied into an Aberdeen publication named Forbes' *Cantus*, first issued in 1662. "Franklin is Fled away" is a song, and the air to this is to be found in *Apollo's Banquet for the Treble Violin*, 1669, also under the title "Ho Hone" in later publications, e.g., *A Collection of Loyal Songs*, 1684, etc. Henry Purcell's "Lesson," for the harpsichord, was published with others in a volume issued by his widow in 1696. Each of these melodies has very much in common with "God save the King," but the fact remains that notwithstanding much structural likeness, not one of them can be accepted as the equivalent of our modern version of "God save the King," which must be considered as a tune apart from these.

Besides the printed melodies mentioned, there are at least two airs in manuscript which must be noticed. One of these, said to be entitled "God save the King," is mentioned as being in a manuscript collection of melodies formerly belonging to the late Mr. Andrew Blaikie, of Paisley. Wm. Chappell, who examined the MS., fixed the date at about 1745, but other writers claimed for it a date fifty or sixty years prior to this. This particular manuscript has disappeared, and until it again comes to light there is little use in discussing it.

The other manuscript has a more important bearing on the question. It is a volume bearing the date 1619, containing compositions by Dr. John Bull, the Elizabethan musician. Picked up in the Netherlands, it came into the library of Dr. Pepusch before the middle of the eighteenth century, afterwards passing into the hands of Dr. Kitchiner, whose son sold it to Richard Clark, author of the before-mentioned *Account of the National Anthem*, 1822. It was still in the possession of Clark's widow in 1878, but of its subsequent history we have no knowledge. At that date (1878) Mrs. Clark refused to let it be seen or copied; but an early transcript had been made by Sir George Smart, and the "Ayre," as it is entitled in the MS., shows a very marked resemblance to our National Anthem. It is, however, a matter of common belief that Richard Clark had tampered with the MS., and this is further borne out by the fact that Kitchiner, who possessed the MS., and described it in his *Loyal and National Songs*, 1823, where he wrote on the origin of the melody, distinctly denies the likelihood of there being any copy of our "God save the King" prior to 1745. Some discredit is thrown on Kitchiner's evidence when it is remembered that he was under the necessity of employing Edward Jones, the Welsh bard, to translate into modern notation an air in the MS. which *was* named "God save the King," though not in the least like our National Anthem. This fact shows that Kitchiner might have easily passed over the "Ayre" without being able to read it as there set down.

Leaving, however, all these questions, Jacobite and other claims, we may devote the rest of the note to the consideration of the air as we ourselves know it.

It is now generally accepted that Henry Carey was the composer of our National Anthem as it now stands, but upon what slight evidence this is admitted will be shown by the following particulars setting forth the claims of

JAMES OSWALD.

The first authentic notice we have of the present National Song is from a paragraph in the *Daily Advertiser* of September 30th, 1745, which reads as follows:—

> "On Saturday last, the audience at the Theatre Royal, Drury Lane, were agreeably surprised by the gentlemen of that house performing the anthem of 'God save the King.' The universal applause it met with, being encored with repeated huzzas, sufficiently denoted in how great an abhorrence they held the arbitrary schemes of our insidious enemies," etc., etc.

The performance above described was doubtless called forth by the reception of the news of the defeat of Sir John Cope's army at Prestonpans a few days previous. Covent Garden and other theatres followed suit, and there are frequent references in the London news-sheets to the song being sung in the theatres.

"God save the King," words and music, appeared in the *Gentleman's Magazine* for October, 1745, published at the end of the month, and as this is the first dated copy of the piece, it is here reproduced verbatim:—

A SONG FOR TWO VOICES.

As Sung at both Playhouses.   From *The Gentleman's Magazine*, Oct., 1745.

1. God save great George our King!   Long live our noble King!   God save the King!
2. O Lord our God,   a - rise,   Scat - ter his en - e - mies,   And make them fall!
3. Thy choic - est gifts in store   On George be pleased to pour,   Long may he reign!

1. Send him vic - to - ri - ous, Hap py, and glo - ri - ous, Long to reign o - ver us, God save the King!
2. Confound their pol - i - tics, Frustrate their kna - vish tricks, On him our hopes we fix, O save us all!
3. May he de - fend our laws, And ev - er give us cause To say with heart and voice, God save the King!

* The harmony in the 4th bar is here apparently wrong. In the *Harmonia* and *Thesaurus* the treble notes are A A B, but the engraving in early copies shows traces that they have originally stood A B C as in the *Gentleman's Magazine*.

In the November number of the same magazine a correspondent contributed another set of verses, commencing "Fame, let thy trumpet sound," as an improvement on the previously printed words.

Under the heading "For Two Voices," the first and second verses, with the music attached, appear on page 22 of a folio musical publication named *Harmonia Anglicana*, published by John Simpson of Sweeting's Alley; not dated. Chappell supposes that this work was published in 1742, but his conclusion is by no means proved, and it is more than probable that the date may be fixed in or near the year 1745. *Harmonia Anglicana* did not long exist under this name, which was removed from the engraved title page plate, and replaced by *Thesaurus Musicus*; the rest of the title was untouched and the contents remained the same. The title page then stood, "A Collection of Two, Three, and Four-Part Songs, several of them never before printed, to which are added some Choice Dialogues, set to Musick by the most Eminent Masters: viz., Dr. Blow, H. Purcell, Handel, Dr. Green, Dl. Purcell, Eccles, Weldon, Leveridge, Lampe, Carey, etc. The whole revis'd, carefully corrected, and figured by a Judicious Master."

While the melody and harmony in this work are precisely as in *The Gentleman's Magazine*, the opening words are "God save our Lord the King," not "Great George our King." Which of the two versions is the earlier will not now be easily discovered, but appearances point to the *Harmonia Anglicana* rather than to *The Gentleman's Magazine*.

With regard to the last-named publication, it is to be observed as negativing Carey's claim, that while Carey's name appears on the title page as one of importance, and is appended in the body of the work to certain airs, yet it does not appear in connection with "God save the King," and the same fact applies to *Calliope*, another work to be presently spoken of. It is therefore evident that Simpson did not regard Carey as the composer, otherwise his name would have been appended to the song as in other cases.

In 1746 John Simpson brought to a conclusion another musical work which had been running in periodical numbers for some years, commencing in 1738. Henry Roberts, an engraver, had first issued it under the title *Calliope; or, English Harmony*, and the first volume is dated 1739. After the work had proceeded a few numbers it appears to have been dropped, until Simpson completed it in 1746. This date is fixed by an advertisement in the book relating to "An Ode on the Return of the Duke of Cumberland from Scotland" (after Culloden), and a "Loyal Song" at page 155, dealing with the Scotch invasion of 1745. We may dismiss from consideration all later copies of "God save the King."

Before 1795 nobody appears to have considered it worthy of inquiry as to who was the composer. In that year George Saville Carey made an application for a pension from the State upon the ground that his father was the composer of the National Anthem. This application was refused, and does not appear to have been ever seriously considered by the Government. George Saville Carey founded his claim upon the following allegations :—

(1) That Dr. Harrington of Bath had told him that Henry Carey had brought the melody to John Christopher Smith in manuscript, and had requested him to help him with the bass, over which he had got into difficulties; Smith himself having told Harrington of this circumstance.

(2) That it was within the knowledge of several people that Carey had sung it at a public dinner held at a tavern in Cornhill, in 1740, on the occasion of Admiral Vernon's victory at Portobello.

These two allegations are *absolutely* the only evidence that has ever been adduced as to Carey's authorship, and these, more than half-a-century after the events, were promulgated in order to uphold a claim for a monetary consideration.

To consider them seriously we may first look at the simple, almost childish bass of the original, as given in *Harmonia Anglicana* and *Gentleman's Magazine*, and ask ourselves if it was likely that Carey, a clever musician of forty years' practice, was likely to have applied for aid in the matter. Secondly, Carey wrote at least two songs in celebration of Vernon's victory at Portobello, and it is quite possible that he may have sung these in public, especially as they would have been distinctly more appropriate to the occasion than "God save the King" at a public dinner in honour of Vernon's victory. It would be scarcely reasonable to ask gentlemen of that wine-bibbing period for particulars as to what happened after dinner, and to the uncertainty of such evidence must be added the weight of fifty-five years of tradition. So much for Carey's claim. In advancing another claim quite new to the public, I admit that nothing is proved, but I venture to say that there is more inherent probability in it than in Carey's.

In 1742 a clever Edinburgh musician, named James Oswald, who was originally a dancing master, left the North for London, and became associated on his arrival there with John Simpson, the publisher of the two early works in which "God save the King" appeared. So far as can be seen, all Oswald's early London work bearing his name was published by Simpson, and there seems to be great likelihood that Oswald did hack work for this London publisher, probably arranging or editing several of his musical publications. The chances also are that Oswald was employed by Simpson in his shop in Sweeting's Alley, near the Royal Exchange; for on the death of Simpson, about 1747, Oswald immediately commenced the trade of musicseller in St. Martin's Lane, where he published his own musical works. Whether such be the case or not, it is very possible that Oswald may have been the "Judicious Master" who "revised and carefully corrected" the pieces in *Harmonia Anglicana*. The figure of James Oswald is shadowy enough, but it is evident from eighteenth century musical publications that he was a notable composer, and that he was patronised by Frederick, Prince of Wales; and by the Princess of Wales, both before and after her husband's death. Oswald dedicated several works to these royal patrons. A peculiarity about James Oswald is that for some reason not now to be discovered he frequently published anonymously and under fictitious names. As, for instance, two sets of sonatas by "I. R., Esq." (generally considered to refer to General John Reid, founder of the Edinburgh music chair), are his. Oswald also published under the name "Dottel Figlio," and while these are established facts, it is suspected that he was also the "San Martini of London," who dedicated to the Princess of Wales a set of sonatas. Even Sir Walter Scott, in *Redgauntlet*, mentions Oswald thus: - "It's no a Scots tune, but it passes for ane; Oswald made it himsel', I reckon. He has cheated mony a ane, but he canna cheat Wandering Willie."

Oswald died in 1769, and William Randall republished by Oswald certain works to which had been affixed fictitious names, such as the "I R. Sonatas," "Queen Mab," etc. In this work Randall says, "Sometime before Mr. Oswald's death he had fitted for the press a correct edition of his works, as well as those which were really such, but had formerly been published under the names of others for reasons not difficult to guess," etc., etc. Had Randall's edition continued, "God save the King" might have found a place in it.

In 1761 James Oswald was appointed chamber composer to the new King George III., a significant fact.

The first direct association of Oswald's name with the tune "God save the King" occurs on a dial plate belonging to the chimes of Windsor Church, which were hung in 1769 under the superintendence of Oswald himself. The dial plate was in existence in 1815, and was then found to bear the names of the eight tunes played by the bells, the one indicating "God save the King" being engraved "Oswald's Are." This fact is mentioned in Clark's *Account of the National Anthem* as from the information of a correspondent, but is silently passed over by Clark and subsequent writers. Tabulating the facts, the conclusion is irresistible that they establish a stronger claim in favour of Oswald than any that has been adduced on behalf of Carey.

(1) "God save the King" is named in 1769 on the dial plate of the chimes of Windsor Church as "Oswald's Are."

(2) In 1761 Oswald was appointed chamber composer to George III over the heads of better-known musicians.

(3) James Oswald was a strong royalist as witnessed by his numerous dedications to the Prince and Princess of Wales.

(4) The numerous fictitious names under which Oswald published prove that he was not anxious to make public claim to much excellent work.

(5) "God save the King" was first published by John Simpson, for whom Oswald at the time of its publication did so much work, and, with the exception of the publisher of the *Gentleman's Magazine* copy, no other publisher appears to have issued the song before 1747, the date of Simpson's death. This would suggest that Simpson may have held a copyright. Single half-sheet copies with the music were issued, but these bear no publisher's or engraver's name, and were probably Simpson's own issue.

(6) Simpson's suppression of Oswald's name, a suppression which was probably intentional, at a time when Scotsmen were in disfavour with English loyalists.

The conclusions to be drawn from the facts above set forth may not make out a very strong case for Oswald, but the claim set up in his favour is at least as good as Carey's, and it is possible that the attention now drawn to the facts may be productive of still stronger evidence.

In concluding this lengthy note it may be pointed out that the slight differences in the air which are observable on comparing an early copy with the now accepted version are due to variations made soon after the first publication of the song.

God save the King.

mf Molto maestoso.

1. God save our gra - cious King, Long live our no - ble King.
2. O Lord our God, a - rise, Scat - ter his en - e - mies,
3. Thy choic - est gifts in store, On him be pleased to pour,

1. God save the King.   Send him vic - to - ri - ous, Hap - py and
2. And make them fall!   Con - found their pol - i - tics, Frus - trate their
3. Long may he reign!   May he de - fend our laws, And ev - er

poco rit.

1. glo - ri - ous, Long to reign o - ver us, God save the King!
2. knav - ish tricks, On Thee our hopes we fix, God save the King!
3. give us cause To sing with heart and voice, God save the King!

Send Home my Long-stray'd Eyes to me.

This beautiful air is by Richard Leveridge, a clever singer and musician, to whom we are indebted for at least two of our most typical National Melodies, "Black Ey'd Susan" and "The Roast Beef of Old England." The poem is by Dr. Donne, and it has another early but less tuneful setting by Anthony Young. This appears on the same half sheet with Leveridge's air, and was engraved during the early part of the 18th century. Leveridge's tune is also inserted in the second volume of his own *Collection*, published in 1727, 8vo. Copies of the words vary a little, and one version is included in *The Hive*, 1724, vol. ii., to which is appended an *Answer*. The tune is used in various early ballad operas, and, with the words, is in *Watt's Musical Miscellany*, vol. i., 1729.

1. But if from you they learnt such ill, To
2. But if it has been taught by thine To
3. That I one day may laugh when thou Shalt

1. sweet - ly smile, And then be - guile,
2. for - feit both Its word and oath,
3. grieve and mourn; For one will scorn

1. Keep the de - cei vers, keep them still.
2. Keep it, for then 'tis none of mine.
3. And prove as false as thou art now.

The Country Parson.

Air—Linco found Damon lying.

Moderato.

mf   *poco rit.*

1. I am a coun - try par - son, I've twen - ty pounds a
2. I mar - ry all the bump - kin swains With - in the par - ish
3. No pol - i - ties per - plex my brain, Or wild, am - bi - tious

1. year, A mare I have to ride up - on, No
2. hounds ; I with the squire go hunt - ing, And
3. flight, No wife have I to trou - ble me, And

The tune was originally fitted to the song, "Linco found Damon lying,' but as this cannot well be sung at the present day, and as the fine sturdy English air deserves modern revival, a song founded on the theme of an early 18th century lyric has been used in its place. The air and song, "Linco found Damon lying" is printed in Walsh's *British Musical Miscellany*, vol. ii. [1734], and in *Calliope*, vol. i., 1739, besides being on the usual engraved half sheets.

1. ills   in   life   I   fear;   A   cot   tage   neat   I
2. fol - low   close   the   hounds;   My   tithes   need   but   the
3. scold   from   morn   to   night;   O'er   flag   ons   of   good

1. live   in,   A   clean - thatch'd   ten   e   ment,   And
2. tak   ing   In   bar   ley,   wheat,   or   hay;   At
3. li - quor   I   mer - ri - ly   can   sing;   While

1. with   the   church   I   preach   in   I'm   ve - ry   well   con - tent.
2. ev' - ry   mer - ry - mak - ing,   I'm   wel - come   as   the   May.
3. I'm   a   coun - try   vic   ar,   I'd   scorn   to   be   a   king.

Love's Votary.

HENRY LAWES.

This famous song by Robert Herrick, which in his *Hesperides*, 1648, is titled, "To Anthea, who may command him anything," obtained new life from the splendid modern setting by J. L. Hatton. Probably Hatton did not know of the original music to the song by Henry Lawes. We reprint Lawes' version from Playford's *Treasury of Music*, 1669. It is there given under the name "Love's Votary," with slight verbal differences from other copies.

How should I your True Love know?

Andante molto espressione.

1. How should I your
2. He is dead and
3. White his shroud as the

1. true love know
2. gone, la - dy,
3. moun-tain snow,

From an-o-ther one?
He is dead and gone,
Lard - ed with sweet flow'rs,

By his cock-le
At his head a
Which be - wept to the

1. hat and staff,
2. grass-green turf,
3. grave did go,

And his san - dal shoon.
At his heels a stone.
With true-love show - ers.

The beautiful ballad air is undoubtedly very old, and is a traditional stage melody set to Ophelia's song in *Hamlet*. Shakespeare no doubt employed an old song for his purpose, and it is not unreasonable to suppose that the air we give has been united to the song prior to his time. John Gay used the tune for words in *The Beggar's Opera*, 1727-8:—"You'll think ere many days ensue," but in all copies of the opera the name of this particular tune is not given, though the old titles of airs are present in other cases. The tune is also set to a song in the ballad opera, *The Generous Freemason*, and in both operas there is an additional refrain of two bars of music fitted to the words, "Twang dang dilly dee," which is supposed to indicate a harper's or crowder's rough symphony between the verses of the ballad. Another curious but excellent version of the air is set in *Love in a Riddle*, 1729, to the words, "My simple heart is fled away." This tune I give in the Appendix.

The Spanish Lady's Love.

1. Will you hear a Span-ish la - dy, How she
2. But at last there came com - mand - ment For to
3. Courteous la - dy, leave this fan - cy, Here comes
4. Then com-mend me to thy la - dy, Bear to

1. woo'd an Eng - lish - man? Gar - ments gay, as rich as
2. set the la - dies free, With their jew - els still a -
3. all that breeds the strife, I in Eng - land have al -
4. her this chain of gold, And these brace - lets for a

We are only able to select four verses of this pretty ballad which may be seen in full in Percy's *Reliques*, vol. ii., 1765, p. 227, and later ballad collections. Percy says that it "probably took its rise from one of those descents made on the Spanish coasts in the time of Queen Elizabeth." He gives it as printed from "an ancient black letter copy corrected in part by the editor's folio MS." Bishop Percy in his later editions hazards certain conjectures as to the hero of the piece. There are in existence several black letter versions, and the ballad is referred to in 17th century works. The tune is used in the ballad operas, *The Quaker's Opera*, 1728, and *The Jovial Crew*, 1731, where it is named "Did you not hear of a Spanish lady?" We have adopted the popular form of the melody as being the more vocal, though it has but very slight difference from the ballad opera copies. There is a tune in *The Skene MS.* named "The Spanish Lady," but while Dauney in his commentary assumes that it belongs to the ballad, there is nothing to confirm the connection. He gives however a valuable traditional version, which we reprint in our Appendix.

1. may be,   Deck'd with jew   els, she had   on: Of a
2. dorn - ed.   None to   do   them in - jur - y.   Then
3. read - y   A sweet wo   man to my   wife.   I'll not
4. to - ken,   Griev - ing that   I was so   bold;   All my

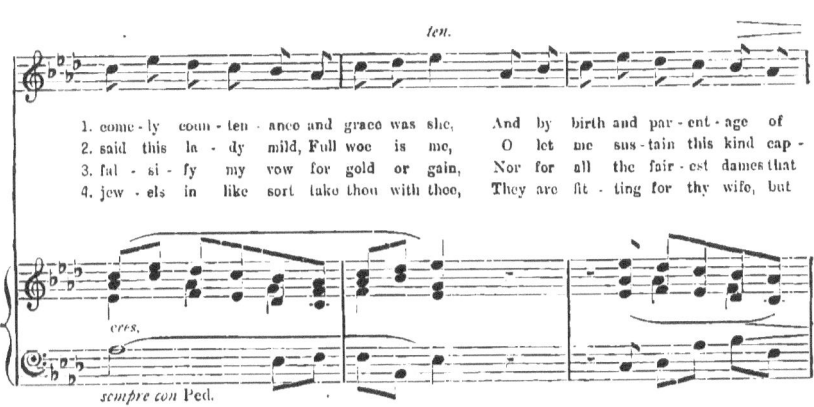

ten.

1. come - ly   coun - ten - ance and grace was she,   And by   birth and par - ent - age of
2. said this la - dy   mild, Full woe   is me,   O let   me sus - tain this kind cap -
3. fal - si - fy   my vow for gold or   gain,   Nor for   all the fair - est dames that
4. jew - els in   like sort take thou with thee,   They are fit - ting for thy wife, but

cres.

sempre con Ped.

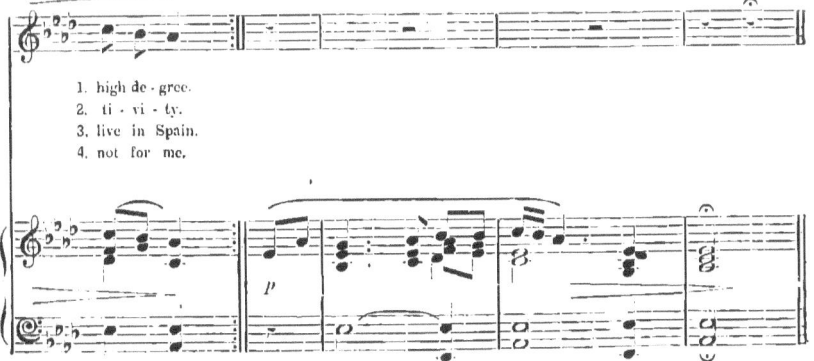

1. high de - gree.
2. ti - vi - ty.
3. live in Spain.
4. not for me.

p

Come, Sweet Lass.

A pretty tune which, under the title "Greenwich Park," is in the second part of the *Dancing Master*, 2nd edition, 1698, p. 33; in the 12th edition of the *Dancing Master*, 1703; 16th edition, 1716, etc. Associated with the words, "Come, Sweet Lass," the air is in *Pills to Purge Melancholy*, vol. i., 1707, and vol. iii., 1719. The tune afterwards got into Oswald's *Caledonian Pocket Companion*, book ii., and from this reason appeared in other Scottish collections, as Aird's *Selection*, iii.; *The Caledonian Muse*, etc. The air was also employed by Gay in *The Beggars' Opera*, 1728, in a song sung by Lucy Lockit. "Come, Sweet Lass," is one of those pseudo-Scottish productions very popular at the end of the 17th century, and was probably written by Thomas D'Urfey, who compiled the collection in which it first appeared.

In Praise of Ale.

A fine old ditty which, with the air, is printed in Joseph Ritson's *Collection of English Songs*, 1783. The song was taken and set to a different tune for Shield's opera of *Robin Hood*, acted 1784, and with the melody as given by Ritson, which we here use, is also in *Calliope; or, The Musical Miscellany*, Edinburgh, 1788.

O Willow, Willow!

1. A poor soul sat sigh - ing by a sy - ca - more
2. He sigh'd in his sing - ing, and made a great

1. tree, Sing wil - low, wil - low, wil - low, With his hand in his
2. moan, Sing wil - low, wil - low, wil - low, I am dead to all

Shakespeare makes Desdemona sing a version of this song in *Othello*, act iv., sc. 3. A setting of the air under the title "All a greene willow," is in a manuscript lute book, dated 1583, in the library of Trinity College, Dublin. The song and air are also in other early manuscripts in the British Museum, and the ballad alone is among the Roxburghe and Pepys' collection of broadsides. From these printed sources Bishop Percy reprinted it in his *Reliques*, 1765. The ballad title is:—"A Lover's Complaint, being forsaken of his love ; To a pleasant tune." The melody we have used is the 16th century one, but the plaintive words have never lacked musical settings. One by Pelham Humphreys originally printed in 1673, is in Stafford Smith's *Musica Antiqua*. There are later ones by Wm. Linley and James Hook ; Hook's composition had much popularity owing to its being sung by Mrs. Jordan, who accompanied herself on the lute. The burden, "Willow, willow," was in frequent use among old song writers.

16

O, Mistress Mine.

The words occur in Shakespeare's *Twelfth Night*, and are either a song written by him for the play, or bodily lifted into it from another source, for it seems uncertain as to whether the play was acted prior to 1596, at which date "O Mistress Mine" was printed with the tune in Morley's *Consort Lessons*. It is also in the 1611 edition of the last-named work, and the tune under its name is in the Fitzwilliam Lute Manuscript. Thomas Morley's *First Book of Consort Lessons made by divers exquisite authors, ... collected by Thomas Morley*, folio, 1599, is a unique volume in the Bodleian Library, Oxford. A copy of the second edition of 1611 is among the books which formed the library of the Sacred Harmonic Society.

We all to Conqu'ring Beauty Bow.

Dr. John Blow.

This song is by Tom D'Urfey, the fashionable Tory poet and song writer, at the close of the 17th century. It was written in honour of the Duchess of Grafton, a patroness of D'Urfey, and the fine air by Dr. John Blow carried it down to a later age. It appeared in D'Urfey's *Third Collection of New Songs*, folio, 1685, under the title, "The Perfection: a new song to the Duchess, set to music by Dr. John Blow." It is also present in *Pills to Purge Melancholy*, Ritson's *English Songs*, 1783, etc. The original song consists of three verses, the second, as given above, has undergone some slight alterations.

18

Cross Purposes.

Allegretto.   *mf*

1. Tom loves Ma - ry
2. Moll gave Hal   a
3. Much as Ma - ry

p   *sf*   *dim.*   *p*

1. pass - ing well, And Ma - ry she loves Har-ry, . . . But Har - ry sighs for bon - ny Bell, And
2. wreath of flow'rs, Which he in am - 'rous fol - ly . . . Consign'd to Bell, and in few hours It
3. Thomas grieves, Proud Hal des-pis - es Ma - ry. . . . And all the flouts which Bell re-ceives From

cres.

1. finds his love mis - car - ry; . . . For bon - ny Bell for Thom - as burns, Whilst Ma - ry slights his
2. came a - gain to Mol - ly; . . . Thus all by turns are woo'd and woo, No tur - tles can be
3. Tom she vents on Har - ry; . . . If one of all the four has frown'd You ne'er saw peo - ple

cres.

1. pas - sion, . . . So strangely freak - ish are the terms Of Cu - pid's fas - ci - na - tion.
2. tru - er, . . . Each loves the ob - ject they pur-sue, But hates the kind pur - su - er.
3. grummer, . . . If one has smil'd it cat - ches round, And all are in good hu - mour.

sf

This quaint little fantasy was popular during the last half of the 18th century, under the name, "Cross Purposes." It is stated in old song books to have been sung at Ranelagh. I have not been able to discover the author of the clever words, or the composer of the music. The air, with the words as "sung by Mr. Beard," are in *Clio and Euterpe*, 1758, vol. i., p. 91, and the air as a country dance under the name, "Tom and Mary," is in Peter Thompson's *Country Dances*, vol. i., in that portion which is apparently the yearly set for 1751. Ritson in 1783 also prints the song and tune, and it is found in many other similar collections.

Beauty in Eclipse.

WILLIAM LAWES.

1. Tell me no more her eyes are like To ris - - ing
2. Say that al - though like to the moon She's heav'n - ly
3. Say that her heart, though cold as snow, Is hard as

1. suns that won - der strike; For if 'twere so, how could it
2. fair, yet chang'd as soon; Else she would con - - stant once re -
3. mar - ble when I woo; Else it would soft - - en and re -

1. be They could be thus e - clips'd to me?
2. main, Ei - ther to pi - ty or dis - dain.
3. lent, With sighs en - flam - - ed, from me sent.

Taken from Playford's *Select Ayres and Dialogues*, book i., 1669. The air is by William Lawes, the talented brother of the better known Henry Lawes.

Come, come, my Lovers.

1. Come, come, my lov - ers, come   a - way!   Let's take our plea - sures while   we may.
2. The pret - ty pearl lends many   a smile,   The sparkling gems our   sight   be - guile.
3. And o - ther pas - sions that   a - rise,   With their soul stir - ring   lul -   la - bies.

The song, with the air "by Mr. Porter," is in *New Ayres and Dialogues composed for Voices and Viols . . . . together with Lessons for Viols or Violin, by John Banister . . . and Thomas Low*, London, 1678, 12mo. The "Mr. Porter" in question is apparently Walter Porter who died about 1659, and much of whose music was printed in the various collections by Playford.

1. Hark! hark! . . . how the mu-sic charms our ears, In-creas-ing
2. Hark! hark! . . . thro' the woodland rings a voice, The ver-dant
3. Hark! hark! . . . such sweet al - lur ing tones Would e'en give

cres.

f *poco rit.*

1. love, in - creas - ing love, ex - pel ling fears,
2. Spring, the ver - dant Spring, bids us re - joice,
3. joy, would e'en give joy to life - less stones.

f *poco rit.* *a tempo.*

ritard.

1. In - creas - ing . . . love, ex - pel - ling fears,
2. The ver - dant . . Spring bids . . us re - joice.
3. Would e'en give . . . joy to . . . life less stones.

ritard.

Jack met his Mother all Alone.

1. Jack met his mo - ther all a - lone, To whom he did smil - ing
2. Then he a - way to Joan did ride, And when he came there did
3. "Why, what's the mat - ter?" Jack re - plied, "With - out an - y more a -
4. With that he went to take his leave, But just as he turn'd a -

1. say, "I'll go and vis - it come - ly Joan, Be - cause it is hol - i -
2. cry, "Sweet jew - el, wilt thou be my bride?" And hear'd a love - sick
3. do, I'd have you know, if hence I go, I can have as good as
4. side, Joan stopp'd and caught him by the sleeve, "I was but in jest," she

The melody to this song is more generally known by the title of another one sung to it: "An old woman poor and blind," and under this heading it occurs in *The Village Op. a, The Fashionable Lady,* and other of the ballad operas. In the several volumes of *Pills* are numerous other songs to the air. The present, "Jack met his mother all alone," is found on early ballad sheets in the Roxburghe and other collections. The theme is a fairly common one among old songs, one printed in Ramsay's *Tea Table Miscellany* and in *The Robin,* 1749, commences, "Young Roger of the Mill."

1. day; And be - ing in my Sun - day clothes, I hope she'll like me
2. sigh; But come - ly Joan be - gan to frown, Said he was much too
3. you; There's Doll, the shep - herd's daugh - ter dear, And Kate of high de -
4. cried; "A kind and lov - ing wife I'll prove, O - bey and love thee

1. well; If Joan be kind, my heart, my mind, To her I will free - ly
2. free; She would not that a home - bred clown Her husband should ev - er
3. gree, Who has at least three marks a year, They're ready to die for
4. too;" "Why then," quoth he, "I here a - gree, To marry with none but

1. tell."
2. be.
3. me."
4. you."

Go from my Window, Go.

Two copies of the air under this same title, arranged respectively by Thomas Morley and by John Munday, are in the manuscript volume of Virginal music now at Cambridge, and commonly, though erroneously named, *Queen Elizabeth's Virginal Book*. The tune is also found in print in several early printed musical works, as : *A New Book of Tablature*, 1596 ; Morley's *First Book of Consort Lessons*, 1599, 1611. It is apparently a folk ballad tune, and portions of the words with parodies are met with in old plays. A few of what appear to be the old lines are quoted in Beaumont and Fletcher's *Knight of the Burning Pestle*, and a ballad, " Goe from the window," was licensed for printing in 1587-8. Chappell quotes also a traditional version. For sufficient reasons we have decided to reject all old copies of the words, and for the purpose of popularizing the exquisite old melody, have adopted the above verses.

Admiral Benbow.

Now Away, my Brave Boys.

1. Now a - way, my brave boys, hoist the
2. Then fare-well for a time, love - ly

1. flag, beat the drum, Let the stream - ers wave ov - er the main; When Old
2. sweethearts, dear wives, Nancy, fear not the fate of True Blue; Tho' we

The above was sung by the character "Captain Dreadnought," in a small musical play, named *True Blue; or, the Press Gang*, acted in 1751. The piece was concocted out of a much earlier one by Henry Carey, entitled, *Nancy; or, the Parting Lovers*, produced in 1739. Several of the songs in *True Blue* were taken from the earlier play, and it is most probable that the song in question was one of these. If this is the case the words and music are probably by Carey, although they are not included among the songs from *Nancy; or, the Parting Lovers*, which are given in *The Musical Century*, 1740. Copies of "Now away, my brave boys" will be found with the music in Fielding's *Vocal Enchantress*, 1783, and in Dr. Kitchiner's *Sea Songs*, 1823; the words alone are in *The Royalty Songster*, 1785.

1. Eng - land she calls us, we mer - ri - ly come, She shan't call a sai - lor in
2. leave you and mer - ri - ly ven - ture our lives, To our fair ones we'll ev - er be

1. vain. Al - rea - dy we seem an Ar - ma - da to chase, Al -
2. true. With spi - rit we go an Ar - ma - da to chase, With

1. rea - dy be - hold the gal - leons; Un - daunt - ed, un - con - quer'd, look
2. rap - ture be - hold the gal - leons: Un - daunt - ed, un - con - quer'd, look

Amidst the Myrtles as I Walk.

As "Love's Sweet Repose," the song, with the air by Henry Lawes, is printed in *The Treasury of Musick*, 1669, *The Musical Companion*, 1673, and many other of Playford's publications. During the 18th century the words set to music by Jonathan Battishill became in great vogue. This latter setting of them is to be found in John Arnold's *Essex Harmony*, vol. II., 1769, and many later glee books. *Apollonian Harmony*, Sibbald's *Glees*, 1783, etc.

Come, Love, let's walk in yonder Spring.

1. Come, love, let's walk in yonder spring, Where we shall hear the blackbirds sing, The robin redbreast
2. In yonder dale grow fragrant flow'rs, With many sweet and sha-dy bow'rs, A pearly brook whose
3. Behold the nymph with all her train Comes tripping thro' the park amain, And in this grove she

1. and the thrush, The nightingale in thorn-y bush, The mavis sweetly car-ol-ling,
2. sil-ver streams Are beautified with Phœbus' beams, Still stealing thro' the trees so fair,
3. here will stay At Barley-break to sport and play, Where we shall sit us down and see

1. This to my love, This to my love con-tent will bring.
2. Because Di-an-a, Because Di-an-a walk-eth there.
3. Fair beauty mix'd, Fair beauty mix'd with chas-ti-tie.

Though the air for this song appears early in the 17th century, in the Scottish Manuscript of Music in Tablature, named the Skene MS., as well as in the Aberdeen Cantus, the structure of the melody proclaims it English. There are some differences in the air as written in the Skene MS. from the one we adopt, which is taken with the words from Cantus. Songs and Fancies to three, four and five parts . . . . Aberdeen, John Forbes, 1682, oblong quarto. The song is also in the earlier editions of 1662 and 1666, and in its original form has five verses.

Trust not the Treason of those Smiling Lookes.

Dr. MAURICE GREENE.

Moderato.

1. Trust not the trea - son of
2. Yet e - ven whilst her cru - ell

1. those smil - ing lookes Un - till ye have their guilefull traines well
2. hands . . them slay, Her eyes looke love - ly, and up - on them

1. tride; For they are like but un - to gol - den hookes That
2. smile, That they take plea - sure in her cru - ell play, And

One of Spenser's sonnets, and included in the musical publication named *Spenser's Amoretti*, set to music by *Dr. Greene*, printed for *Jas. Walsh, in Catherine Street in the Strand*, circa 17.5.40, oblong folio.

1. from the fool - ish fish their baytes doe hide. So she with
2. dy - ing doe themselves of paine be - guile. O might - ie

1. flat - t'ring smyles weake harts doth guide . . . . Un - to her love, and tempt
2 charme which makes men love their bane, And think they die with plea - sure,

1. to their de - cay: Whom, be - ing caught, she kills with cru - ell
2. live with paine! — O might - ie charme which makes men love their

1. pride. And feeds at plea sure on the wretch - ed prey.
2. bane, And think they die with pleasure, live with paine!

The Three Ravens.

For note to this song see Appendix.

Now is the month of Maying.

Thomas Morley.

A pastoral which has been popular from its first appearance in print down to our own time. The air is by Thomas Morley, perhaps the most talented of the Elizabethan musicians. It was printed in his *First Booke of Balletts to five Voyces*, printed in 1595; the work was dedicated to Queen Elizabeth's minister, Sir Robert Cecil. John Playford republished the song many times in the 17th century, and it also appears in the Aberdeen *Cantus*, 1682, etc. During the 18th century it stood pre-eminent as a part-song, and is included in most books of catches and glees. The tune was used by Thomas Linley as a finale to his opera, *The Duenna*, 1776, with the words, "Come now for jest and smiling."

C

The Message.

HENRY PURCELL.

1. Ye birds that sing sweet - ly, come, list - en to me, And
2. And ask her up - on him a thought to be - stow, One

1. take to fair Phil - lis a mes - sage with ye; Be - low in the
2. glance of her eyes that so won-drous - ly glow; But pray for some

One of the many fine lyrics by Henry Purcell. This great musician was one of a musical family, his father, uncle, brother, and son having made their mark in the art. He was born in 1658, and died at Westminster, November 21, 1695, in the middle of a brilliant career. The above air appeared in *The Indian Queen*, to words beginning, "They tell me that you mighty powers."

The Angler's Song.

HENRY LAWES.

1. Man's life is but vain, For 'tis sub - ject to pain And
2. But we'll take no care When the wea - ther proves fair, Nor

1. sor - row, and short as a bub - ble; 'Tis a hodge podge of busi - ness, And
2. will we vex now though it rain; We will ban - ish all sor - row, And

1. mon - ey and care, And care and mon - ey and trou - ble.
2. sing till to - mor - row, And an - gle and an - gle a - gain.

Old Izaak Walton in his *Compleat Angler*, 1653, introduces the song thus:—"Gentlemen, these were a part of the thoughts that then possessed me, and I have made a conversion of a piece of an old catch and added more to it, fitting them to be sung by us anglers. Come, master, you can sing well you must sing a part of it, as it is here in this paper." Then follows the song with the music, one part of which is printed upside down as was then the fashion for the placing of part-songs. The arrangement thus made rendered it more convenient for the singing of two or three people from the one book. A wiseacre some little time ago informed the public through the press that the first edition of Walton's *Compleat Angler* could be known by "the mistake which the printer had made in imposing one half of the music upside down."!! The tune is by Henry Lawes, and is also in *Select Ayres and Dialogues*, 1659, *Musick's Delights on the Cithren*, 1666, Playford's *Musical Companion*, 1667, and 1672-3, etc. The words are understood to be by John Chalkhill.

Tom Tinker's my True Love.

Con spirito.

1. Tom Tin - ker's my some
2. At night by some
3. Tom Tin - ker's half
4. Tom Tin - ker is

1. true love and I am his dear, And I am con - tent - ed his bud - get to
2. barnyard or low - ly - ing wood We light our camp - fire if pro - ven - der's
3. gip - sy — no need to say that, You see by his elf - locks and big slouch-ing
4. wel-come wher - e'er he may rest, He sings an old song and drinks ale of the

1. bear; From ham - let to vil - lage, from mar - ket to fair, We cheer - ful - ly
2. good; The farm - er may grum - ble, the keep - er may curse, Tom Tin - ker the
3. hat; His lit - tle black pipe he sticks in its hand, And long are his
4. best; To mend you a ket - tle, to clout you a pan, Or quaff your brown

1. trudge it, for lit - tle's our care.
2. poach - er is ne - ver the worse.
3. fin - gers though dir - ty his hand,
4. stin - go Tom Tinker's your man.

For note to this song see *Appendix.*

On a Day—alack the Day!

Thomas Chilcot.

1. On   a   day— a - lack   the   day!
2. Air,   quoth   he,   thy   cheeks   may   blow,
3. Do   not   call   it   sin   in   me,

The words are by Shakespeare, and occur in *The Passionate Pilgrim* and in *Love's Labour Lost*. The melody is by Thomas Chilcot, a clever Bath musician who was organist of the Abbey Church. He published about 1745-50 *Twelve English Songs, the words by Shakespeare and other celebrated poets,* from which the present is taken. Chilcot died in 1766. The song has been also set by Bishop and others.

1. Love, whose month is ev - - er May,
2. Air, would I might tri - umph so!
3. That I am for - sworn for thee,—

1. Spied a blos - som, pass ing
2. But, a - lack! my hand is
3. Thou for whom e'en Jovo would

1. fair, Play - - ing in the wan - - ton air:
2. sworn Ne'er to pluck thee from thy thorn;—
3. swear Ju no but an Eth - i - op were;

1. Through the
2. Vow, a -
3. And de -

con espress.   poco rit............................   p

1. vel - vet leaves the wind, All un - seen, 'gan
2. lack! for youth un - meet, Youth so apt to
3. ny him - self for Jove, Turn ing mor - tal

1. pass - age find, That the lov - - er, sick to
2. pluck a sweet, Vow, a lack! for youth un -
3. for thy love, And de - ny him - self for

1. death, Wished him - self the hea - ven's breath,
2. meet, Youth so apt to pluck a sweet.
3. Jove, Turn - - ing mor - - tal for thy love.

Last time.

Where the Bee sucks.

THOMAS AUGUSTINE ARNE.

(Piano accompaniment arranged from a contemporary score.)

Allegro spiritoso.

Where the bee sucks, there lurk I: In a cow-slip's bell I

One of Dr. Arne's most beautiful melodies, set to Ariel's song in the *Tempest*. Arne's tune was among his earlier productions, and was probably first issued about the year 1746. Besides being on contemporary half sheet music, it is included in *Clio and Euterpe*, vol. i., 1758, and *The Delightful Pocket Companion for the German-Flute*, circa 1746. Previous settings of the words had been made by Robert Johnson, early in the 17th century, and by Purcell.

lie: There I couch when owls do cry, when owls do

cry, when owls do cry, On a bat's back do I

fly, ... do I fly, Af-ter sun-set, mer-ri-ly,

mer-ri-ly, Af-ter sun-set, mer-ri ly. . .

The Miller of the Dee.

This lyrical expression of self confidence was first sung on the stage by John Beard, who took the character of Hawthorn in *Love in a Village*, acted in 1762. The libretto of the piece was by Isaac Bickerstaffe, and its music was selected from a variety of sources. "The Miller of the Dee" in the opera has but the first verse, and there is presumptive evidence that it had been an old song bodily placed there. The tune named "The budgeon, it is a fine trade," was used in several earlier ballad operas, such as *The Fashionable Lady*, 1730, *The Devil to pay*, 1732, etc., and Chappell quotes a verse from a song, "The budgeon it is a delicate trade," in a collection of canting songs printed in 1723. He supposes that "budgeon" is from the thieves' word "budge," to steal into a house, but with more probability we may assume that "The budgeon it is a fine trade" has sung the pleasures of a wandering tinker's life, and that the word in question is but another one for "budget," a tinker's bag of tools. The full song, "The Miller of the Dee," is found in *The Convivial Songster*, 1782, Dale's *English Songs*, and other collections. In Nathaniel Gow's Third *Repository* the tune is marked "very old." I believe several mills on the rivers Dee in Scotland and Wales lay claim to being the veritable mill sung of in the song. The modern corruption of the words into "I care for nobody, no, not I, *for* nobody cares for me," alters the whole sentiment of the song. In Surrey and Sussex a version of the air has been traditionally known to the harvest-home song, "Here's a health to our master," and a major setting of the tune to another, "The Jolly Woodcutter." This latter will be found in the present volume.

1. morn till night, no lark so blithe as he. . . . . . . And
2. sta - tion now for an - y one in life. . . . . No
3. larms his fears, nor Win - ter's sad de - lay. . . . . . No
4. made for glee, and time is on the wing. . . . . . This

1. this the bur - den of his song for ev - er used to
2. law - yer, sur - geon, or doc - tor e'er had a great from
3. fore - sight mars the mil - ler's joy, who's wont to sing and
4. song shall pass from thee to me, a - long this jo - vial

1. be, ... I care for no - bod - y, no, not I, if
2. me, ... I care for no - bod - y, no, not I, if
3. say, ... Let o - thers toil . . from year to year, I
4. ring, ... Let heart and voice . . and all a - gree to

Last time.

1. no - bod - y cares for me. . . . .
2. no - bod - y cares for me. . . . .
3. live . . from day to day. . . . .
4. say, . . . Long live the King. . . . .

It is not that I Love You less.

CHARLES YOUNG.

1. It is not that I love you less
2. In vain, a - las! for ev - 'ry thing
3. But vow'd I have, and nev - er must

1. Than when be - fore your feet I lay,
2. Which I have known be - long to you,
3. Your ban ish'd ser vant trou - - ble you;

The song, of which our space only permits us to use a portion, is by Edmund Waller, and is named in his *Poems on Several Occasions,* "The Self Banished." Waller, born in 1605, died in 1688, and very worthily upheld the character of the poetry of an earlier age, some of his songs reaching a high standard. We need but recall to the reader's memory, "Go, lovely rose," and his dainty piece, "On a girdle," ("That which her slender waist confined.") The charming piece of melody set to the song we select is by Charles Young, the father of the gifted singer, Cecilia Young, who married Dr. Arne. It is taken from *British Melody,* 1739, folio.

1. But to pre · vent the sad in · crease
2. Your form does to my fan · cy bring,
3. For if I break you may mis · trust

1. Of hope · less love, I keep a · way,
2. And makes my old wounds bleed a · new,
3. The vow I made to love you too,

1. But to pre · vent the sad in · crease
2. Your form does to my fan · cy bring,
3. For if I break you may mis · trust

1. Of hope · less love I keep a · way.
2. And makes my old wounds bleed a · new.
3. The vow I made to love you too.

Come you not from Newcastle?

For note to this song see Appendix.

To a Lady Weeping.

The music is by Henry Lawes, and published in his *Ayres and Dialogues for one, two, and three voyces*, 1653, folio. The words are by "Mr. Cartwright." Henry Lawes was one of the best musicians of his day, and a thorough Englishman. It was he, who to ridicule the growing fashionable taste for Italian vocal music—really not understood by its enthusiastic hearers,—set to music the contents table of an Italian song book, and palmed it off as an Italian song! Henry Lawes was born in 1595, near Salisbury, and died in 1662. William Lawes, whose works also still live in the estimation of musicians, was his brother.

Though your Strangenesse fretts my Heart.

JOHN WILSON.

Andante espressione.

1. Though your strangenesse
2. When an-oth-er

1. fretts my heart, Yet may not I com-plaine, You perswade me 'tis but art, That
2. holds your hand, You sweare I have your heart; When my ri-valls close doe stand, And

1. se-cret love must feigne. I an-oth-er you af-fect, 'Tis but a show t'a-
2. I stand farre a-part, They en-joy you, ev-'ry one, Yet must I seeme your

1. voy'd sus-pect, Is this faire ex-cus-ing? O no, all is a-bus - ing.
2. friend a-lone; Is this faire ex-cus-ing? O no, all is a-bus - ing.

This is taken from *Cheerful Ayres or Ballads first composed for one single voice, and since set for three voices, by Dr. John Wilson,* Oxford, 1060. Dr. John Wilson was a clever musician in much repute during the middle of the 17th century. His songs, "When Troy town," "From the fair Lavinion Shore," "Cast your caps and cares away," "In the merry month of May" (this last reproduced in the present volume) have all been notable long past the age they were written for. Wilson was born in 1594, and died in 1673. A large number of his songs were reprinted by John Playford. Dr. Rimbault wrote a pamphlet to prove that John, or Jack Wilson was a singer on the early Shakesperian stage, and is the "Jack Wilson" mentioned in one of the stage directions in the folio of 1623. He is thought to have been the composer of many of the early airs to Shakespere's songs.

As I Walked Forth one Summer's Day.

For note to this song see Appendix.

Here's a Health unto His Majesty.

JER. SAVILE.

Here's a health un - to his Ma - jes - ty, With a

fa, la, la, la, la, la, la. Con ver - sion to his

This noble and spirited song was (so far as the melody is concerned), the production of Jeremy or Jeremiah Savile, a composer of much strength, during the 17th century. It is first found in John Playford's publications, including *The Musical Companion*, 1667 and 1672-3, where it is arranged for three voices. The song as there printed has but one verse, but in modern copies another is added, and "confusion to his enemies" stands in place of the original "conversion to," etc. Savile was also composer of the glee known as "The Waits," or "Fal la, la," the performance of which was always the closing number at the meetings of all old glee societies.

en - e - mies, With a fa, la, la, la, la, la, la; And

he that will not pledge this health, I wish him nei - ther

wit nor wealth, Nor yet a rope to hang him - self, With a

I do Confess Thou'rt Smooth and Fair.

HENRY LAWES.

1. I do con - fess thou'rt smooth and fair. And
2. I do con - fess thou'rt sweet, yet find Thee

1. I might have gone near to love thee,
2. such an un thrift of thy sweets;

The music is by Henry Lawes, and was probably first printed in Playford's *Select Ayres and Dialogues*, 1659, being reprinted in *The Treasury of Musick*, 1669. The song is there named "To his forsaken mistress," and the words are generally attributed to Sir Robert Ayton, who died in 1638. After its appearance in Watson's *Collection of Scots Poems*, 1705-11 (Ayton being a Scotsman by birth), the song became frequent in Scotch collections, and Robert Burns rewrote it for Johnson's *Museum*, vol. iv. Hejset it to the tune generally known as the "Cuckoo's Nest," which is structurally a hornpipe, and decidedly unsuited to the words. There are four verses in the original, of these we only reprint the first two.

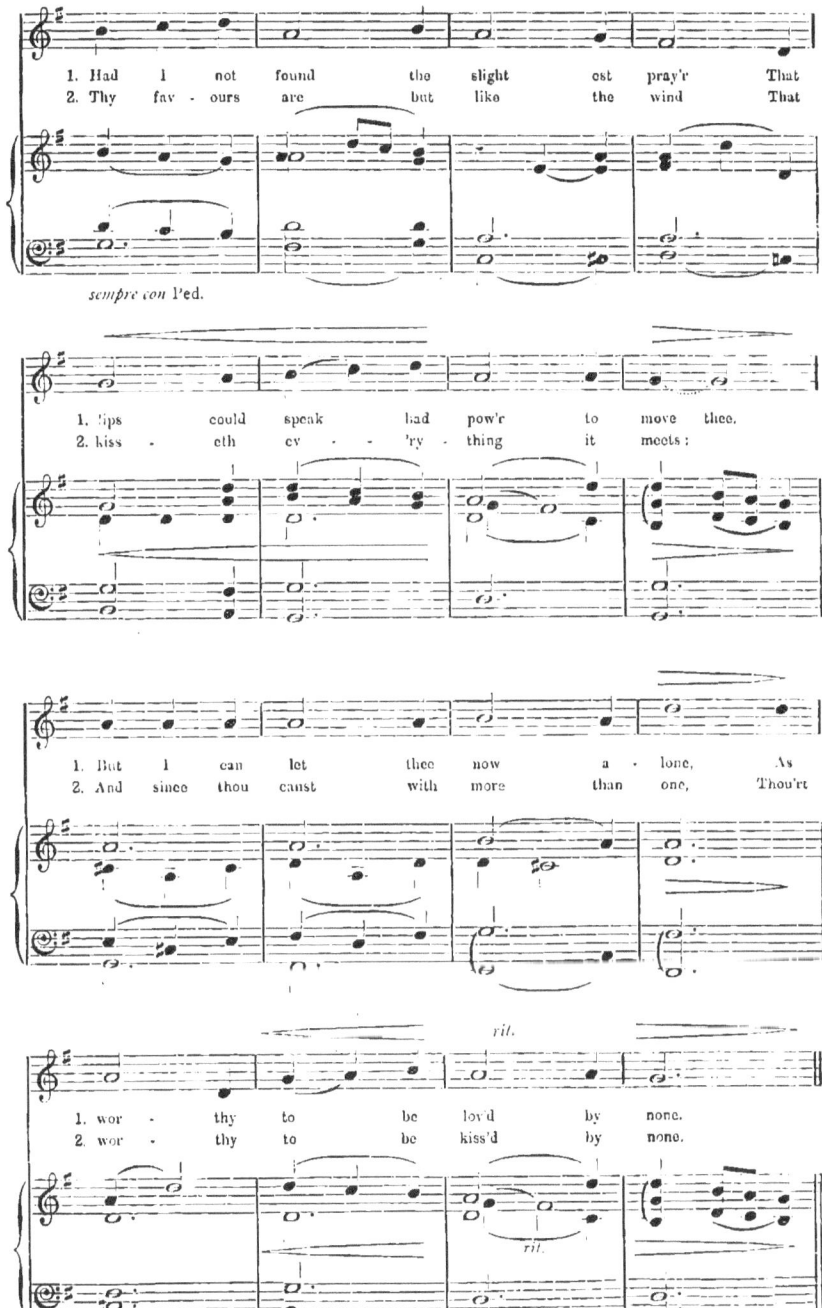

sempre con l'ed.

1. Had I not found the slight est pray'r That
2. Thy fav - ours are but like the wind That

1. lips could speak had pow'r to move thee.
2. kiss - eth ev - - 'ry - thing it meets:

1. But I can let thee now a - lone, As
2. And since thou canst with more than one, Thou'rt

rit.

1. wor - thy to be lov'd by none.
2. wor - thy to be kiss'd by none.

rit.

The Mermaid.

The tune of this fine old forecastle ditty was first put into print by William Chappell, although it had been much sung among sailors and others prior to his time. Copies of the words varying in length and in wording are to be seen in the quaint little song garlands of which the British Museum possesses such a fine collection. The above version is taken from a ballad sheet in the present writer's library. The chorus, "When the stormy winds do blow," seems to have been a sort of tag to many an old sea song even as early as the 17th century.

1. comb and a glass in her hand, her hand, her hand, With a comb and a glass in her hand.
2. night they will weep for me, for me, for me, And this night they will weep for me.
3. night a wi-dow she'll be, she'll be, she'll be, And this night a wi-dow she'll be.
4. sunk to the bottom of the sea, the sea, the sea, So she sunk to the bottom of the sea.
5. look to the bottom of the sea, the sea, the sea, She may look to the bottom of the sea.

f CHORUS.

Oh, the storm-y winds do blow, ... And the rag-ing seas do

roar, While we poor sai-lors go up to the top, And the

land lub-bers lie down be-low, be-low, be-low, And the land-lub-bers lie down be-low.

Golden Slumbers Kiss Your Eyes.

1. Gol · den slum · bers
2. Caro is hea · vy,

1. kiss your eyes, Smiles a · wake you when you rise,
2. there · fore sleep, You are care, and care must keep,

1. Sleep, pret · ty wan · tons, do not cry, And I will sing a
2. Sleep, pret · ty wan · tons, do not cry, And I will sing a

1. lul · la · by, Rock them, rock them, lul · la · · by.
2. lul · la · by, Rock them, rock them, lul · la · · by.

We select the above as one of the few early English songs written as lullabies. It occurs as a song in *The Pleasant Comedy of Patient Grissil*, quarto, printed in 1603; the comedy is by Haughton Chettle and Dekker. As the tune to the song is irrecoverably lost, we have followed Chappell's lead, and adapted it to the air which is variously named " May Fair," " The Willoughby Whim," "O Jenny, O Jenny, where hast thou been?" This latter title is the name of the tune as given in the early ballad operas of 1725, 1730, etc , and forms the first line of " The Willoughby Whim," a song in the first volume of *Pills*, 1719. The tune in a far less simple form appears as " May Fair" in the 1703 and 1719 editions of the *Dancing Master*. In that of 1716 it has the sub-title "Or, Grief a-la-mode." In the *Beggar's Opera*, 1727-8, the tune is set to the song, "O Polly, you might have toyed and kissed," and Scottish collections have it to the song, " My mither says I maunna."

In the Merry Month of May.

JOHN WILSON.

1. In the mer - ry month of May, On a morn by break of day,
Forth I walked the wood so wide, When as May was in her pride, There I spied all a-lone, all a - lone, Phil - li - da and Cor - i - don.

2. Much a - doe there was, God wot, He would love but she could not,
He said his love was to woo, She said none was false to you, He said he had loved her long, She said love should take no wrong.

3. Cor - i - don would have kissed her then, She said maids must kiss no men,
Till they kiss for good and all; Then she bade the shep - herd call All the gods to wit - ness truth, Ne'er was loved so fair a youth.

4. Then with many a pret - ty oath, Yea and nay and faith and troth,
Such as sil - ly shepherds use When they would not love a - buse, Love which had been long de - lud - ed Was with kis - ses sweet con - cluded.

This delightful pastoral is by Nicholas Breton, an Elizabethan poet. It was sung as a morning greeting to Queen Elizabeth in one of her progresses in 1591, "by three excellent musicians, who being disguised in ancient country attire, did greet her with a pleasant song of Corydon and Phillida, made in three parts of purpose, the song as well as the work of the ditty, or the aptness of the notes thereto applied, pleased her Highness after it had been once sung to command again, and highly to grace it with her cheerful acceptance and commendation. It was entitled, 'The Plowman's Song; In the merry month of May.'"—*Nichol's Progresses*. Many madrigal and glee composers have set the words, including Michael Este, in his *Madrigals to 3, 4, and 5 parts*, London, 1604 (4to). Henry Youll in his *Canzonets to three voyces*, 1608, gives another setting, and Dr. John Wilson, whose tune we adopt, prints his in *Cheerful Ayres*, Oxford, 1660. This is the one most frequently reprinted. Another composer who set the song was Mr. Rogers, and his air as well as Wilson's is in Playford's *Musical Companion*, 1672. More recent is T. Linley's setting, which is given in Linley's *Posthumous Works*. A varied version of the words is by Dr. Percy in his *Reliques*.

We be Three Poor Mariners.

The above song and air are in *Deuteromelia; or, the second part of Musicke's Melodie,* 1609, and since that time in a great number of glee books and on sheet and half sheet music, generally arranged for three voices. A version of the fine tune under the name "Brangill of Poictu" is in the *Skene MS.* The "Branle" or "Braule" was a French dance much in favour in the 16th and the 17th centuries, and the words of "We be three poor mariners" seem to indicate that the song was sung while dancing, or that the dance occurred between the verses. Curiously enough street children sing to a dance some fragmentary ditty which appears from similarity of words and tune to be a survival of the older song. "The Brangill of Poictu" from the *Skene MS.* is given in our Appendix.

The Maiden's Complaint.

THOMAS AUGUSTINE ARNE.

This song is from Dr. Arne's *Masque of Comus*, performed at Drury Lane in 1738. The piece was one of the early important works composed by Arne, and so tuneful are its numbers that many of them have held in favour until almost the present day. "By the gaily circling glass," "Would you taste the noon-tide air?" and the one we have here selected, have never waned in their popularity. The *Masque* was adapted from an early one written by John Milton, and performed at Ludlow Castle in 1634. The adaptation was made by Dr. Dalton, who wrote the several new songs, including "How gentle was my Damon's air." Mrs. Arne was the first public singer of the song on the stage.

beau-ties to re-sign, And yet the cru-el task is mine.

Andante amoroso.

p con espress.

sempre con Ped.

p con espress.

On ev 'ry hill, in

p

poco rit.

p

p

ev 'ry grove, A - long . . . the mar — gin of . . . each

stream, Dear con - scious scenes of form er love . . I

mourn, and Da mon is . . my . theme. The hills, . the

groves, the streams re main, But Da mon there . . . I.

seek . . in vain, Tho hills. the groves, the streams re -

main. . . But Da - mon there . I seek . . in vain.

From hill, from

dale   each   charm   has   fled,   Groves, flocks, and   foun   tains

please . . no   more, . .   Each flow'r in   pi   ty   droops . . its

head, . . All na - ture does . . my . . loss . . de - plore;

All, all re - proach the faith - less swain, Yet Da mon

still . . I . . seek . . in vain, All, all re - proach . . the

faith - less swain, Yet Da - mon still . . I seek . . in vain.

E

The Free and Accepted Mason.

This song has been sung on the installation of a new member into the Freemason fraternity for nearly two hundred years. The first trace to be found of the air in print is in *Pills to Purge Melancholy*, 1719, vol. ii., p. 230, where it is set to a song entitled "On the Queen's progress to the Bath." As "Freemason's Health," the tune alone appears in the third volume of the *Dancing Master*, circa 1726-7, and again under the same heading in one of Walsh's early dance books without date. Next the song and air is in *Watt's Musical Miscellany*, vol. iii., 1730, and the tune in his editions of the ballad operas—*The Village Opera*, *The Lover's Opera*, etc. The *Gentleman's Magazine* for October, 1731, has the first stanza of the song as by "Mr. Birkhead." In later times the air became known as "The Freemason's March" and as "The Merry Masons." Under the former title, an altered version of the tune is in *Aird's Selection*, book i. The song is of course frequently printed in Masonic song books, and is included in an American publication, *The Masonick Minstrel*, 1816.

Wherever I am or Whatever I doe.

PELHAM HUMPHREY.

A song with many musical settings, the earliest to be found being the one here printed by Pelham Humphrey, a graceful composer and a lutenist during the middle of the 17th century. He was born in 1647, and died 1674. He was a singer and "master of the children" at the Chapel Royal, Windsor. John Playford published in his various books many of Humphrey's compositions. The words of the above song, united to another air, are in *Pills*, 1707, vol. i., and in vol. iii. of the 1719 edition. Another setting is by Charles Froud, an organist of Cripplegate Church; this is to be seen in *Calliope, or English Harmony*, 1739, vol. i.

On the Brow of Richmond Hill.

HENRY PURCELL.

This is one of the lesser known songs by Henry Purcell. In *Pills to purge Melancholy*, it is headed, "An Ode to Cynthia walking on Richmond Hill, set by Mr. Henry Purcell." Richmond Hill has inspired many poets and musicians.

Love - ly Cyn - thia, pass - ing by, With bright - er glo - ries blest my eye;

Ah! then in vain, in vain, said I, The fields and flowers do shine;

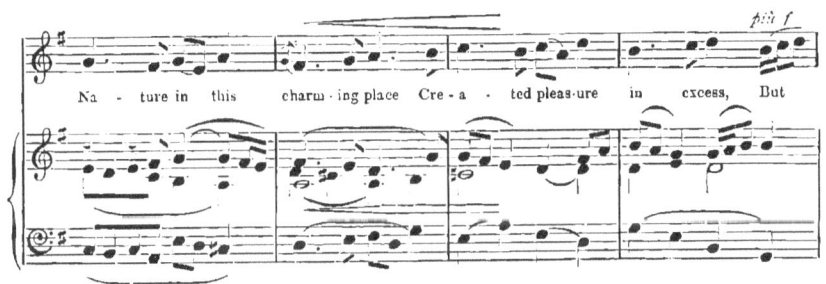

Na - ture in this charm - ing place Cre - a - ted pleas - ure in excess, But

all are poor to Cyn - thi - a's face, Whose fea - tures are di - vine.

Jog on, Jog on.

‡ Hent: to seize, or to hold.

The first four lines is a snatch of song sung by the tuneful Autolycus in *A Winter's Tale*, act iv. The pedlar's entire song as here given is in *The Antidote against Melancholy*, 1661. Regarding the tune above printed, and now always associated with the words, it is assumed by Chappell that from its title, "Jog on," in the *Dancing Master*, 1650 to 1665, it is the one originally fitted to the words. This is undoubtedly very likely, but it must be remembered that in the later editions of the *Dancing Master*, 1670-1690, the same tune has the heading, "Jog on, my honey," (see Appendix), and that this line does not occur in the Shakespearian song. A version of the tune under the name "Hanskin" is in the *Fitzwilliam Virginal Book*, an early musical manuscript of great value and importance. In *Pills to purge Melancholy*, 1707 and 1719, there are several ballads set to this air, two being on the Spanish Armada.

When that I was a Little Tiny Boy.

1. When that I was a little tiny boy, With a hey, ho, the wind and the rain, A fool-ish thing was but a toy, For the rain it rain-eth ev-'ry day, With a hey, ho, the wind and the rain, And the rain it rain-eth ev-'ry day.

2. But when I came to man's e-state, With a hey, ho, the wind and the rain, 'Gainst knave and thief men shut their gate, For the rain it rain-eth ev-'ry day, With a hey, ho, the wind and the rain, And the rain it rain-eth ev-'ry day.

3. But when I came, a-las! to wife, With a hey, ho, the wind and the rain, By swagg'ring I could nev-er thrive, For the rain it rain-eth ev-'ry day, With a hey, ho, the wind and the rain, And the rain it rain-eth ev-'ry day.

4. Long, long a-go the world be-gun, With a hey, ho, the wind and the rain, But that's all one, our play is done, And we'll strive to please you ev-'ry day, With a hey, ho, the wind and the rain, And the rain it rain-eth ev-'ry day.

The song is in the epilogue to Shakespeare's *Twelfth Night*. Chappell who prints the tune, says that it had passed down on the stage traditionally, and that it was generally considered as the composition of a person named Fickling. This is not likely to be correct, for the air has every appearance of being a melody coeval with the words. I have in my own library a folio publication of *New Songs in the Pantomime of the Witches, The celebrated Epilogue in the Comedy of Twelfth Night, ... composed by J. Vernon*, published by John Johnston, circa 1769. This contains the words and air as sung by Vernon himself at Vauxhall, who appears to have rightly, (or more probably) wrongly claimed the composition of the air himself.

Here's to the Maiden of Bashful Fifteen.

Con spirito.

1. Here's to the maid-en of
2. Here's to the charmer, whose
3. Here's to the maid with a
4. Let them be clumsy, or

1. bashful fifteen,   Here's to the wi-dow of   fif · ty;   Here's to the flaunting ex-travagant quean, And
2. dimples we prize,   Now to the maid who has none,   sir;   Here's to the girl with a pair of blue eyes, And
3. bo-som of snow,   Now to her brown as a   ber · ry;   Here's to the wife with a face full of woe, And
4. let them be slim,   Mar-ry! I care not a   fea · ther!   Fill a pint bumper, nay, fill to the brim, And

1. here's to the housewife that's thrif · ty.
2. here's to the nymph with but one, sir.
3. here's to the dam-sel that's mer · ry.
4. e'en let us toast all to · ge-ther.
Let the toast pass,   drink to the lass,   I warrant she'll prove an ex-

cuse for the glass;   Let the toast pass,   Drink to the lass,   I warrant she'll prove an ex-cuse for the glass.

Sung in Sheridan's comedy, *The School for Scandal*, first acted in 1777. All old copies of the song bear the title, "The General Toast," and it was engraved on half sheets as "sung by Mr. Vernon." The fine air was adapted by Thomas Linley, from a very old dance tune named "Half Hanykin." Under this title the dance is found in the first (1650), and all early editions of Playford's *Dancing Master*, a copy from the 4th edition being given in the Appendix. "Here's to the maiden" was such a popular favourite that the words were printed on pottery beer mugs, etc.

Will Cloris cast her Sun-bright Eye?

The air is by John Goodgroom, a musician of the 17th century. He was born 1630, and died 1704. The dainty little song is printed in John Playford's *Select Ayres and Dialogues*, 2nd book, 1669, and in his *Musical Companion*, 1673, besides occurring as a lesson in several editions of *The Introduction to the Skill of Musick*.

Harvest Home.

Love me little, Love me long.

Moderato.

mf

1. Love me lit - tle,   love me long   Is the bur-den   of my song,   Love that is too
2. Winter's cold or   summer's heat,   Autumn's tempest   on it beat,   It can nev - er

1. hot and strong   Burneth soon   to waste.   Still, I would not   have thee cold, Nor too
2. know de - feat,   Nev - er can   re - bel.   Such the love that   I would gain, Such

1. backward, nor too   bold;   Love that last - eth   till 'tis old   Fad - eth not   in haste.
2. love, I   tell thee plain,   Thou must give, or   woo in vain,   So,   to thee,   fare-well.

The air is the old tune, "Mad Robin," copies of which occur in several editions of the *Dancing Master*—11th, 1701; 12th, 1703; 16th, 1716, etc.—and the air is also used for songs in the ballad operas, *Polly*, 1728, *The Lovers' Opera*, 1729, and others. The words and air which Mr. Chappell so happily placed together, thus united now form one of our most charming national lyrics. Chappell gives the words as from a manuscript of the time of James I., then in the possession of Mr. Payne Collier. In *The Book of English Songs*, 1851, the song is stated to have been printed in 1569-70 on a black letter broadside.

With Tuneful Pipe and Merry Glee.

Another of Dr. Maurice Greene's compositions. The words have had several different musical settings, one of which is in *Watts' Musical Miscellany*, vol. i., and another, more recent, was sung at Vauxhall about 1790. Watts' tune was used in many of the early ballad operas.

Club your Firelocks.

Alla marcia.

1. Club your
2. We'll re -
3. Cross
4. And

1. fire - locks, my lads, let us march to the coasts, To try whether Monsieur will
2. mind them (if hap - ly their mem - 'ries are bad) What drub - bings and dressings they
3. quick - ly the chan - nel! why all this de - lay? We long to re - turn you the
4. what though the Spaniards have join'd with the Frogs? The world soon shall find we can

1. stick to his boasts, For Par - blew! he cries, me vill
2. for - mer - ly bad When Bri - tain's rous'd Li - on stretch'd
3. vi - sit you pay. In us you will find of po -
4. thrash both the dogs. Ha - van a we'll put in our

A lyric expressive of an average Englishman's unreasoning contempt, during the Georgian era, for Frenchmen. The tune is good, and the song vigorous. It appears to have been called up by one of the many threatened invasions, and without the melody, made its appearance in *The Universal Magazine* for July, 1779, under the title, "The Jolly Soldiers; a new song." United to the tune, it is in *College; or, The Musical Miscellany*, Edinburgh, 1788. There are six verses in the original.

The Happy Beggars.

HENRY CAREY. (?)

Moderato e poco energia.

f

mf

1. Tho' beg - ging is an hon - est trade which wealth - y knaves des -
2. Tho' for - eign - ers have swarm'd of late and spoil'd our beg - ging
3. Let heav - y tax - es great - er grow to make our ar - my
4. What tho' we make the world be - lieve that we are sick or

mf

cres.

f

1. pise, Yet rich men may be beg - gars made, and
2. trade, Yet still we live and drink good beer tho'
3. fight, Where 'tis not to be had, you know, the
4. lame? 'Tis now a vir - tue to de - ceive, our

cres.

Both in words and music this has every appearance of being by Henry Carey. His name is added in an old hand-writing on one copy, but I have not found it ascribed to him in print. The song is to be found in Walsh's *Merry Musician*, vol. i., 1716, and in *Pills to purge Melancholy*, vol. vi., 1719. Later copies are in the illustrated volumes, *British Melody*, folio, 1739 ; *Universal Harmony*, 1745; *Calliope*, vol. ii., circa 1746. In the *Muse's Delight*, Liverpool, 1754, the same air is given to the song, and stated to be "set by Mr. Eaton." Who Mr. Eaton was I have not been able to discover, but it must be noted that the editor of the *Muse's Delight* has made many wild guesses in that work, and in earlier collections the song and air are published anonymously.

The Lass with the Delicate Air.

A pretty song which has lately been revived. It is generally understood to be the composition of Dr. Arne, but this is a mistake. It was that of his talented son, Michael Arne, a precocious musical genius whose works under the signature, "Master Arne," were issued at a very early date. He was born 1741, and died 1786. "The Lass with the delicate air" came into fashion about 1782, and appears in the *Universal Magazine* with the music, in August of that year. It is also in *Vocal Music*, Thompson's *Violin Tutor*, circa 1763, and in song books without music, such as, *The Humming-bird*, *The Masque*, 1767, etc. In this latter named work the composer's name is mentioned—"set by Mr. Michael Arne and sung by Miss Wright at Ranelagh." The lady named was afterwards the wife of Michael Arne. Samuel Lover, in *Handy Andy*, makes one of his female characters warble "The Lass with the delicate air."

The Merry Cuckoo, Messenger of Spring.

MAURICE GREENE.

The merry cuck - oo, mes-sen - ger of Spring, his trum pet shrill hath thrice al - rea-dy sound - ed, That warnes all lov - ers waite up - on the King, Who now is coming forth with garland crown ed.

The words are by Edmund Spenser from his *Amoretti*, a series of twenty-five sonnets written by the Elizabethan poet, and before the middle of the 16th century set to music by Dr. Maurice Greene [1695-6 to 1755]. John Walsh, the publisher of Handel's works, issued these in oblong folio, with an exquisitely designed and engraved title page, and the book was reprinted much later in the same century by Harrison & Co. Maurice Greene stands, musically, very high among his contemporaries.

her   that   most   it   ought.   But   she   his   pre   cept

proud - ly dis - o - beyes,   and   doth his i - dle   mes   sage   set   at

nought,   Therefore,   O   Love,   un - lesse she turne to   thee,

E'er cuck - oo   end,   e'er cuck - oo   end,   let   her   a reb - ell   be.

Love will find out the way.

1. The Phœnix.

For note to this song see Appendix.

As Down in the Meadows I Chanced to Pass.

1. As down in the mea - dows I chanc - ed to pass, Oh,
2. Oh, why does my lov'd one prove false and un - kind, Ah,
3. She fin - ished her song, and then rose to be gone, When

1. there I be - held a young beau - ti - ful lass: Her age, I am sure, it was
2. why does he change like the wa - ver - ing wind From one that is loy - al in
3. o - ver the com - mon comes jol - ly young John; He told her that she was the

A pretty lyric which came into vogue during the first quarter of the 18th century. With the first line beginning "'Twas down in a meadow," it appears in Walsh's *Merry Musician; or, a Cure for the Spleen*, vol. ii., *circa* 1728. Next, under the title, "Susan's Complaint," it is found in Watts' *Musical Miscellany*, vol. i., 1729, and with the name, "Down in a meadow," the air is given in *Polly*, 1729, to the song, "The sportsmen keep hawks." The air has to a slight extent an Irish flavour, but the six-eight measure h a frequently a knack of imparting this with no stronger authority to back it. The song is here slightly shortened from the original version.

1. scarce · ly fif · teen, And she on her head wore a gar · land of green; Her
2. ev · 'ry de · gree? Ah, why does he change to an · oth · er from me? For
3. joy of his life, And if she'd con · sent he would make her his wife. She

1. lips were like ru · bies, and as for her eyes, They spar · kled like dia · monds or
2. now he has left me for Fan · ny the fair, Em · ploys all his wish · es, his
3. could not re · fuse him, so to church she went—Young Wil · ly's for · got and young

1. stars in the skies; And as for her voice, it was
2. thoughts and his care, And says all the kind things he
3. Su · san con · tent: Most men are like Wil · ly, most

ten.

1. charm · ing and clear, And she sang a song for the loss of her dear.
2. once said to me, No lad in the world was so lov · ing as he.
3. wo · men like Sue, If men will be false, why should wo · men prove true?

colla voce.

The Hunt is Up.

1. The hunt is up, the hunt is up, And
2. Be - hold the skies with gold - en dyes Are
3. The sunne is glad to see us clad All

1. it is well nigh day; And Har - ry, our king is
2. glow - ing all a - round, The grasse is greene and
3. in our lust ie greene, And smiles in the skye as

Another of our now popular songs which we are principally indebted to the late Mr. William Chappell for resuscitating. The tune is in Playford's *Musick's Delights on the Cithren*, a small book in tablature, from which we have translated the present copy. The words are given by Mr. Chappell from a manuscript then in the possession of Mr. Payne Collier, and the song there has the title, ' The Kinge's Hunt is uppe." A tune in the Fitzwilliam Virginal book is called "The Hunt is up," but this is not the present one; in fact the phrase was so common for a hunting ditty that much confusion appears to have existed among different copies. "The Hunt is up" is mentioned as a dance tune in *The Complaint of Scotland*, 1549, and there are also some religious parodies. The song from Mr. Collier's manuscript is considered to be by one Gray, a favourite of Henry VIII.

1. gone hunt - ing, To bring his deere to
2. so are the treene, All laugh - ing at the
3. he ris - eth hye, To see and to be

1. baye. The east is bright with morn ing light, And
2. sound. Tho hor ses snort to join the sport, Tho
3. scene. A - wake, all men, I say o - gen, Be

1. dark ness it is fled, The mer - ie horne wakes
2. dogges are run ning free, The woddes re - joice at
3. mer - ie as you maye, For Har - ry, our king, is

1. up the morne, To leave his i - dle bed.
2. all the noise Of hey tan - ta - ra tee - ree!
3. gone hunt - ing, To bring his deere to baye.

Youth's the Season made for Joys.

The sprightly little song with the air is given in the *Beggar's Opera*, 1727-8, the tune in the old editions being marked "Cotillon." Macheath sings the song and prefaces it with the following:—" Ere you seat yourselves, ladies, what think you of a dance! *(Enter Harper.)* Play the French tune that Mrs. Slammekin was so fond of (a dance à-la-ronde in the French manner): near the end of it this song and chorus." From this and from the character of the tune itself it seems likely that it was a French cotillon then in vogue in the fashionable world, though Gay's words, and its place in the *Beggars' Opera* have sufficiently naturalised it.

Gather ye Rosebuds.

WILLIAM LAWES.

Moderato.

p

con Ped.

rit.

p

1. Gath-er ye rose - buds while ye   may,   Old Time   is   still   a   fly - ing,
2. The glorious lamp of heav'n, the   sun,   Tho high - er   he   is   get - ting,
3. That age is best   that   is   the   first,   When youth and blood are   warm - er,
4. Then be not coy,   but use   your time,   And while ye   may - go,   mar - ry;

poco rit.

1. And   this same flow'r which smiles to - day   To - mor - row   will   be   dy - ing.
2. The   soon-er will   his   race   be   run,   And near - er   he's   to   set - ting.
3. But   be - ing spent the worse and worst   Times still suc - ceed   the   form - er.
4. For   hav - ing lost but once   your prime,   You may for   ev - er   tar - ry.

poco rit.

The immortal words are by Robert Herrick, and are published in his *Hesperides; or, the works both Humane and Divine of Robert Herrick, Esq.*, 1648. The old title runs, "To the Virgins, to make much of Time." The air is by William Lawes, the older brother of Henry Lawes. William was musician to Charles I., and was killed at the siege of Chester in 1645. He no doubt composed the air to the sonnet while it was yet in manuscript form. His air was first published with the words in Playford's *Select Musicall Ayres and Dialogues*, folio, 1652, as well as the later edition of 1659. It was after this frequently reprinted by Playford, and appears in his *Musick's Delight on the Cithren*, 1666, *The Musical Companion*, 1672-3, and in most of his editions of *The Introduction to the Skill of Musick*. It is also in Forbes' *Cantus*, 1682, and in the Leyden and Blaikie MSS., as well as in nearly every glee book published since Playford's time.

The Rose-buds in June.

Andante con espressione.

1. Here the
2. Our
3. Our
4. Now the

p

poco rit.

con l'ed.

1. rose - buds   in   June,   and   the   vio - lets   are   blow - ing,   The
2. shep - herds   re - joice   in   their   fine   heav - y   fleec - es,   And
3. clean   milk - ing   pails   they   are   fouled   with   good   ale,   At   the
4. sheep   shear - ing's   ov   er   and   har - vest   draws   nigh,   We'll   pre -

1. small   birds   they   war - ble   on   ev' - ry   green   bough,   Here's the
2. frisk - y   young   lambs   which   their   flocks   do   in - crease,   Each
3. ta - ble   there's   plen - ty   of   cheer   to   be   found ;   We'll
4. pare   for   the   fields   our   strength for   to   try ;   We'll

A delightful folk song and melody, taken from a thin folio volume of this class of song, collected by the late Rev. John Broadwood, in Surrey and Sussex, and published by him anonymously in 1843. This work may be said to be practically the first English collection of peasant song and folk melodies published as such, and for the avowed purpose of rescuing traditional English songs in their primitive state. The collection consisted of but 16 songs, but his niece, Miss Lucy Broadwood, added to this number from her store of similar songs obtained in the same district, and the work was then republished. We are indebted to Miss Broadwood for the loan of the very scarce original volume.

1. pink and the li - ly, and the daf - fy down dil - ly,
2. lad takes his lass all on the green grass,
3. whis - tle and sing and dance in a ring,
4. reap and we'll mow, we'll plough and we'll sow,

To a -

dorn and per - fume those sweet mea - dows in June. If it

weren't for the plough the fat ox would go slow, And the

lads and the bonny lass - ies to the sheep-shear - ing go.

colla voce.

rit.

There was a Maid went to the Mill.

1. There was a maid, and she went to the mill, Sing
2. The mill-er kissed her, a-way she went, Sing
3. He danced and sang while the mill went clack, Sing

1. trol-ly, lol-ly, lol-ly, lol-ly, lo, The mill turned round, but the maid stood still, Oh, oh,
2. trol-ly, lol-ly, lol-ly, lol-ly, lo, The maid was pleased, and the miller con-tent, Oh, oh,
3. trol-ly, lol-ly, lol-ly, lol-ly, lo, He cheered his heart with a cup of old sack, Oh, oh,

1. ho! oh, oh, ho! oh, oh, ho! did she so?
2. ho! oh, oh, ho! oh, oh, ho! did he so?
3. ho! oh, oh, ho! oh, oh, ho! did he so?

The song appears in the ballad opera, *The Jovial Crew* (acted 1781), as well as in a later adaptation of the opera, *The Ladies' Frolic*, 1770. Both these musical plays were versions of one named *The Jovial Crew; or, the Merry Beggars*, acted in 1641, and it is possible that the song may belong to the latter date. The air is also that to a song in *Pills to purge Melancholy*, vol. v., p. 13, beginning "There was an old woman."

A Swain in Despair.

FRANK.

1. A swain in de - spair Cried, "Wo - men ne'er trust: A las! they are all Un - kind or un - just." A maid who was by, Soon thus did re - ply: "The men we all find More false and un - kind."

2. "Ex - cept me," he cried, "And me," she re - plied; "Then try me," said he; "I dare not," said she. The swain did pur - sue, Each al - ter'd their mind, She vow'd he was true, He swore she was kind.

From the sixth and last volume of D'Urfey's *Pills to purge Melancholy*, 1720, where it is given as "A song set by Mr. Frank."

G

Hark! hark! the Joy-inspiring Horn.

RICHARD BRIDE.

A hunting song popular during the latter part of the 18th century. A sheet copy of it with the music, *circa* 1770, informs us that it was "set" or composed by Richard Bride, and was sung by Mr. Dearl at the Grotto Gardens. This place of amusement was owned by one Finch, and the gardens were situate on the south side of the Thames, near the King's bench prison, part of their site being now occupied by the Borough Road Station. Richard Bride was a music publisher who succeeded Henry Waylett, at Exeter Change in the Strand. Copies of the song with the music occur in Horsfield's *Vocal Music*, 1775, Fielding's *Vocal Enchantress*, 1783, and many other works.

It was a Maid of my Countrie.

The song was first unearthed by Joseph Ritson from an Elizabethan MS. in the Cotton library. It is really a long poem extending to thirteen verses, and scarcely suited in its entirety to be reproduced here. The MS. directs it to be sung to "Donkin Dargeson." The tune, "Dargeson; or, The Sedany," is in Playford's *Dancing Master* from 1650 to 1693, and was the air for country or rustic dancing where the performers commenced by being in a single line, not facing each other as generally. The melody is interminable, and a version of it is also given to "Oft have I ridden upon my grey nag," in *Pammelia; or, Musick's Miscellanie*, 1609. Edward Jones prints a somewhat similar tune in his *Musical and Poetical Relics of the Welsh Bards*, 1784, which he names "The Melody of Cynwyd." He apparently noted this down traditionally. Jones' tune has a distinct Irish flavour, and appears to be far more modern than "Dargeson."

1. mar - vell'd to see the tree so green. At last she ask - ed
2. fall on me to keep me green. Yea, quoth the maid, but
3. more and more my twigs grow green. But an' they chance to

1. of the tree, How came this fresh - ness un - to thee, And
2. when you grow You stand at hand at ev - 'ry blow Of
3. cut thee down, And take thy branch - es in - to town, Then

1. ev - 'ry branch so fair and clean. I mar - vel that ye grow so green.
2. ev - 'ry man for to be seen, I mar - vel that ye grow so green.
3. they will nev - er more be seen, To grow a - gain so fresh and green.

The Dumb Wife Cured.

1. There was a bon-ny blade Had marry'd a country maid, And
2. She could brew and she could bake, She could sew and she could make, And
3. To the doc-tor he did bring, And he cut her chatt'ring string, At
4. To the doc-tor then he goes, And thus he vents his woes: O

1. safe-ly con-duct-ed her home, home, home; She was neat in ev-'ry part, And she
2. she could sweep the house with a broom, broom, broom; She could wash and she could wring, And do
3. lib-er-ty he set her tongue, tongue, tongue; Oh! her tongue be-gan to walk, And
4. doc-tor, you have me un done, done, done, For my wife she's turn'd a scold, And her

The song with the above air appears in all editions of *Pills to purge Melancholy*, from 1698 to 1719, and is even now known traditionally in country places—in Yorkshire to a tune quite different from the early printed one here given. The melody is a version of "I am the Duke of Norfolk," or "Paul's Steeple," printed under the latter named title in the first and other editions of Playford's *Dancing Master*, 1650, etc. The tune is one of the numerous branches of the primal theme of "John Anderson, my jo." Versions and survivals of the melody are found in Irish, English, and Scottish folk tunes; even to-day we may recognise it in the American song, "When Johnny comes marching home," and in the more modern edition of that tune set to a popular comic song.

He that will not merry, merry be.

Spiritoso.

1. He that will not mer-ry, mer-ry be With a gen-er-ous bowl and
2. He that will not mer-ry, mer-ry be And take his glass in
3. He that will not mer-ry, mer-ry be With a com-pan-y of jol-ly

1. toast, May he in Bride-well be shut up, And
2. course, May he then have to drink small beer, Ne'er a
3. boys, May he be plagued with a scold-ing wife, To con-

Song and air from the ballad opera, *The Jovial Crew*, printed in 1731. The old name of the tune is there given as "Three merry men of Kent." Chappell mentions that in a work called *Folly in print*, 1667, there is a song entitled "Three merry boys of Kent." The song from *The Jovial Crew* is only part of a much earlier lyric, the whole of which is reprinted in Dixon's *Songs of the Peasantry of England*, p. 209.

cres.

1. fast bound to a post.
2. pen - ny in his purse.
3. found him with her noise.

Let him be mer - ry,

mer - ry, mer - ry there, And we will be mer - ry, mer - ry here, For

who can know where we may go To be mer - ry an - oth - er

year, brave boys, To be mer - ry an - oth - er year?

Gipsy Song.

For note to this song see Appendix.

The Pretty Ploughboy.

1. As I was a-walk-ing one morn-ing in Spring, I heard a pretty ploughboy and so sweetly he did sing, And as he was a-singing, oh! these words I heard him say: "There's no life like the ploughboy's in the sweet month of May."

2. The lark in the morning she will rise up from her nest, She'll mount the white air with the dew all on her breast, And with the pretty ploughboy, oh! she'll whis-tle and she'll sing, And at night she'll re-turn to her nest back again.

3. If you walk in the fields an-y pleas-ure to find, You'll see what the ploughman en-joys in his mind: The corn he sows grows, and she flow-ers all do spring, And the ploughman's as hap-py as a prince or a king.

4. When his day's work is done that he has had to do, Per-haps to some wake or fair he will go; There, with a sweet lass, oh, he will dance and sing, And at night he'll re-turn to his home back again.

The song and air were taken down by Mr. Frank Kidson from the singing of a ploughman in North Yorkshire, and is by permission reprinted from his *Traditional Tunes*, 1891. The two verses there printed make a Yorkshire version of a song obtained traditionally by Robert Burns the poet (see Cromek's *Reliques*, 1808), but there is a lengthy copy of the song in a garland in the British Museum, from which we take the third and fourth verses.

The Jovial Beggar.

1. There was a jov-ial beg - gar, He had a wooden leg, Was lame from his cra - dle, And
2. Oh, sev - en years I begg'd For my old mas - ter Wild, He taught me the beg - ging When
3. Of all the oc - cu - pa - tions, A beg - gar lives the best, For when he's a - wea - ry He'll
4. I fear no plots against me, I live in op - en cell, Then, who'd be a king, When the

1. forc - ed for to beg.
2. that I was a child.
3. lie him down and rest.
4. beg-gars live so well.

And a - beg - ging we will go, we'll go, we'll go, And a -

beg - ging we will go.

A very popular 18th century tune used for almost all classes of lyrics. The melody, however, dates back to the preceding century, and the song itself is attributed to Richard Brome, who wrote a play named *The Jovial Crew* in 1641, from which the later ballad opera was adapted. A black letter broadside in the Bagford collection has the song, "The Jovial Beggar," with the heading, "The Beggars' Chorus in *The Jovial Crew*." The song, however, does not appear in the original edition of the play, but it is possible it may have been interpolated in the acting. "The Jovial Beggar" with the air is given in Playford's *Choice Ayres and Songs*, fifth book 1684, p. 2; in 180 *Loyal Songs*; in all editions of *Pills*, etc. The tune is also present in many of the early ballad operas. When Henry Fielding wrote the words, "The Dusky Night," he intended them for this tune with the refrain. "A-hunting we will go." Other songs to the air have burdens "A-sailing we will go," "A-hawking we will go," "A-fishing we will go," etc., etc. Near the end of the 18th century a ditty commencing "Come bustle, bustle, drink about, and let us merry be,' became associated with the melody.

Who can Resist my Celia's Charms?

Andantino.   *p*   TREVERS.

1. Who can re- sist . . my Ce- lia's charms? Her beau- ty wounds, her
2. Love seems to pro- mise, in . . her eyes, A kind . . and last- ing
3. In vain a thou- sand ways . . I strive To keep . . my faint- ing

1. wit . . . dis - arms: When these their might - y for - ces
2. ago . . . of joys: But have a care, . . their trea - son
3. hopes . . a - live; My love can nev - er find . . . re -

p

poco rit.

1. join, . . What heart's so strong . . but must . . re - sign?
2. shun, . . I . . look'd, be - liev'd, . . and was . . un - done.
3. ward, . . Since pride and beau - ty are . . her guard.

poco rit.

The song is from the farce, *Duke and no Duke*, by N. Tate, 1685. Set to a lengthy piece of music by "Sen Baptist," it is also in Henry Playford's *Theater of Music*, first book, 1685. In Watt's *Musical Miscellany*, vol. v., 1731, another air (the one given above), is used for the words, "set by Mr. Trevers."

Since Phillis swears Inconstancy.

Entitled "'Fair Phillis,' set by Mr. James Hart," in the sixth volume of *Pills*, 1720. James Hart, according to Brown and Stratton's excellent *British Musical Biography*, 1897, was a gentleman of the Chapel Royal, and a chorister of Westminster, who, born in 1647, died in 1718.

I made Love to Kate.

Con spirito.

1. I made love to Kate, Long I sigh'd for she, Till I heard of late, She'd a mind to me; I
2. As I fond-er grew, She began to prate, Mar-ry you I will, You shall mar-ry Kate; At
3. For a dance, she said, She was wondrous sick; Har-ry danc'd with Sue, Molly with young Dick; Then

1. met her on the green, In her best array, So pret-ty she did seem, She stole my heart away! O
2. that I laugh'd and said, Still I lov'd her more, My love should nev-er end, Up-on my knees I swore; A-
3. Kate she led the game, First in ev-'ry joke, And mer-ri-ly we play'd All un-der yon-der oak; And

1. then I kiss'd the maid! Was I much to blame? Had you been in my place, Why, you had done the same!
2. gain I kiss'd my Kate, Was I much to blame? Had you been in my place, Why, you had done the same!
3. at the rise of moon Kiss'd, and thought no shame, Had you been in my place, Why, you had done the same!

As "Woo'd an' Married an' a'," this tune has been claimed as a Scottish one, but while dates of Scotch and English publication are about equal, it must be pointed out that there are very marked differences between the two airs. "I made love to Kate" appears to have been sung by Mr. Beard at Ranelagh, and with this statement it was printed on half sheets, the plate afterwards being used in a folio edition of *The Jovial Crew; or, the Merry Beggars,* circa 1760. "Woo'd an' Married an' a'" was printed in *Bremner's Reels,* 1759. The song and air "I made love to Kate," as "A New Song sung by Mr. Beard at Ranelagh," appears in the December supplement to *The Universal Magazine,* 1759, and afterwards in *Clio and Euterpe,* vol. iii., 1762; *Edinburgh Musical Miscellany,* vol. ii., 1793; *The Songster's Companion,* circa 1800, and many other works. The verses have had to be slightly modified to suit modern taste.

A Kiss I Begged.

John Gamble,

Andante espressione.

1. A kiss I begg'd, and thou did'st join thy lips to mine;
2. Ah, once a - gain I pray thee raise thy lips to mine;

1. Then, as a - fraid, snatch'd back their treasure, and mock'd my plea - sure. A - gain, my
2. Why should their sweetness go un - tast-ed, their treas - ure wast - ed Up - on the

1. dear - est, for in this Thou on - ly gav'st de - sire, and not a kiss.
2. wan - ton, i - dle air, While I, thy lov - er, wait in mute des - pair?

The air is by John Gamble, and is found in *Ayres and Dialogues to be sung to the theorb-lute or basse-viol, by John Gamb'e,* published by John Playford in 1657, folio. It is also reproduced in *New Ayres and Dialogues composed for Voices and Viols . . . . . London,* printed by M. C. for H. Brome, 1678, 12mo. Gamble was a violinist in the private band of Charles II. It is stated that he died in 1657.

As May in all her Youthful Dress.

The air is by a Yorkshire composer named Samuel Akeroyde, whose works are found in many of the publications of Henry Playford and elsewhere at the end of the 17th century. The present song appears in The Theater of Music, first book, 1685, and afterwards in Pills, vol. i., 1707, and vol. iii., 1719.

The Country Fair.

Spiritoso.

1. In the
2. In the

1. pleas-ant month of May, When the mer-ry, merry birds be - gan to sing, And the
2. mid - dle of the sport, When the fid - dle went brisk, and glass went round, And the

1. blos - soms fresh and gay Usher'd in the wel - come Spring— When the
2. pret - ty nymphs for court With their merry feet beat the ground, Lit - tle

The words are by Thomas D'Urfey, and appear with the tune in *British Melody; or, the Musical Magazine*, 1739, there headed with a pictorial illustration. The melody, whose composer does not seem to be now known, is also used for a song in the ballad opera, *The Jovial Crew*, 1731. D'Urfey's words have had to be slightly modified to suit modern taste.

1. long cold win-ter's gone, And the bright en-tic-ing moon In the
2. Cu-pid, arm'd un-seen, With a bow and dart stole in, With a

1. ev-'ning sweet-ly shone— When the bonny men and maids tripp'd it on the grass At a
2. con-q'ring air and mien, And emp-tied his bow thro' the nymphs and swains. Ev'ry

1. jol-ly coun-try fair. When the maids in their best ap-pear, We re-
2. shep-herd and his mate Soon felt this pleasing fate, Dame

1. solv'd to be free, with a fid-dle and a she, Ev'ry shep-herd and his lass.
2. Ven-us stood by and watch'd the darts fly, Love reign'd o'er all the plains.

A Song of a Wedding.

Sir John Suckling's famous and dainty "Song of a Wedding" has so many verses that we must refer the reader to other sources for the entire poem, our scheme only allowing us to print as much as will comfortably lie under the music. The present copy of the tune is taken from an early engraved half sheet, but it is in *A Choice Collection of Two Loyal Songs*, 1685, and in all editions of *Pills to purge Melancholy*, from 1699 to 1710, also in *The Convivial Songster*, 1782. The words are said to have been occasioned by the marriage of Lord Broghill with Lady Margaret Howard, and were printed among Sir John Suckling's poems in 1646. A great number of political and other parodies were written in the same metre and to the same tune.

Maids are Grown so Coy of Late.

Words and tune from the fourth volume of *Pills to purge Melancholy*, 1719, where they are headed "The Silly Maids." It has been necessary to slightly alter a few lines of the song.

When I was Bound Apprentice.

1. When I was bound apprentice In
2. As me and my comrade Was
3. As me and my comrade Was
4. Success to ev'ry gentleman That

1. famous Lincolnshire, ... Full well I serv'd my master For
2. setting of a snare, ... 'Twas then we spied the gamekeeper, For
3. setting four or five, ... And taking on 'em up again We
4. lives in Lincolnshire, ... Success to ev'ry poacher That

This now well known song was printed from traditional sources by the late William Chappell in his *National English Airs*, 1838, though Messrs. D'Almaine & Co. had shortly before this issued the air in sheet form with a song by J. R. Planché, named "In the Springtime of the year." During the forties the tune became immensely popular, and was much whistled and sung in the streets and in country alehouses. It is frequently to be met with in collections of airs for the accordion or for the early concertinas. How old the tune itself is would be difficult to definitely fix. Chappell informs us that it was on one occasion sung by several hundred voices before George IV. at Windsor. J. H. Dixon in his *Songs and Ballads of the Peasantry*, speaks of having seen a copy of the words printed at York in date about 1776. Traditional copies of the song, united to another tune, have "Northamptonshire" instead of "Lincolnshire."

Strephon of the Hill.

Poco allegretto.

Dr. ARNE.

1. As once I sat be - neath a shade, Be-
2. He tapp'd my shoul - der, snatch'd a kiss, I
3. Con - sent, O love - ly maid! he cried, Nor
4. Ob - serve the doves on yon - der spray, See
5. We went to church with heart - y glee, O

1. side a purl - ing rill, Who should my sol - i - tude in - vade But
2. could not take it ill; For noth - ing sure is done a - miss By
3. aim thy swain to kill; Con - sent this day to be the bride. Of
4. how they sit and bill; So, sweet, your time will pass a - way With
5. Love, pro - pi - tious still! May ev - 'ry maid be bless'd like me With

1. Stre - phon, but Stre - phon, but Stre - phon of the hill?
2. Stre - phon, by Stre - phon, by Stre - phon of the hill.
3. Stre - phon, of Stre - phon, of Stre - phon of the hill.
4. Stre - phon, with Stre - phon, with Stre - phon of the hill.
5. Stre - phon, with Stre - phon, with Stre - phon of the hill.

f poco rit. e dim.

In the *Universal Magazine* for September, 1754, there is a song, of which the above is probably a parody, named "Polly of the Plain, a new song sung by Mrs. Chambers at Mary-le-Bon Gardens." The song we print above is in many song books (without music), of the latter part of the 18th century, such as *The Humming Bird*, circa 1775; *The Minstrell*; *The Bull-Finch*, 1780, etc. In these works the air is stated to be by Dr. Arne. In Bew's edition of *Vocal Music*, circa 1781, the air is present but without composer's name. The first verse here omitted, commences "Let others Damon's praise rehearse."

Comely Swain, why sitt'st thou so?

JOHN PLAYFORD.

This is a part song by "Honest John Playford," and it appears in his *Musical Companion*, 1672. The original only consists of the first four lines, exclusive of the chorus. John Playford was the greatest, almost the only, publisher of music from 1650 to nearly the beginning of the 18th century. To him we are indebted for a mass of fine English music which, but for his enterprise, would probably have never seen the light. He seems to have won the respect and friendship of the best musicians of his time, and well earned the general epithet "Honest," so lovingly applied to him. He was Clerk to the Temple Church, near where he had his shop, and was succeeded in business by his son Henry. His eldest son John set up as music printer, but he died young. The elder Playford was born in 1623, and died about 1693-4. He was the composer of many psalm tunes and part songs, and author of an excellent *Introduction to the Skill of Music*, which held its place for nearly eighty years.

Colin's Complaint.

The words of this well known song were written by Nicholas Rowe (born 1673; died 1718), who in it is supposed to allude to his own suit with the Countess Dowager of Warwick, who bestowed her hand on Joseph Addison in 1716. Rowe's poem, which consists of seven verses, occurs in *Pills*, vol vi., 1720, set to the air, and from the first appearance of the poem it has been the subject of innumerable parodies. The old air to which the song is adapted has the name, "Grim King of the Ghosts," from the first line of an early ballad first set to it. The tune was used for "Can love be controlled by advice?" in the *Beggars' Opera*, in *The Devil to Pay*, and others. To a song beginning, "On the bank of a river so deep," the air is included in Watts' *Musical Miscellany*, vol. i., 1729. In Hogg's *Jacobite Relics* there is also a song, set to the tune, "By the side of a country kirk wall."

The Spotted Cow.

1. One morn - ing in the month of May, As from my cot I stray'd, . . . Just
2. "No more complain, no long - er mourn, Your cow's not lost, my dear, . . . I
3. And in the grove we spent the day, And thought it pass'd too soon, . . At

1. at the dawn - ing of the day I met a charm - ing maid, . . . Just
2. saw her down in yon - der bourne, Come, love, I'll show you where, . . I
3. night we home - ward bent our way, When bright-ly shone the moon, . At

A folk melody which, united to these words, was once popular in Yorkshire. The present is taken from (by permission) Kidson's *Traditional Tunes,* 1891, and is one of two versions of the melody there printed; it was noted down at Calverley, near Leeds. The words alone are in Fairburn's *Everlasting Songster, circa* 1825, and are also frequently found on ballad sheets.

1. at the dawn-ing of the day I met a charm-ing maid. . . . "Good
2. saw her down in yon-der bourne, Come, love, I'll show you where." . . "I
3. night we home-ward bent our way, When bright-ly shone the moon. . . . If

1. morn-ing fair maid, whith-er go So ear-ly? Tell me now." . . . The
2. must con-fess you're ve-ry kind; I thank you, sir," said she. . . . "You
3. I should cross the flow-'ry vale, Or go to view the plough, . . . She

1. maid re-plied, "Kind sir," she said, "I've lost my spot-ted cow;" . . . . The
2. will be sure her there to find, Come, sweet-heart, go with me; . . . . You
3. comes and calls, "Ye gen-tle swains, I've lost my spot-ted cow;" . . . . She

1. maid re-plied, "Kind sir," she said, "I've lost my spot-ted cow."
2. will be sure her there to find, Come, sweet-heart, go with me."
3. comes and calls, "Ye gen-tle swains, I've lost my spot-ted cow."

All in a Garden Green.

Moderato. / poco rit.

1. All in a garden green Two lo - vers sat at ease, As they could scarce be seen a mong, A-
2. Quoth he, Most love-ly maid, My troth shall aye en - dure, And be thou not, not a - fraid, But

1. mong the leaf - y trees. They long had lov'd y - fere, And no long-er than tru - ly,
2. rest thee still se - cure. My love shall be the same, It nev - er shall de - cay,

1. In that time of the year, In that time of the year Be - twixt May and Ju - ly.
2. But shine without all blame, But shine without all blame Tho' bo - dy turn to clay.

A song and tune of Elizabeth's reign, which occur in a manuscript. The air was employed for other songs, as: "An excellent song of an outcast Lover," to "All in a Garden Green," printed in an old song book with the quaint title, *A Handefull of Pleasant Delites*, 1584. This has been reprinted by Professor Arber, and is an interesting record of popular songs during the Elizabethan era. The air for "All in a Garden Green" is found in the *Fitzwilliam MS.* (*Queen Elizabeth's Virginal book*, as erroneously called), and is printed in editions of Playford's *Dancing Master*, 1st edition, 1650; 2nd, 1652; 3rd, 1665, and several later ones. In Walsh's *Country Dancing Master*, the air is named "The Green Garden," as it also is in Wright's *Country Dances*, vol. i.

The Dairymaid.

1. praise of a dai-ry I pur-pose to sing, But all things in or-der, first God save the King And the
2. first of fair dai-ry-maids, if you'll believe, Was Adam's own wife, or great-grandmo-ther Eve, Who
3. vir-tues of milk there is more to be muster'd, The charming delights both of cheese-cakes and custard. If to

1. Queen, I may say, That ev-'ry May-day Has ma-ny fair dai-ry-maids, all fine and gay. As
2. oft milk'd a cow, as well she knew how, Tho' but-ter was not then as cheap as 'tis now; She
3. wakes you re-sort you can have no sport. Un-less you give custards and cheesecake to for't, And

1. sist me, fair dam-sels, to fin-ish my theme, In-spir-ing my fan-cy with straw-ber-ry-cream.
2. hoard-ed no but-ter nor cheese on her shelves, For but-ter and cheese in those days made themselves.
3. what's the Jack pudding that makes us to laugh, Un-less he hath got a great cust-ard to quaff?

The fine old air has been the vehicle for a great number of ballads, frequently political ones. Its name, "Packington's Pound," or "Pagginton's Pound," is supposed to have arisen from one Sir John Packington (born 1549, di d 1624-5), having made a large pond near his house, which pond encroaching on the public highway, gave ri-e to a satirical ditty sung to this air. The tune is a fine specimen of 16th century English melody, and it fortunately did not share the oblivion its original ballad words have suffered. The melody is in the *Fitzwilliam Virginal book ;* in *A New Book of Tablature,* published by Wm. Barley in 1501; in Playford's *Select Ayres,* 16 9, and many other later publications. Gay used it for a song in the *Beggars' O era.* The present ballad, "The Dairymaid," is found with the music in Playford's *Musical Companion,* part second, 1687, and there are a great number of songs printed with the air in the several volumes of *Pills,* 1707 to 1719, etc.

Sweet are the Charms of Her I Love.

RICHARD LEVERIDGE.

The air is by Richard Leveridge, and the words by a writer named Barton Booth. With the song, it is printed in Watts' *Musical Miscellany*, vol. ii., 1729; Bickham's *Musical Entertainer*, vol. i., 1737; *British Melody*, 1739, folio; Ritson's *English Songs*, 1783, and the tune was used for songs in the ballad operas: *Fashionable Lady* and *Village Opera*. Leveridge, one of our finest song composers, was a bass singer who retained his voice and sang in public for many years. He was born in 1670, and died in 1758. A collection of Leveridge's songs, engraved by Thomas Cross, on single folio leaves, was published about 1695; it is now very rare. A better known work, in two volumes, beautifully engraved, is dated 1727.

1 Soft as the down . . . . of tur - tle . . . dove,
2 Con - stant as glid - - ing wa - ters . . . roll.

1. Gen - tle as wind which ze - - - phyr blows, Re -
2. Whose swell - ing tides o - bey . . . . . . the moon, From

1. fresh ing . as . . . . . de scend ing rains, To
2. ev 'ry . . oth - - er char mer free, My

1. sun burnt climes . . and thirst y plains.
2. life . . . and love . . . . shall fol - low thee.

There were Three Travellers.

A copy of the ballad is in the Bagford collection entitled, "The Jovial Companions; or, the Merry Travellers who paid their shot wherever they came without ever a stiver of money. To an excellent North Country tune." An early parody of this exists as "A new ditty to an old tune of 'Three Travellers,'" among the *Harleian MSS.*, and the air and song are in *Pills*, vol. vi., 1720. A somewhat similar song is found on ballad sheets under the name, "The Adventures of a Penny." This, with a tune, exists tradition-ally in Yorkshire.

Barbara Allen's Cruelty.

1. In Scar - let town, where I was born, There was a fair maid
2. All in the mer - ry month of May, When green buds they were
3. So slow - ly, slow - ly she came up, And slow - ly she came
4. When he was dead and laid in grave, Her heart was struck with
5. Fare - well, she said, ye vir - gins all, And shun the fault I

1. dwell - ing. Made ev - 'ry youth cry, Well - a - day! Her
2. swell - ing, Young Jem - my Grove on his death - bed lay For
3. nigh him, And all she said, when there she came, Young
4. sor - row: Oh, mo - ther, mo - ther, make my bed, For
5. fell in; Hence-forth take warn - ing by the fall Of

1. name was Bar b'ra Al - len.
2. love of Bar b'ra Al - len.
3. man, I think you're dy - ing.
4. I shall die to - mor - row!
5. cru - el Bar b'ra Al - len.

Forty or fifty years ago there were few more popular songs in country districts than "Barbara Allen." A great number of different traditional melodies to the ballad have been recovered, some of which will be found printed in *Traditional Tunes: a collection of ballad a ra ch 'ty obtained in Yorkshire and the South of Scotland, by Frank Kidson*, 1891. The set of the tune given above is one taken down by Dr. Rimbault from north country singing, and first printed in his *Musical Illustrations of Percy's Reliques*, 1850. The ballad itself is very old, and traditional versions vary considerably in length and wording. The Scottish copy, which has quite a different tune of its own, commences, "It was in and about the Martinmas time." From lack of space we have here to abbreviate the English version; it can be seen in full in Percy's *Reliques*, and most ballad books.

Robin Hood and Little John.

For note to this song see Appendix.

While O'erhead the Storm is Howling.

Air—"Of all the Comforts I Miscarried."

Con energia.

mf

1. While o'er - head the storm is howl - ing, Think we sai - lors are a - fraid?
2. What if some - times boat - swains blus - ter? What if pur - sers filch our grog?
3. When to Nan - cy back re - turn - ing, An - chor'd then on Eng - lish ground,

1. What if skies with clouds are scowl - ing, Sure - ly sail - ing is our trade?
2. Does that keep us from a mus - ter For to thrash the Span - ish dog?
3. Mon - ey in our pock - ets burn - ing, How we fling the shin - ers round!

The original air for this song is found in *Pills to purge Melancholy*, vol. ii., 1719, p. 137, under the title, "The Curtain Lecture: a New Song"; it is in the form of a dialogue, and begins "Of all the comforts I miscarried." With the first line as title it is used as an air for songs in the ballad operas, *The Devil to pay*, and *Momus turned Fabulist*. With the names, "Of all the Comforts; or, Whitechapel Mount," the melody is given in the *Dancing Master*, vol. ii., 1719. As the original song is totally unfit for present day singing, modern words have been written for the air.

Spring Song.

1. Thou calm - ray'd Spring, whose bloom - ing face Leads
2. To thee their snow - y blos - soms owe Each

1. on the year re new'd, Thou or - na - ment, thou
2. fu - ture fruit - ful tree, The birds that charm their

The song and air are taken from a folio publication entitled, *A Collection of English Songs sung by Miss Falkner at Marybon-Gardens, Mr. Beard, Mr. Lowe, Mrs. Arne at Ranelagh and Vauxhall Gardens, composed by the most eminent masters,* with no printer's name or date, but prior to 1763. The same words were, at a later period (circa 1780-90), set to music by Edward Light in a little volume of guitar music which he issued about that time.

Chevy Chase.

Air—"In Pescod Time."

1. God pros - per long our
2. The chief - est harts in
3. With fif - teen hun - dred
4. At last these two stout

1. no ble King. Our lives and safe - ties all, . . A
2. Che - vy Chase, To kill and bear a - way, . . The
3. bow - men bold, All cho - sen men of might, . . Who
4. earls did meet, Like cap - tains of great might, ... Like

"Chevy Chase" is above all others the ballad of the English people. During and before the 18th century it must have been much sung and recited among country people. Writers like Addison and Goldsmith have referred to it in terms of warm eulogy and affection. There is an earlier ballad of "Chevy Chase," but the better known one commencing, "God prosper long our noble King" may be referred back to the reign of Charles II., if not before. A ballad so much sung was naturally set to many different airs. One was "In Pescod Time," another, "Flying Fame," and perhaps the most frequently of all, "Rogero." The air we have used is "In Pescod Time," a ballad tune to be found in several old MSS. of Queen Elizabeth's reign, and in Anthony Holborne's *Cithara Schoole*, 1597, a rare, if not unique work which was one of the treasures of the old Sacred Harmonic Society's Library. The tune must not be confounded with "Gathering Pescods." The above is merely a selection of verses from the lengthy ballad.

1. woe - ful hunt - ing once there did In Che - vy Chase be -
2. tid - ings to Earl Doug - las came In Scot - land where he
3. know full well in time of need To aim their shafts a -
4. li - ons moved, they laid on loud, And made a cru - el

1. fall; . . To drive the deer with hound and horn Earl
2. lay, . . Who sent Earl Per - cy pres - ent word He
3. right; . . . . The hounds ran swift - ly through the wood, The
4. fight; . . . . . God save the king, and bless the land, In

1. Per - cy took his way; The wife may rue that's
2. would pre - vent his sport, The Eng lish earl not
3. nim - ble deer to take, And with their cries the
4. plen - ty, joy and peace, . And grant hence - forth that

1. left for - lorn[1] The hunt ing of that day. . .
2. fear ing this Did to the woods re - sort. . . .
3. hills and dales An ech o shrill did make. . . . . .
4. foul de - bate Twixt no ble - men may cease. . . . . .

[1] In the original ballad the line stands, "The child may rue that is unborn."

Black Sloven.

Hunting Song.

1. Last Val - en - tine's Day, when bright Phœ - bus shone clear   I
2. "Hal - lo, in - to cov - ert!" old An - tho - ny cries;   No
3. Our hounds and our hor - ses were al - ways as good   As
4. The day's sport being o - ver, the horns we will sound, To

1. had not been hunt - ing for more than a year. Tal - ly ho, tal - ly ho, tal - ly
2. soon - er he spoke, but the fox, sir, he spies. Tal - ly ho, tal - ly ho, tal - ly
3. ev - er broke cov - ert or dash'd thro' the wood. Tal - ly ho, tal - ly ho, tal - ly
4. jol - ly fox - hunt - ers let ech - oes re - sound. Tal - ly ho, tal - ly ho, tal - ly

During the 18th century the florid hunting song was strongly in evidence. It always contained classic allusions to Diana or Aurora, and finished up with complicated musical passages devoted to the imitation of the hunting horn, and fitted to numberless "tally ho's." Kelly in his *Reminiscences*, vol. i., p. 222, gives an amusing account of an English lady singer at Vienna, startling the Emperor by the shrieking out of "Tally ho!" in such a song as above alluded to, the Emperor being unable to comprehend the meaning of the word. "Black Sloven" is one of the best of these 18th century hunting lyrics. It was engraved as a half sheet song about 1775, and appears in Fielding's *Vocal Enchantress*, in 1783.

1. ho, tal - ly ho! I mount-ed Black Slov-en, o'er the road made him bound, For I
2. ho, tal - ly ho! This be - ing the sig - nal, he . . then crack'd his whip— "Tal-ly
3. ho, tal - ly ho! Old Rey - nard runs hard, but must . cer - tain - ly die, "Have
4. ho, tal - ly ho! So fill up your glass-es and . . cheer - ful - ly drink To the

1. heard the hounds chal lenge and horns sweet - ly sound,—Tal - ly ho, tal - ly ho, tal - ly
2. ho!" was the word, and a - way we did leap, – Tal - ly ho, tal - ly ho, tal - ly
2. at you, old To - ny," Dick Daw - son did cry,— Tal - ly ho, tal - ly ho, tal - ly
4. hon - est true sportsmen who nev - er will shrink,—Tal - ly ho, tal - ly ho, tal - ly

cres.

1. ho, tal - ly ho, tal - ly ho, tal - ly ho, tal - ly ho: .
2. ho, tal - ly ho, tal - ly ho, tal - ly ho, tal - ly ho: . .
3. ho, tal ly ho, tal - ly ho, tal - ly ho, tal - ly ho! . .
4. ho, tal - ly ho, tal - ly ho, tal - ly ho, tal - ly ho! . .

Talk not so much to me of Love.

Robin Hood and the Bishop of Hereford.

1. O some they do talk of bold Rob - in Hood, And
2. Rob - in Hood dress'd him - self in shep - herd's at - tire, With
3. "You are brave fel - lows all," the Bish - op he said, "The
4. Then Lit - tle John took the Bish - op's cloak, And
5. Rob - in Hood took the Bish - op by the hand, And

1. some of the ba - rons bold; But I'll tell you of the Bish - op of
2. six of his men al - so; When the Bish - op of Her - e - ford
3. King of your doings shall know; And make ye there - fore haste, and
4. spread it up - on the ground; And from the Bish - op's
5. caus - ed the horn to play; And he made the old Bish - op to

1. Her - e - ford, How they robb'd him of all his gold.
2. he pass - ed by, They a - bout the fire did go.
3. come with me, For be - fore the King you shall go."
4. port - man - teau He took three hun - dred pound.
5. dance in his boots, And glad he could so get a - way.

This air, with a ballad of twenty-one verses attached, is in a volume of half-sheet songs in the British Museum, press mark, G 311. The sheet was engraved and published by Thomas Straight about 1780, but it is evidently from a much earlier copy. Ritson in his Robin Hood Ballads gives two different ones of the adventures of the bishop with Robin Hood's men; one of these, similar to the one on the music sheet, is here in part adopted.

Dulce Domum.

Andante molto maestoso.   *mf*

1. Sing a
2. Lo! the
3. See, the
4. Oh! what
5. Greet our

f e poco rit.   *mf*

cres.

1.	sweet	mel - o - dious	meas - ure,	Walt	en -
2.	joy	ful hour ad	van - ces,	Hap -	py
3.	year	the mea dow	smil - ing,	Let	us
4.	rap -	ture! oh! what	bliss - es,	When	we
5.	house -	hold gods with	sing - ing,	Lend,	O

cres.

1.	chant - ing lays a - round;	Home's a	theme re - plete	with
2.	sea - son of de - light!	Fes - tal	songs and fes -	tal
3.	then a smile dis - play!	Ru - ral	sports our pain	be -
4.	gain the love - ly gate!	Moth - er's	arms and moth -	er's
5.	"Morn - ing Star," thy ray!	Why should	light, so slow -	ly

Attributed, so far as the melody is concerned, to John Reading, who was organist at Winchester College and Cathedral from 1681 to probably the date of his death, 1695. Reading was also composer of an Election Grace. "Dulce Domum," sung in Latin, has been from time immemorial the breaking-up song of the College at the Whitsun holidays, and from there has spread to similar institutions. Many translations of the old Latin words have been made, the one we adopt being the most popular; another very similar is in *The Gentleman's Magazine* for 1796. The story goes that the song was composed by a student named Turner, who, while his fellow scholars went home at a holiday time, was chained to a tree for some misdemeanour, and that he died in captivity. On the evening preceding the holidays, the scholars with the choir and organist, used to march round this tree singing "Dulce Domum." A writer in *Notes and Queries*, in 1854, stated that the tree then was standing. It is evident that the pretty legend is scarcely likely to be correct. The tune, words, and sundry other items were published in *Harmonia Wykhamica*, 1811 (and in the earlier edition). The song and tune are also in Imle's *English Songs*, and other collections. The present must not be confounded with another, "Dulce Domum," a song written by Braham in the beginning of the 19th century.

1. pleas - ure!   Home!   a   grate - ful   theme   ro -
2. dan - ces   All   our   to - dious   toil   re -
3. guil - ing,   Ru - ral   pas - times   call   a -
4. kiss - es   There   our   bless'd ar - ri - val
5. spring - ing,   All   our   prom - ised   joys   do -

1. sound.
2. quite.
3. way.   Home, sweet home! an am - ple treas - ure; Home, with
4. wait.
5. lay.

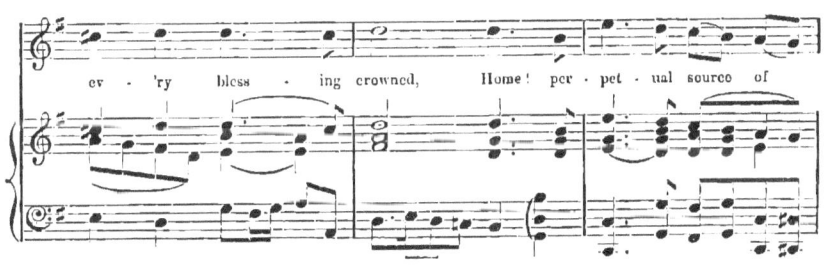

ev - 'ry bless - ing crowned, Home! per - pet - ual source of

pleas - ure! Home! a no - ble strain re - sound!

K

Come, here's to Robin Hood.

1. Come, here's to Rob·in Hood Of the mer·ry green·wood, And a
2. Bold Rob·in oft gave chase To the monks with sul·len face, Till he
3. When·e'er he fill'd his can, He would drink to Ma·ri·an To that

1. bless·ing on his name; Tho' with shaft and bow He de·
2. made them drop their gear; And their hearts would quake, And their
3. kind and love·ly maid; And he vow'd her smile Would the

Messrs. Chappell & Co. kindly give permission to use the above excellent words written by Mr. John Oxenford. They are fitted to an early dance air which, appearing among the *New tunes for the treble Violin*, at the end of the 1665 edition of Playford's *Dancing Master*, is there named "The Lady Frances Neville's Delight." The air is also in the later editions of these *New Dances* ("Apollo's Banquet"), and in *Musick's Delight on the Cithren*, 1666. The melody is so vocal that it can scarcely have been a dance tune pure and simple, but the original words up to the present remain undiscovered. John Oxenford wrote another song to the air, "Hope the Hermit," and while this had a large degree of popularity, yet it is by no means so suited to the bold melody as his later Robin Hood song.

f

1. part - ed long a - go, Un - per - ish - ing shall be his fame. Like a
2. lust - y limbs would shake, If gal - lant Rob - in Hood was near. Like that
3. worst of cares be - guile, While tip - pling in the green - wood shade. As tho'

1. no - ble soul He doat-ed on his bowl, And a gob - let of the best love we. So tho'
2. yeo - man brave, We hate a cant-ing knave As the ver - y worst of com - pa - nie. So tho'
3. bowl we pass, Each quaff to his lass, Vowing none to be so fair as she. So tho'

ff Chorus.

1. bold Rob-in's gone, Still his heart lives on, And we drink to him with three times three.
2. bold Rob-in's gone, Still his heart lives on, And we drink to him with three times three. So tho'
3. bold Rob-in's gone, Still his heart lives on, And we drink to him with three times three.

bold Rob-in's gone, Still his heart lives on, And we drink to him with three times three.

The Leather Bottél.

1. When I sur-vey the world a-round, The
2. Now what do you say to these cans of wood? Oh
3. At morn the hay-mak-ers sit them down, To
4. And when the bot-tle at last grows old, And

1. won - drous things that do a - bouud, Tho ships that on the
2. no, in faith, they can - not be good, For if the bear - er
3. drink from bot - tles of ale nut - hrown; In sum - mer, too, when
4. will good li - quor no lon - ger hold, Out of the sides you

The words are from a black letter ballad sheet, printed in the 17th century, copies of which are among the Roxburghe and other collections of broadsides. The now popular tune was originally published by William Chappell in his *National English Airs*, 1838, and again twenty years later in his *Popular Music*; it had been noted down as a traditional ballad air. That this ballad of the "Leather Bottél" was traditional in Yorkshire about a hundred years ago the writer of the present note can vouch for, as it was a favourite song of his grandfather about the years 1800-10. There were other traditional ballads in praise of the leather bottle (see Dixon's *Ballads and Songs of the Peasantry of England*, p. 203, and *English County Songs*, p. 66, "The good old leathern bottle"). The song similar to the one on the broadside is given in the 1707 and the 1719 editions of *Pills to purge Melancholy*, with an air attached which is reproduced in the Appendix. Following it, to the same tune, is another in praise of the black Jack, commencing:—

"'Tis a pitiful thing that now-a-days, sirs,
Our poets turn Leathern bottle praisers,
But if a Leathern theme they did lack,
They might better have chosen the bonny black Jack."

It need scarcely be noted that a leather bottle for the purpose of carrying spirits on a journey was in use till quite recent times. The black Jack was a black leather jug of varied form for alehouse use, frequently mounted in pewter or silver.

1. sea do swim, To keep out foes that none come in; Well
2. fall by the way, Why, on the ground your li - quor doth lay! But
3. wea - ther is warm, A good full drink will do them no harm; Then
4. make a clout To mend your shoes when they're worn out; Or

1. let them all say what they can, 'Twas for one end— the
2. had it been in a leath - er bot - tél, Al - though he had fall'n, all
3. lads and las - ses be - gin to tat - tle, What would they be with -
4. take and hang it up - on a pin, 'Twill serve to put nails and

poco cres.

1. use of man.
2. had been well.
3. out this bot - tle.
4. odd things in.
So I wish him joy, wher - e'er he dwell, That

first found out the leath - - - - - er bot - tél. . . .

f

The Dusky Night rides down the Sky.

One of our finest hunting songs, the words of which were written by Henry Fielding for a ballad opera named *Don Quixote in England*, acted at the Haymarket in 1733, and originally set to the old air, "There was a jovial beggar," printed in the present volume. The above air to "The Dusky Night" first became associated with the words about 1760-70, and appeared with them on half sheets. One of these early copies shows that the song was introduced by Mr. Farrell in *The Beggars' Opera*. As a "New Favourite Hunting Song," the song and the present air are printed in John Arnold's *Essex Harmony*, vol. ii., 2nd edition, 1777; in Hew's *Vocal Music*, circa 1781; Fielding's *Vocal Enchantress*, 1783; *The Musical Miscellany*, Perth, 1786, and many later song books. The air as a country dance is in Skillern's *Dances* for 17.0 ; Longman and Broderip's *Country Dances*, vol. ii., and in numerous violin and flute tutors of the period. In the *Musical Miscellany*, printed at Perth in 1786, a song entitled "Father Paul" is set to the air, commencing "While grave divines preach up dull rules." In the Rev. James Plumptre's *Collection of Songs*, Cambridge, 1805, a harvest home, and a gleaning song are set to the tune.

The Blossom of the Year.

Air—"Gathering Peascods."

Moderato.

1. How plea - sant is it in the blos - som of the year To
2. And as I wan - der in the blos - som of the year, By

1. stray and find a nook, When nought doth fill the hol - low
2. crys - tal wa - ters flow, Flow'rs sweet to gaze on as the

The old air, "Gathering Peascods," appears in all editions of the *Dancing Master* from 1650 to 1690. The first two bars are practically the same as "All in a garden green," given in the present volume. As nothing seems to have been known about the original words (not unlikely the name is but a fanciful dance tune title), Mr. Chappell got J. A. Wade the musician to write new verses for it. These are used here, and Chappell's version of the air employed, although it must be pointed out that he has by no means closely followed Playford's setting, and there does not appear to be any other old printed copy extant. For comparison the *Dancing Master* tune is given in the Appendix.

1. of the list - 'ning ear, Ex - cept the mur-m'ring brook; Or
2. song of birds to hear, Spring up wher - e'er I go! The

cres.

1. hind in neigh b'ring grove, That in sol - i - tude doth love To
2. vi - o - let a - grees With the hon - ey - suck - le trees, To

1. breathe his lone - ly hymn! Lost in their min gled song, I
2. shed their balms a - round! Thus from the bus y throng, I

poco rit.

1. care - less roam a - long, From morn to twi - light dim.
2. care - less roam a - long, 'Mid per - fume and sweet sound.

Shepherd, saw thou not?

1. Shepherd, saw thou not my fair, love-ly Phy-lis, Walk-ing on you mountain, or in yon-der plain?
2. Shepherd, I have seen thy fair, love-ly Phy-lis, Where her flocks are feeding by the riv-er-side.
3. Thus I do des-pair, love her I shall nev-er; If she be so coy, lost is all my love.

1. She is gone this way to Di-an-ac's fountain, And hath left me wounded with her high dis-dain.
2. Ah, I much ad-mire, she is fair ex-ceed-ing; In sur-pass-ing beau-ty, should surpass in pride.
3. But she is so fair, I will love her ev-er! All my pain is joy, which for her I prove.

Another English song and melody appearing in Scottish manuscripts and printed works. As in the case of Scottish airs first being found in English books the structure of the tune alone must decide its nationality. The air is a version of the old English melody, "Crimson Velvet." As "Shepherd, saw thou not?" it is in the *Skene MS.* and in the *Straloch lute book*, which has the date 1627. G. F. Graham fortunately made a copy of a part of this manuscript, the original being now lost, and Graham's first transcript is now among the valuable musical treasures possessed by Mr. T. W. Taphouse of Oxford. Graham's second copy is in the Advocates' Library. The words and air of "Shepherd, saw thou not?" are in Forbes' *Cantus*, 1662, 1666, and 1682.

1. Ay, she is so fair and with-out com-pare, Sor - row comes to sit with me.
2. But, a-lace! I find they are all un - kind, Beau - ty knows her pow'r too well;
3. If I should her love, and she should de - ny, Hea - vy heart with me would break.

1. Love is full of fear, love is full of care; Love with-out this can - not be.
2. While they list they love, when they please they move; Thus they turn their heart to hell.
3. Tho' a-gainst my will, tongue, thou must be still, For she will not hear thee speak.

1. Thus my pas-sions pain me, and my love hath slain me, Gen-tle shepherd, play a - part;
2. Where their fair eyes gleaming, like to Cu-pid's dancing, Rules well for to de-ceive us.
3. Then with kiss-es move her, they shall show I love her; Love-ly love, be thou my guide.

poco rit.

1. Pray to Cu-pid's mother, for I know no oth - er That can ease me of my smart.
2. With vain hopes de-lud-ing, still their praise con-cluding, Thus they love, thus they leave us.
3. But I'll sore complain me, she will still dis-dain me, Beau-ty is so full of pride.

Good-morrow, Gossip Joan.

The song, "Good-morrow, gossip Joan,' under the title, "The Woman's Complaint to her Neighbour," is in *Pills*, vol. vi., 1720, and it is in the present volume abbreviated from this rather long version. In *The Merry Musician; or, a Cure for the Spleen*, vol. ii., *circa* 1728, a song called "Happy Dick" is placed with the melody, and this again occurs in Watt's *Musical Miscellany*, vol. iv., 1730; later in the century, "Happy Dick" completely superseded "Gossip Joan." In *The Beggars' Opera*, the sprightly duet between Polly and Lucy, "Why, how now, Madam Flirt?" was set to the melody, which was also employed in other ballad operas of the period.

Fair Hebe.

Lyrics (from the score):

1. Fair He-be I left with a cau-tious de-sign, To es-cape from her charms, and to drown them in wine; I tried it, but found when I came to de-part, The wine in my head, but love still in my heart.

2. I re-pair'd then to Reas-on, in-treat-ed her aid, Who paus'd on my case, and each cir-cumstance weigh'd, Then grave-ly pro-nounc'd in re-turn to my pray'r, That He-be was fair-est of all that was fair.

3. That's a truth, re-plied I, I've no need to be taught, I came for your coun-sel to find out a fault. If that's all, quoth Reason, re-turn as you came, To find fault with He-be would for-feit my name.

Chappell placed these clever old words to a traditional tune belonging to the ballad, "Polly Oliver's Ramble," but considering that one of the original tunes to "Fair Hebe" is so excellent, to make such a change seemed unnecessary. There are two distinct old melodies to the song, one appearing in the June supplement to the *Universal Magazine* for 1752 as "Fair Hebe, a new song sung by Mr. Beard at Ranelagh Gardens." This is also in the *Gentleman's Magazine* for August, 1752, *Clio and Euterpe*, vol. i., 1758, and in other places. The air gradually gave place to another and a finer one, reproduced above, which has every appearance of being the composition of Dr. Arne or of his son. This later melody was printed in Horsfield's *Vocal Music*, vol. i., *circa* 1770-72, as well as in a numerous array of flute, harpsichord, and violin tutors published by the Thompsons, Dale, Longman, and other music publishers of the period. In Dalrymple's *Collection of English Songs*, 1796, and elsewhere, the verses are attributed to Lord Cantalupe.

Fairest Isle.

John Dryden wrote the words in honour of England for the opera, *King Arthur; or, the British Worthy,* where the song is sung by the character Venus.   Purcell wrote the music of the opera, which was first produced in 1691, and the air is among this great musician's finest compositions.   In 1770, *King Arthur* was again revived, with alterations, omissions, and additions by Dr. Arne, who, however, wisely retained "Fairest Isle."   Mrs. Scot sang it at this representation.   The song with the music is printed in the first volume of Purcell's *Orpheus Britannicus,* 1695.

1. choose . . her dwell - ing, And . for - sake . . her Cy - prian groves.
2. kind . . dis - dain - ing, Shall . be all . . the pains . . you prove.

1. Cu - pid from his fav - 'rite na - tion, Care . and en vy
2. Ev - 'ry swain shall pay his du - ty, Grate ful ev 'ry

1. will . . . . re move Jea - lous - ie, that poi sons
2. nymph . . . shall prove; And as these ex - cel . . . . in

cres.   *f rit.*

1. pas sion, And . . des - pair . . that dies . for . . love.
2. beau ty, Those . shall be . . . re - nown'd . for . love.

cres.   *f rit.*

O Rare Turpin.

Moderato e con energia.

1. On
2. Says
3. As
4. This

1. Hounslow Heath as I rode o'er I spied a law-yer rid-ing before, "Kind
2. Tur-pin, "He'd ne'er find me out, I've hid my mon-ey in my boot;" The
3. they rode by the pow-der mill Tur-pin com-mands him to stand still, Said
4. caus'd the law-yer much to fret, To think he was so fair-ly hit; And

1. sir," said I, "Aren't you a-fraid Of Tur-pin, that mis-chiev-ous blade?"
2. law-yer says, "There's none can find, My gold is stitch'd in my cape be-hind."
3. he, "Your cape I must cut off, My mare she wants a sad-dle cloth."
4. Tur-pin robb'd him of his store, Be-cause he knew he'd lie for more.

1. O rare Tur-pin he-ro, O rare Tur-pin, O!
2. O rare Tur-pin he-ro, O rare Tur-pin, O!
3. O rare Tur-pin he-ro, O rare Tur-pin, O!
4. O rare Tur-pin he-ro, O rare Tur-pin, O!

William Chappell noted this traditional ballad air with the song, from the singing of Charles Sloman in 1840, and it was published in *Popular Music of the olden time*. The ballad occurs on broadsides, and at least two different traditional tunes are sung to the song in Yorkshire. I have copies of these, but they are quite different from the Sloman version which is here given. Readers of *Pickwick* will remember how Sam Weller sang a similar ballad of Dick Turpin, which by the way Dickens took from *Galeties and Gravities*, vol. ii., 1825, a work "by one of the authors of the *Rejected Addresses.*" The above words are merely a selection from the lengthy ballad.

The Knight and Shepherd's Daughter.

1. was a shep-herd's daugh-ter Came tripping on the waye; And
2. mor-rowe to you, beauteous maide, These words pro-nounc-ed hee; O
3. sett her on a milk-white steede, Him-self up-on a graye; He
4. when he came un-to the place Where marriage rites were done, She
5. mar-rye me or not, Sir knight, Your pleasure shall be free; If you

1. there by chance a knighte shee mett, Which caus-ed her to stay.
2. I shall dye this daye, he sayd, If thou'lt not mar-ry me.
3. hung a bu-gle round his necke, And see they rode a-way.
4. proved her-self a duke's daughter, And hee but a squire's sonne.
5. make me la-dye of one good town, I'll make you lord of three.

The long ballad has had here to be abbreviated. It is old, and found on black letter broadsides in the Roxburgh and other collections of broadsides. It is printed in Percy's *Reliques*, and in most other ballad books. There are Scottish versions under the title, "Earl Richards." Traditional variants have also recently been noted down, one of which with a Yorkshire tune is printed in Kidson's *Traditional Tunes*, 1891. The present air is in Playford's *Dancing Master*, 1650, and in later editions under the title, "The Shepherd's Daughter." There is also another name for the air by which it was known late in the 17th, and early in the 18th centuries.

To Arms, Jolly Grenadiers.

Moderato e con energia.

1. To arms, to arms, to arms, my jol - ly gren - a - diers!
2. March on, march on, to where the thun-d'ring can - on roar! The
3. See how, see how, see how they fly be - fore . . us! See

1. Hark how the drums do . . roll . . it a - long! To horse, to horse, to
2. bat - tle is be - gun, my boys, as you may plainly see; Stand firm, be bold, and
3. how they are scat - ter'd all o - ver the plain. Pur - sue! pur - sue! our

Taken from Dr. Kitchiner's collection of *Loyal and National Songs of England*, where it has probably in turn been transcribed from a music sheet of the 18th century. The tune is one of the many 18th century Marches, Quicksteps, etc., named after the popular Marquis of Granby. It will be found in several of the old flute and violin tutors under the title, "The Marquis of Granby's March."

1. horse, with val - iant good . . cheer; We'll face the haugh - ty foe, be they
2. it shall soon be o'er,— We shall soon . . gain the field, boys, of
3. coun - try will a - dore . . us, In tri - umph and in peace, boys, when

1. ev - er so strong. Let not your cour-age fail you, be val - iant, stout and bold, And
2. our en - e - my. The squad - rons ap - pear, boys, and if they dare but stand, Boys,
3. we re-turn a - gain. Then lau - rels let your glo - ry crown and for your ac-tions bold, The

CHORUS.

1. it shall soon a - vail . you, my gallant hearts of gold.
2. nev-er fear, but mind . . well the word of command. } Hur-rah ! my val - iant coun-try-men, a -
3. hills shall ech-o all a round, my gallant hearts of gold.

gain I say, Hur-rah! 'Tis brave-ly done, the day is won, Hur-rah! hur-rah! hur-rah!

Black-Ey'd Susan.

For note to this song see Appendix.

Richard of Taunton Dean.

Allegro moderato.

1. Last New-year's Day as I've heard say, Young Richard he mounted his dap-pled grey, And he
2. Miss Jean she came with-out de-lay To hear what Dicky had got to say, I sup-
3. Sup-pose that I would be your bride, Pray, how would you for me provide? For
4. Why, I can plow and I can sow, And some-times to the mar-ket go With
5. Nine-pence a day will nev-er do, For I must have silks, and sat-ins too, Nine-
6. Dick's com-pliments did so delight, They made the fam-il-y laugh out-right, Young

1. trotted a-long to Taun-ton Dean, To court the par-son's daughter Jean. ⎫
2. pose you know me, Mis-tress Jean, I'm hon-est Richard of Taunton Dean. ⎪
3. I can nei-ther sew nor spin, Pray, what will your day's work bring you in? ⎬ Singing
4. gaf-ter John-son's straw or hay, And earn my nine-pence ev-'ry day. ⎪
5. pence a day won't buy us meat; Ad-zooks, says Dick, I've a sack of wheat. ⎪
6. Richard took huff, no more would say, He kick'd up old Dobbin and rode a-way. ⎭

dumble dum dear-y, dumble dum dear-y, dumble dum dear-y, dumble dum dee.

Popularly known as "Dumble Dum Deary," from the first line of the chorus. The tune has served as the vehicle for many a political or satirical effusion, all having similar nonsensical verses as a burden. The present song in different forms has been united to the melody for probably a hundred years. Sometimes it is "Richard of Dalton Dale," and in an Irish case, "Dicky of Ballyman" (see J. H. Dixon's *Ballads and Songs of the Peasantry*). There is also a Yorkshire traditional version beginning:—

"Last Michaelmas day, a year or more,
I was where I ne'er was before;
It was in love slap up to the chin,
And you're the beauty that's tumbled me in."

The tune has been frequently printed, especially during the forties, by Duncombe and other music publishers of similar type. The song is abbreviated here for lack of space.

The Sun from the East.

One of the many hunting songs current during the 18th century. These in general (though in many cases fine specimens of English melody), were of very extended compass and full of florid graces, frequently having a recitative prefixed. The songs must have even taxed the healthy lungs of the sturdy fox and hare hunting squires of the period. Now-a-days it is pretty certain that anything like an adequate rendering of most of them would be beyond the powers of the ordinary amateur. The specimens of this kind of English song which we have selected have been chosen with the above fact before us. "The Sun from the East" was sung in the opera, Apollo and Daphne, acted in 1734, and is from an early engraved half sheet. Other copies of the song and air are in Dale's English Songs, Fielding's Vocal Enchantress, 1783.

Since from my Dear Astrea's Sight.

HENRY PURCELL.

By Henry Purcell, and sung in *The Prophetess; or, the History of Dioclesian,* produced in 1690. The song was reprinted in the first volume of *The Orpheus Britannicus,* 1698.

soul has nev-er, never, nev-er, has nev-er, never, never known de-

light, Un-less it were to mourn, to

mourn, un-less, un-less it were to mourn. But

oh! a-las, a-las, With weep-ing eyes, and

bleed ing, bleed ing heart, I lie, Thinking on

her, on her, Whose ab sence 'tis that makes me wish to

die, die, die, die, makes me,

makes me wish to die, die, die.

Queen Eleanor's Confession.

Moderato.

1. Queen El-ean-or was a sick wo-man, And a-fraid that she should
2. Then when they came be-fore the queen, They fell on their bend-ed
3. The first vile thing that e'er I did, To you I'll not do-
4. The next vile thing that e'er I did, To you I now will
5. The king pulled off his fri-ar's coat, And ap-pear-ed all in

1. die, And she sent for two fri-ars out of France, To
2. knee; A boon! a boon! our gra-cious queen, That you
3. ny, I made a box of poi-son strong, To
4. tell, I poi-son-ed fair Ros-a-mond, Who in
5. red, She shrieked and cried, and wrung her hands, And

1. speak with her speed-i-ly.
2. sent so has-ti-ly.
3. poi-son King Hen-ry.
4. Wood-stock bow'r did dwell.
5. said she was be-tray'd.

The very beautiful ballad air was first printed in the Appendix to Motherwell's *Minstrelsy*, 1827, under the title, "Earl Marshall," the name for a Scottish version of the ballad. It is said by Rimbault to have been noted down by Andrew Blaikie, of Paisley, a musical antiquary. Rimbault also mentions that he himself has frequently heard the tune in Derbyshire and Staffordshire. The full ballad will be found in Percy's *Reliques*. We can but give a brief snatch of it here.

The Collier's Rant.

Allegro.

1. As me and my mar - row was gan - ning to wark, We
2. As me and my mar - row was put - ting the tram, The
3. Oh, mar - row! oh, mar - row! oh, what dost thou think? I've

1. met with the dev - il, it was in the dark. I up with my pick, it
2. lowe it went out and my mar - row went wrang. Oh, you would have laugh'd had
3. bro - ken my bot - tle, and spill'd all my drink! I lost all my shin - splints a -

From Topliff's *Selection of the most popular Melodies of the Tyne and Wear*, circa 1812-1815. It is also in Sir Cuthbert Sharp's *Bishoprick Garland*, and the words alone in Ritson's *Northumberland Garland; or, Newcastle Nightingale*, 1793, as well as in other places. The song itself is purely a Northumbrian pitman's ditty, and it has evolved from the pit itself. The technical allusions will be easily understood even by those not conversant with the workings of a north country colliery.

The Woodcutter.

1. health un-to the jol-ly wood-cut-ter, That lives at home at ease, He
2. health un-to our mas - ter, The found - er of the feast; I

1. takes his work a slight in hand, And he leaves it when he please; He
2. wish him well with all my heart, That his soul in heav'n may rest: That

Taken from the folio collection of *Old English Songs as now sung by the peasantry of the weald of Surrey and Sussex,* made by the Rev. John Broadwood. The air is a major set of the "Miller of the Dee" (see present volume), and, with the above words, has been sung as a harvest home song in the southern counties for a long time.

1. takes the withe and he winds it, And he lays it on the ground, . . A -
2. all his works may pros per, What - ev - er he takes in hand ; . . . For

f CHORUS.

1. round the fag-got he binds it, Drink round, brave boys, drink round! Drink
2. we are all his ser vants, And all at his com - mand. So

1. round, brave boys! drink round, brave boys! Till it does come to me, . The
2. drink, boys, drink! so drink, boys, drink! And see you do not spill, . For

1. long - er we sit here and drink, The mer - ri - er we shall be.
2. if you do you shall drink two, For it is our mas - ter's will.

My Mind to Me a Kingdom is.

WM BYRD.

1. My mind to me a king-dom is, Such per-fect joys there-in I find; That it ex-cels all oth-er bliss The world af-fords or grows by kind; Tho' much I want that most would have, Yet still my mind for-bids to crave.

2. No prince-ly pomp, no wealth-y store, No force to win the vic-to-ry, No cun-ning wit to salve a sore, No shape to feed a lov-ing eye: To none of these am I in thrall—For why? my mind to me is all.

3. Con-tent I live with this my stay, I wish no more than may suf-fice; I press to bear no might-y sway, Look, what I want my mind sup-plies; Thus do I tri-umph like a king, Con-tent with that my mind doth bring.

These verses form part of a well known poem, attributed on the authority of an ancient manuscript in the Bodleian library, to Sir Edward Dyer in the reign of Elizabeth. The song is set to music by William Byrd in *Psalms, Sonnets, and Songs of Sadness and Pietie*, made into music of five parts, 1588, and is quoted by Ben Jonson in "Every Man out of his Humour," 1599. The present tune with the words is reprinted from *Pills*, vol. iv., 1719. The full words are to be seen in Percy's *Reliques*, and in many other works.

The Perils of the Isle.

Air—"Ne Kirree fo'n Sniaghtey."
("The sheep under the snow.")

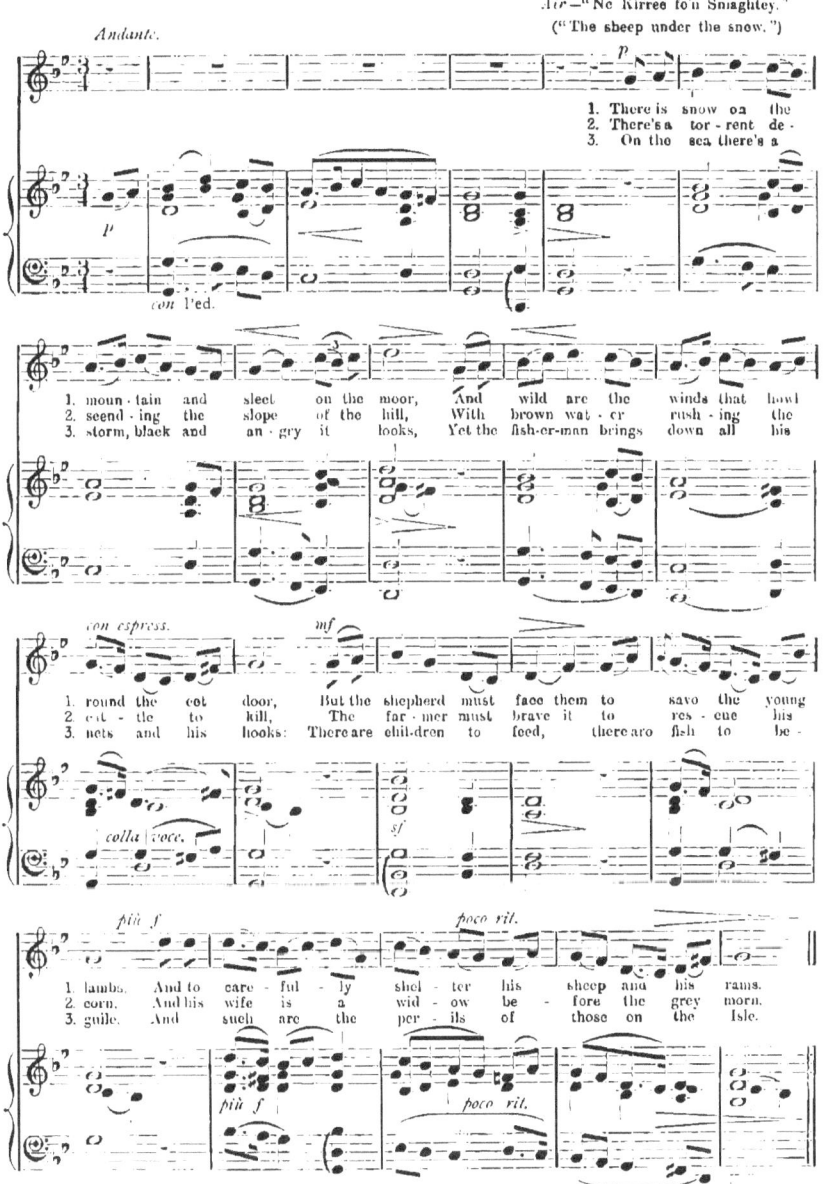

1. There is snow on the moun-tain and sleet on the moor, And wild are the winds that howl round the cot door, But the shepherd must face them to save the young lambs. And to care-ful-ly shel-ter his sheep and his rams.

2. There's a tor-rent de-seend-ing the slope of the hill, With brown wat-er rush-ing the cat-tle to kill, The far-mer must brave it to res-cue his corn. And his wife is a wid-ow be-fore the grey morn.

3. On the sea there's a storm, black and an-gry it looks, Yet the fish-er-man brings down all his nets and his hooks: There are chil-dren to feed, there are fish to be-guile. And such are the per-ils of those on the Isle.

The air is one of those peculiar to the Isle of Man, and there are several published versions of it. The one here selected is taken from the first attempt at a collection of Manx airs, published in 1820, under the title, *Mona's Melodies*, edited by C. St. George. In that work the original Manx words are only indicated by the title of the air. In the present case the stanzas published in *Mona Melodies* do not in the least degree bear upon the subject of the Manx original. We have therefore substituted a song especially written, which (so far as the first verse goes) is more in keeping with the early Manx words.

M

Ah! the Sighs that come fro' my Heart.

Mr. William Chappell printed this song and air from a manuscript of the reign of Henry the Eighth, now in the British Museum. The MS. also contains other specimens of secular songs of the period, and is especially valuable in fixing the character of English song and melody at this time. The contents of the manuscript include both words and music of "Western Wynde, when wilt thou blow?" and "Blow thy horn, hunter!"

I prithee, send me back my Heart.

The verses are by Sir John Suckling (born 1613; died 1641), and the melody is by Henry Lawes. The air and two verses of the song are printed in John Playford's *Treasury of Musick*, 1669, where strangely enough the words are set down to the authorship of "Dr. Hughes."

The Oak and the Ash.

1. North country lass up to London did pass, Al · though with her na · ture it did not a gree, Which
2. faia would I be in the North coun · tree, Where lads and the las · ses are mak · ing ot hay, There
3. maid · en I am, and a maid I'll re-main, Un · til my own coun · try a · gain I do see, For
4. fare-well my dad · dy, and farewell my mammy, Un · til I do see you I · noth · ing but mourn. Re ·

1. made her re-pent and so oft · en lament, Still wishing again in the North for to be.
2. should I see what is pleasant to me; A mischief light on them en · tic'd me away.
3. here in this place I shall ne'er see the face Of him that's al · lot · ted my love for to be.
4. memb'ring my brothers, my sisters, and oth · ers, In less than a year I hope to return

Oh the

oak and the ash and the bonnie iv · y tree Flourish'd bravely at home in my own country.

A version of the tune under the name, "Quodling's Delight" (reprinted in our Appendix) is in the Fitzwilliam Virginal book. Under the title, "Goddesses," another variant is in the first and all early editions of the *Dancing Master*. The ballad is of great length, and was a popular one during the 17th century, being printed on black letter broadsides, in the Roxburghe and other collections. There were also certain parodies of it extant at this time. Sir Walter Scott, in *Rob Roy*, puts a fragment of the ballad into the mouth of one of his characters.

Near Woodstock Town.

1. Near Woodstock town, in Oxford-
2. "Alas," quoth she, "my love's un-
3. The la-dy round the mea-dow

1. shire, As I walk'd forth to take the air, To view the fields and meadows round, Methought I
2. kind, My sighs and tears he will not mind, But he is cru-el un-to me, Which caus-es
3. ran, And gath-er'd flow - ers as they sprang; Of ev - 'ry sort she there did pull, Un - til she

1. heard a dole-ful sound. Down by a crys - tal ri - ver-side A gal-lant bow - er I es-
2. all my mi-ser - y. Soon aft-er he had gain'd my heart, He cru-el-ly did from me
3. got her a-pron full. The green ground ser - ved as a bed, And flow'rs a pil - low for her

1. pied, Where a fair la - dy made great moan, With many a sigh and bit - ter groan,
2. part; An - oth - er maid he did pur-sue, And to his vows he bids a - dieu."
3. head; She laid her down and noth-ing spoke, A - las, for love her heart was broke!

The ballad is an early one, and of great length. It is printed in full in Chappell's *National English Airs*, 1838, and in his *Popular Music*. We can only give a few of the verses here. It is also named "The Oxfordshire Tragedy," and the tune is employed for songs in *The Cobbler's Opera*, 1729, *The Village Opera*, 1729, and *Silvia*, 1731. As printed in editions of these operas the tune varies a little. In the last named opera the air is in common time.

To all you Ladies now at Land.

RICHARD LEVERIDGE.

Con spirito.

1. To all you la-dies now at land, We men at sea en-
2. Then if we write not by each post, Think not we are un-
3. The king, with won-der and sur-prise, Will swear the seas grow
4. And now we've told you all our loves, And like-wise all our

1. dite, But first would have you un-der-stand, How
2. kind, Nor yet con-clude our ships are lost, By
3. bold, Be cause the tides will high-er rise, Than
4. fears, In hopes this dee-lar 'a-tion moves Some

Pepys mentions in his diary under the date January 2nd, 1664-5, that he took to my Lord Brouaker's, "a ballet made from the seamen at sea to the ladies in town." This was in all probability the celebrated and clever poem, "To all you ladies now at land," which, it is stated, was written by Charles, afterwards Earl of Dorset, the night before an engagement. As the engagement alluded to took place in July, 1665, it is thought that Pepys' entry contradicts this statement, but the entry is vague, and we have no proof as to its referring to Lord Dorset's ballad after all. The song with an air was engraved on half sheets about 1710-20, and this tune has a slight "taste" of the "British Grenadiers," and other similar melodies. A version of it, with the words as "A Ballad by the late Lord Dorset when at sea," is given in *Pills*, vol. vi., 1720; it is also set to a parody (of which there have been hundreds), in *Watt's Musical Miscellany*, vol. iii., 1730, and many other places. About 1727-9 another song came into vogue (with an air by Richard Leveridge), "The Faithful Mariner," beginning "To you who live at home at ease"; this was published in vol. iii. of the *Merry Musician*, and in Walsh's *British Musical Miscellany*, 1734. As Leveridge's air is so superior to the one printed in *Pills* and on the engraved sheets, we have taken his and united it to a few verses of Lord Dorset's long ballad, which by the way is contained in full in most collections of English ballad and lyric poetry.

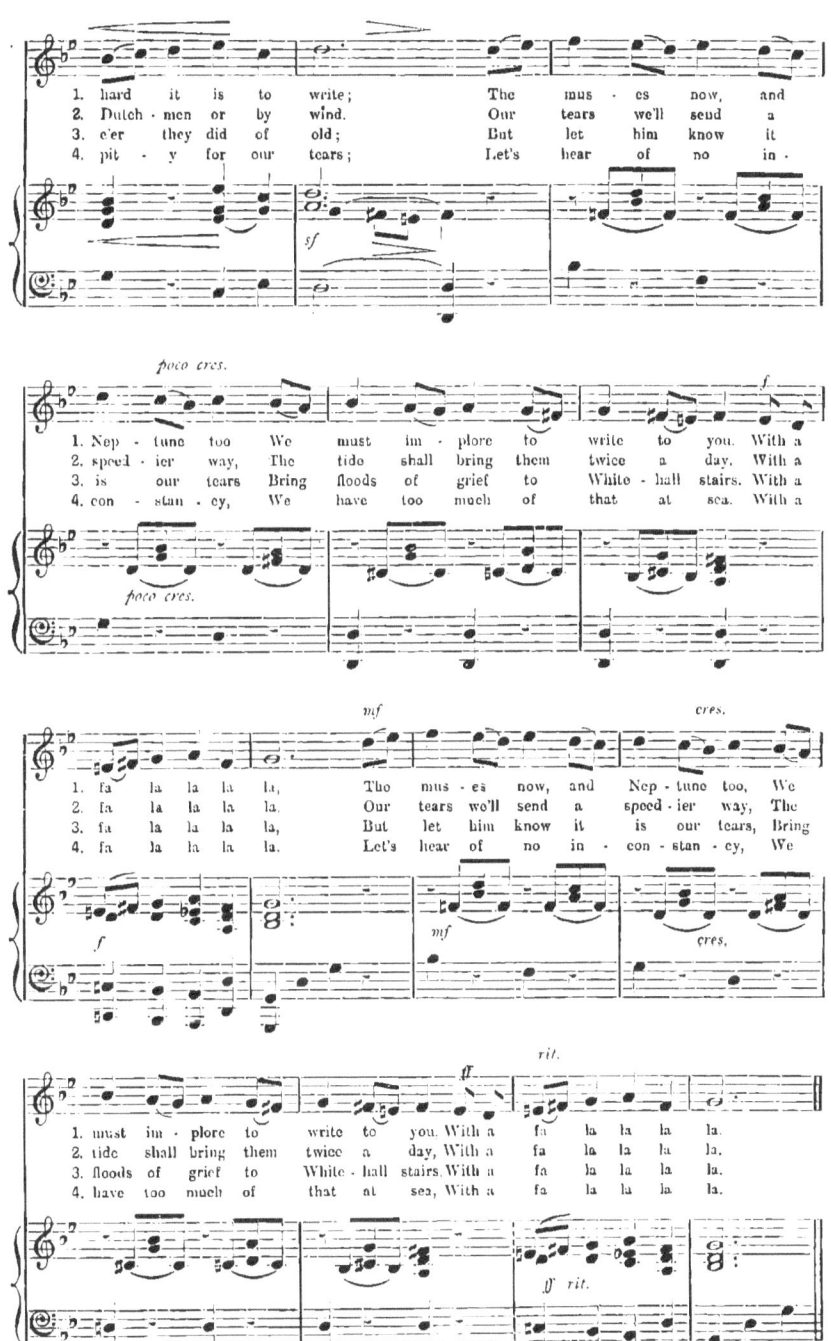

Come and Listen to My Ditty.

1. Come and list-en to my dit-ty, All ye jol-ly hearts of gold, Lend a bro-ther tar your pi-ty, Who was once so stout and bold; But the ar-rows of Cu-pid, A-las! have made me rue, Sure true love was ne'er so treat-ed As I am by scorn-ful Sue.

2. When I first saw my pret-ty crea-ture, The de-light of land and sea, No man ev-er saw a sweet-er, I'd have kept her com-pa-ny; I'd have fain made her my true love, For bet-ter or for worse, But, a-las! I could not per-suade her For to steer the marriage course.

3. Long I won-der'd why my jew-el Had the heart to use me so, Till I found by of-ten sound-ing She'd an-oth-er ve in tow. So fare-well, hard-heart-ed Su-key, I'll my for-tune seek at sea, And try in more friend-ly quar-ter, Since in yours I can not be.

The tune has been generally associated with sailors' songs. The above lyric, which has much the appearance of a traditional folk song, is called "The Sailor's Complaint." It is present in Walsh's *British Musical Miscellany*, vol. iv., 1733-4, Bickham's *Musical Entertainer*, 1737, *The Universal Musician*, 1738, etc. Prior to this the verses had been used for a sailor ballad beginning, "O how happy are young lovers," and with this first line as a heading the song is printed in several ballad operas, as *The Squire's Wedding*, 1729, *Silvia*, 1731, etc. It was also used for Charles Coffey's "Welcome, brother debtor"—see *Bickham*, vol. ii., 1738, *Calliope*, 1739, and other works. In 1754 the "Sailor's Complaint" gave up its tune to George Alexander Steven's fine sea song, "Cease, rude Boreas," published in that year by John Sadler in *The Muses Delight*. "The Storm," as this latter song was generally named, was one of Charles Incledon's great successes. We have not reproduced all the numerous verses of "Come and Listen to My Ditty."

Once I Loved a Maiden Fair.

A seventeenth century ballad and tune generally titled "Maiden Fair." The melody is given in a number of Playford's publications. In the first (1650) edition of *The Dancing Master*, and many later editions, *Musick's Delight on the Cithren*, 1663, *Introduction to the Skill of Music*, 1664 (and all later editions), Greeting's *Pleasant Companion for the Flagolet*, 1680, etc. The ballad is among the Roxburghe Collection, and a song published in 1651 is directed to be sung to the tune, "Once I loved a maiden fair." Chappell, who first brought the tune into modern revival, appears to have taken some liberties with it, and his version much resembles Savile's "Here's a health unto His Majesty." I give Playford's copy in the Appendix.

Joy to the Person of my Love.

Andante espressione.

1. Joy to the per - son
2. Thou - sand for - tunes

1. of my love, Al - though she me dis - dain, Fix'd are my thoughts and
2. full to her share Tho' she re - ject - ed me, And fill'd my heart full

1. may not move, But yet I love in vain. Shall I lose the sight of my
2. of de - spair, Yet shall I con - stant be; For she is the dame my

The air is in the *Skene MS.* in the Advocates' Library, Edinburgh. The manuscript is written in a four-line tablature for a small kind of lute, and there is some dispute as to its precise age. It may, however, be readily granted that the period was between 1625 and 1650. "Joy to the Person of my love" is also found in all three editions of John Forbes' *Cantus*, printed at Aberdeen in 1662, 1666, and 1682. This work may claim to be the first collection of secular music printed in Scotland. For his enterprise poor Forbes suffered confiscation, fine and imprisonment, under the law of printing without a license. The above song is also in the *Leyden and Blaikie MSS.*, both of which date about the latter part of the 17th century.

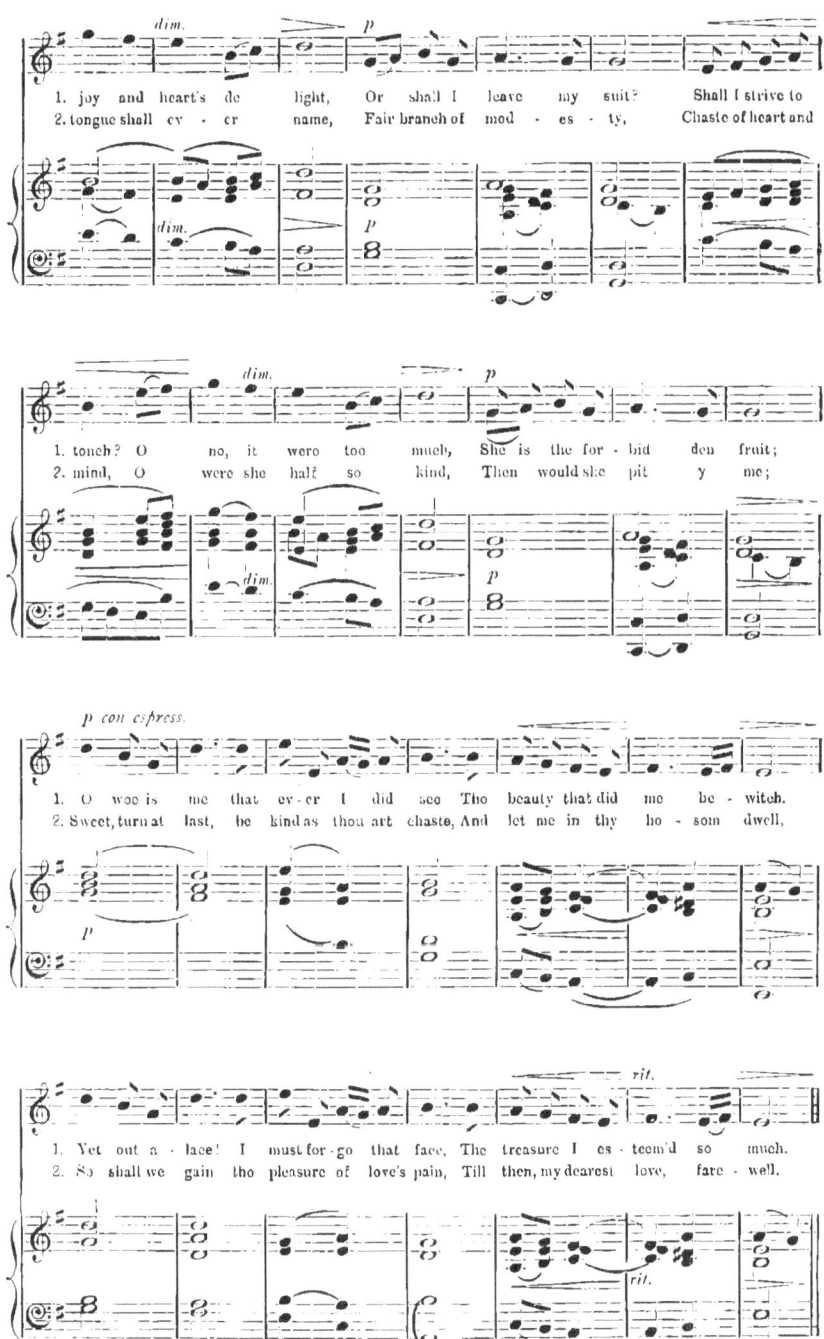

188

The Cheshire Man.

A song in praise of the Cheshire cheese, from a thin folio publication issued by Edward Jones, the gatherer of Welsh melodies. The book named *Cheshire Melodies* was printed in 1798, and is adorned by a fine engraving showing the defeat of the Spaniard and triumph of the Cheshire man and his cheese. The music is in our present volume arranged to include a "Cheshire Round," the dance once peculiar to that county and to Shropshire. The structure of these rounds is similar to that of the ancient triple time hornpipes, and many different ones are included in the contents of the early dance books. The one here used is from Jones' work above named.

Moderato.

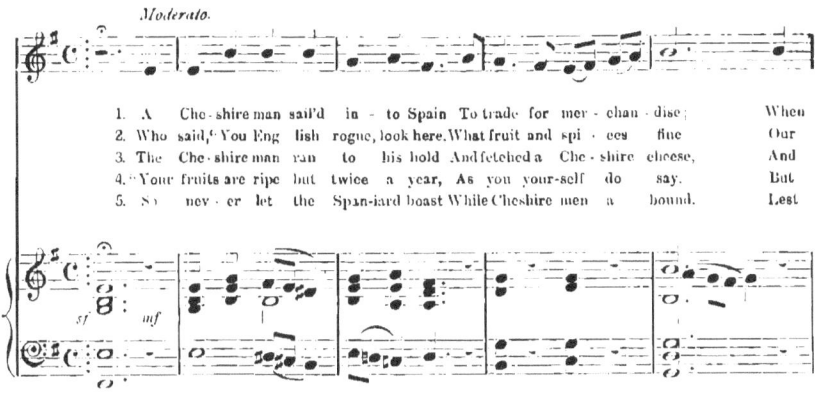

1. A Cheshire man sail'd in - to Spain To trade for mer - chan - dise; When
2. Who said, "You Eng - lish rogue, look here, What fruit and spi - ces fine Our
3. The Che - shire man ran to his hold And fetched a Che - shire cheese, And
4. "Your fruits are ripe but twice a year, As you your-self do say. But
5. So nev - er let the Span-iard boast While Cheshire men a - bound. Lest

1. he ar - riv - ed from the main, A Span-iard him es - pies, . . . A
2. land pro - du - ces twice a year! Thou hast not such in thine, . . . Thou
3. said, "Look here, you dog, be - hold, We have such fruit as these, . We
4. such as I pre - sent you here Our land brings twice a day, . . Our
5. they should teach him to his cost To dance a Che - shire round, . To

Con spirito.

1. Span-iard him es - pies.
2. hast not such in thine."
3. have such fruit as these.
4. land brings twice a - day."
5. dance a Cheshire round.

Phillis.

These well-known words seem to have first seen the light in *A Royal Garland of New Songs*, 12mo., black letter, in the Pepys collection. They have been attributed to a playwright named Southerne, as they appear in his play, the *Disappointment; or, the Mother in fashion*, acted 1684; but Southerne himself there states that the song was written by Colonel Sackville. The song is printed in Henry Playford's *Theater of Music*, first book, 1685, as one of three from the play above named. The music is signed Capt. Pack, and this, with the song, is reprinted in *Pills*, vol. iv., 1719. On an early sheet (circa 1700), in my own possession another air by "Mr. Dau" is united to the words.

1. vow, But durst not think of love: . . . .
2. lies, Her eyes dart on - ly fire: .

1. Till beau - ty, charm - ing ev - 'ry sonse, An ea - sy con - quest
2. Be - tween ex - tremes I am un done, Like plants too north - ward

1. made; . . . . . And shew'd the vain - ness of do -
2. set; . . . . . . Burnt by too vi - o - lent a

1. fence When Phil - lis does in - vade. . . . .
2. sun, Or chill'd for want of heat. . . . .

What shall I do? I am undone.

Song and air from the sixth volume of *Pills to purge Melancholy*, 1720, with the title, "The Unfortunate Lover, set by Mr. Willis." It may be surmised as to what relation the above Mr. Willis was to Mrs. Willis, a singer at the end of the 17th century.

Tippling John.

Ye Shepherds, give ear to my Lay.

William Jackson.

Andante espressione.

1. shep - herds, give ear to my lay, And take no more
2. faith - less and I am un - done, Ye that wit - ness the
3. woods, spread your bran - ches a - pace, To your deep - est re -

1. heed of my sheep, They've noth - ing to do but to
2. woes I en - dure, Let rea - son in - struct you to
3. cess - es I fly: I would hide with the beasts of the

The music is the composition of William Jackson, the organist of Exeter Cathedral, born 1730, died 1803. The song and melody appear in one of his early sets of *Twelve Songs*, folio, *circa* 1760. William Jackson was a notable figure in the world of music, literature and art of his time, being an essayist and a landscape painter, besides having musical gifts of a high order. Many of his songs and canzonets attained much popularity. He was also the composer of a successful opera, *The Lord of the Manor*, acted 1780-1.

My Love bound Me with a Kisse.

ROBERT JONES.

1. My love bound me with a kisse, That I should no long-er stay,
2. Had she bid me goe at first It would ne'er have griev'd my heart,

1. When I felt so sweete a bliss I had lesse pow'r to
2. Hope de-laide had beene the worst, But ah! to kisse and

A pretty song composed by Robert Jones, who was a lute player of repute during the Elizabethan period. Jones was author of a number of musical works, including five books of *Ayres* published between 1601 and 1611, with a book of Madrigals dated 1607. The present song is found in his *Second Booke of Songs and Ayres set out to the lute*, . . . composed by Robert Jones, printed by P. S. for *Mathew Selman*, 1601, folio. It was reprinted in 1799 in *The Vocal Magazine*, Edinburgh, vol. iii., and a few years after this in J. S. Smith's *Musica Antiqua*.

1. part a - way. A - las! a - las! a - las! that
2. then to part. But ah! But ah! how deepe it

1. wo - men doth not know. Kiss - es make men loath to goe!
2. strucke, speake, Gods, you know, Kiss - es make men loath to goe!

1. A - las! a - las! a - las! that wo - men doth not
2. But ah! but ah! how deepe it strucke, speake, gods, you

1. know, Kiss es make men loath to goe!
2. know. Kiss es make men loath to goe!

Here's to Thee, my Boy.

Drinking Song.

HENRY CAREY.

A drinking song by Henry Carey published on a half sheet engraved by J. Cluer, Bow Churchyard, *circa* 1725. The song and air also appear in *Watt's Musical Miscellany*, vol. iv., 1730; Bickham's *Musical Entertainer*, vol. ii., 1738; and in *The Convivial Songster*, 1782.

The Arch Denial.

THOMAS AUGUSTINE ARNE.

The song with its melody was first published in the fifth number of *The Agreeable Musical Choice; an entire new Collection of Songs with the duet in Harlequin Sorcerer*, sung by Mr. Lowe and Mrs. Lampe; never before printed, composed by Mr. Arne, folio, Walsh, circa 1755. From here it was copied into *Apollo's Cabinet*, Liverpool, 1757, Hyde's *Miscellaneous Collection*, 1798, etc. Mr. Arne became Doctor Arne in 1759. *The Agreeable Musical Choice* was one of a series of publications published by Walsh between 1750 and 1760; some of these were collections of songs by Arne and others by Boyce.

Bucks a-Hunting Go.

1. How sweet is the horn that blows in the morn, Young bucks a-hunt-ing
2. The fox he leaps o-ver the hedg-es so high, The hounds all af-ter him
3. How sweet is my home, my low lit-tle cot, Let my sta-tion be high or

1. go; . How sweet is the horn that blows in the morn, Young bucks a-hunt-ing
2. go; The fox he leaps o-ver the hed-ges so high, The hounds all af-ter him
3. low; . How sweet is my home, my low lit-tle cot, Let my sta-tion be high or

By permission, from Frank Kidson's *Traditional Tunes; a collection of ballad airs chiefly obtained in Yorkshire and the south of Scotland*, 1891. The tune was commonly sung on the borders of Staffordshire, Cheshire and Shropshire, between 1820 and 1840, and the words are in early song garlands printed by T. Evans and by J. Pitts. Variants of the song and air are also known in other parts of England. One of these, engraved and printed on a half sheet, by Skillern, circa 1786, contains a version of the words set to similar music; it is headed, "Sweet Tally Ho; a favourite song."

1. go, . . . Young bucks a - hunt - ing go.
2. go, . . The hounds all af-ter him go.
3. low, . . Let my sta-tion be high or low.

All my fan - cy dwells up-on Nan - cy Whilst I sing tal - ly ho, . . . Whilst

I sing tal - ly ho;

All my fan - cy dwells up-on Nan - cy. Whilst I sing tal - ly ho.

Rosalinda.

BUTLER.

Moderato.

con Ped.

1. sung my pas - sion to the wind, And told it
2. winds at - tend my mourn - ful songs, And ech o

1. to the floods, Since Ro - sa - lin da proves un -
2. back my sighs, The gush - ing stream be - wails my

A duo melody with the words from an engraved music sheet of about 1762. It is entitled, "Rosalinda, set by Mr. Butler." Biographical dictionaries are silent regarding this particular Mr. Butler.

1. kind,   Fare · well   the   fields   and   woods.   Those   field's   and
2. wrongs,   And   mur · mur · ing   re · plies: Call   home   thy

1. woods   which   charmed   my   sight   When   Ro · sa
2. thoughts,   de · lud · ed   swain,   Thy   flocks   de ·

1. lin · da   smil'd,   But   since   her   frowns   my
2. mand   thy   care,   Those   songs   which   feed   but

1. vows   re · quite   They   seem   a   bar · ren   wild.
2. her   dis · dain,   Pas · tor · a   dies   to   hear.

The Merry Gregorians.

"The Merry Gregs" was the punning title of a social and convivial society existing in London before 1738, and more properly named "The Gregorians." One of its members was Henry Carey, who wrote the above piece named in his *Musical Century*, 1740, "The Gregorian Constitution Song; Words and Music by Brother Carey." It also appeared in the second volume of Bickham's *Musical Entertainer* under the name, "The Merry Gregs." Bickham heads the song with a humorous engraving representing a party of singers in wigs, along with some boys, all lustily singing, "O save us all," a lyric from Carey and Lampe's burlesque opera, *The Dragon of Wantley*. Carey's name does not here appear as author of the music, nor does it on an engraved half-sheet copy of the song in my possession. The tune of "The Merry Gregs" occurs three times in Carey's *Musical Century*; once as above, again to a song on church and dissent, "The Union of Parties," and again headed "Chorus to the Honest Yorkshire Man." Carey's play bearing this name was acted in 1735.

Fair Sally.

MAURICE GREENE.

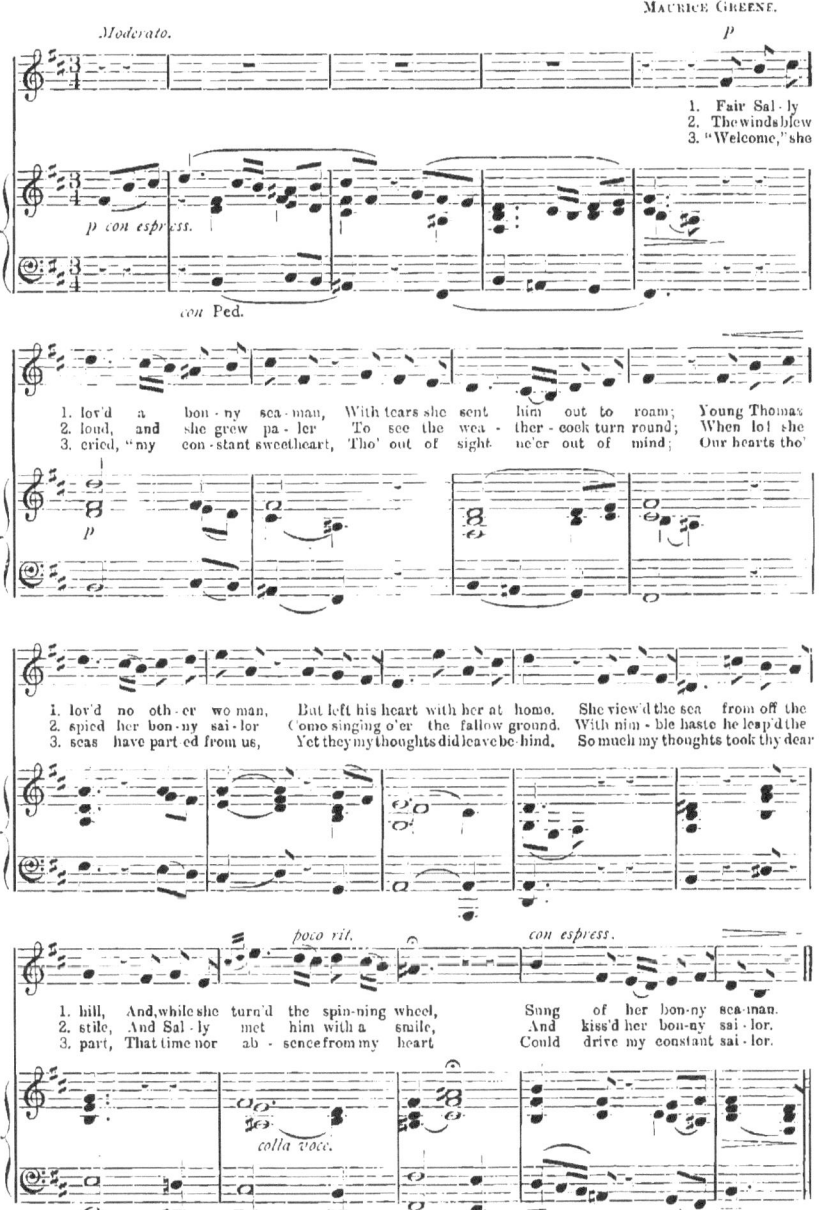

1. Fair Sal - ly lov'd a bon - ny sea - man, With tears she sent him out to roam; Young Thomas lov'd no oth - er wo man, But left his heart with her at home. She view'd the sea from off the hill, And, while she turn'd the spin-ning wheel, Sung of her bon-ny sea-man.

2. The winds blew loud, and she grew pa - ler To see the wea - ther cock turn round; When lo! she spied her bon-ny sai - lor Come singing o'er the fallow ground. With nim - ble haste he leap'd the stile, And Sal - ly met him with a smile, And kiss'd her bon-ny sai - lor.

3. "Welcome," she cried, "my con - stant sweetheart, Tho' out of sight ne'er out of mind; Our hearts tho' seas have part - ed from us, Yet they my thoughts did leave be-hind. So much my thoughts took thy dear part, That time nor ab - sence from my heart Could drive my constant sai - lor.

This pretty song, so far as the tune is concerned, is the composition of Dr. Maurice Greene. Probably its earliest appearance in a collection was in 1739, at which date it was included in *Calliope; or, English Harmony*. It was afterwards printed in *Universal Harmony*, 1745, *The Muse's Delight*, 1754, and in a great number of other works during the 18th century. It is to be noted that the first few bars of "Fair Sally" are practically identical with the generally accepted version of "Black Ey'd Susan."

Jockey to the Fair.

1. 'Twas on the morn of sweet May-day, When Na - ture paint - ed all things gay, Taught birds to sing and lambs to play, And deck'd the mea - dows fair, Young
2. Tho' cheer - ful par - ish bells had rung, With eag - er steps he trudg'd a - long, Sweet flow'r - y gar - land round him hung, Which shep - herds us'd to wear; He
3. "My dad and mam are fast a - sleep, My broth - er's up and with the sheep; And will you still your prom - ise keep, Which I have heard you swear? And
4. "Be - hold the ring!" the shep - herd cried, "Will Jen - ny be my charm - ing bride? Let Cu - pid be our hap - py guide, And Hy - men meet us there!" Then

A popular favourite, probably first sung at Vauxhall or some similar public garden. It was in great vogue about 1779 and 1780, and Chappell refers to the song being in *Vocal Music*, 1772. I am unable to verify this date, although the song is present in the edition issued by J. Bew, which was advertised as "just published" in 1781. There seems much uncertainty as to the dates of some editions of *Vocal Music*. The words of the song are in several Scottish song books—in *St. Cecilia; or, the Lady and Gentleman's Harmonious Companion*, 1779; its later edition of 1782; *The Scots Vocal Miscellany*, 1780; Ding's *Songster's Favourite*, circa 1785, etc. The air alone is in Skillern's *Twenty-four Country Dances for 1790*, and in Aird's *Selection*, vol. ii., 1784. Longman and Broderip and other publishers also published the song and air on engraved half-sheets. In its original form the air is of more extended compass and not so vocal as the present traditional set which has been its recognised form for half a century. The late Dr. Charles Mackay wrote a song to the air, "Amid the new-mown hay," which had some slight degree of popularity.

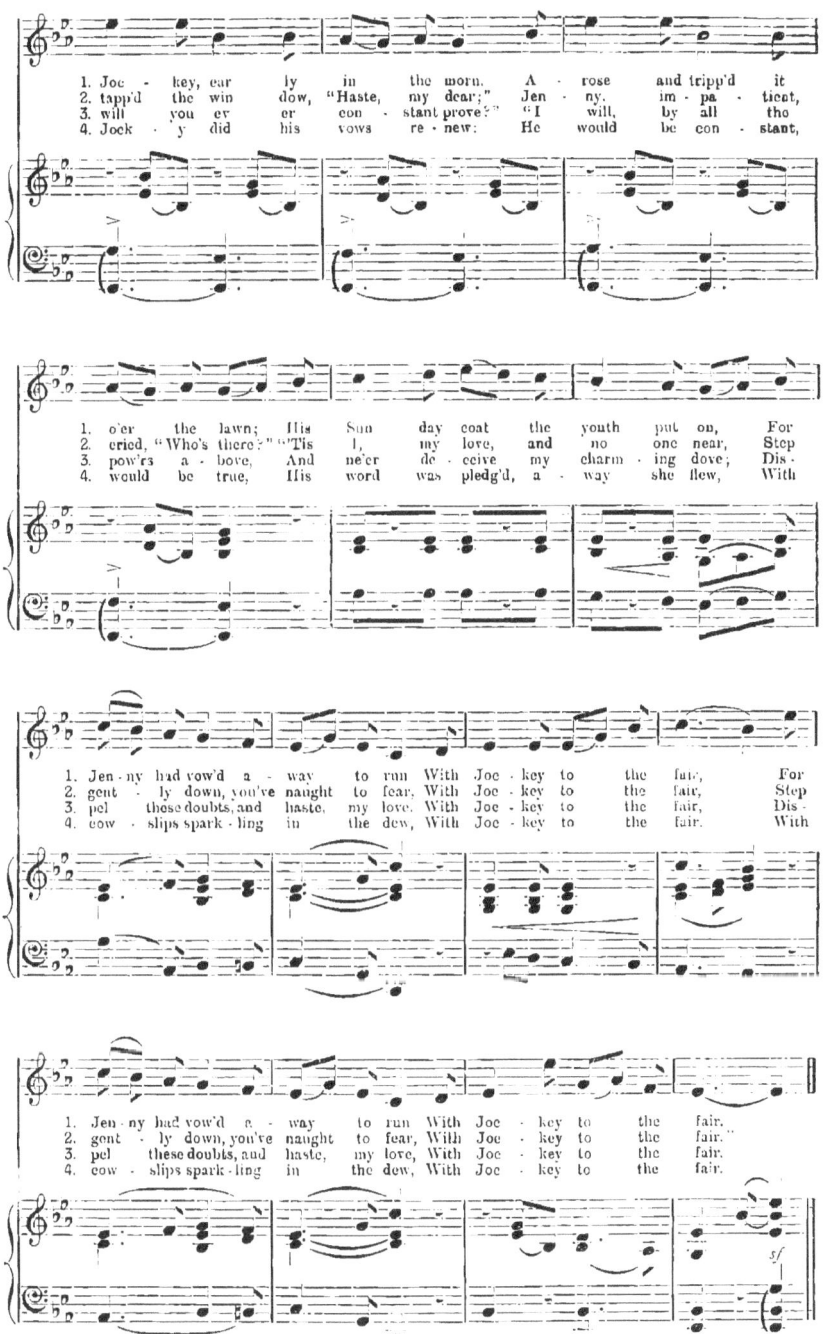

1. Joc - key, ear - ly in the morn, A - rose and tripp'd it
2. tapp'd the win - dow, "Haste, my dear;" Jen - ny, im - pa - tient,
3. will you ev - er con - stant prove?" "I will, by all tho
4. Jock - y did his vows re - new: He would be con - stant,

1. o'er the lawn; His Sun - day coat the youth put on, For
2. cried, "Who's there?" "'Tis I, my love, and no one near, Step
3. pow'rs a - bove, And ne'er de - ceive my charm - ing dove; Dis -
4. would be true, His word was pledg'd, a - way she flew, With

1. Jen - ny had vow'd a - way to run With Joc - key to the fair, For
2. gent - ly down, you've naught to fear, With Joc - key to the fair, Step
3. pel these doubts, and haste, my love, With Joc - key to the fair, Dis -
4. cow - slips spark - ling in the dew, With Joc - key to the fair. With

1. Jen - ny had vow'd a - way to run With Joc - key to the fair."
2. gent - ly down, you've naught to fear, With Joc - key to the fair."
3. pel these doubts, and haste, my love, With Joc - key to the fair.
4. cow - slips spark - ling in the dew, With Joc - key to the fair.

When Daisies Pied.

THOMAS AUGUSTINE ARNE.

Another of Dr. Arne's Shakespearian settings, the words being taken from *Love's Labour Lost.* A collection of Dr. Arne's music to songs from Shakespeare's plays would form a volume of English lyrics not to be surpassed, within its limits, for musicianly skill and melodic beauty.

Phillida Flouts Me.

Allegretto.

1. O what a plague is love, I can-not bear it, She will in-constant prove, I greatly fear it;
2. At the fair t'other day, As she pass'd by me, She look'd an-oth-er way And would not spy me;
3. She has a cloth of mine, Wrought with blue Cov-en-try, She keeps it as a sign Of my fi-del-i-ty;

1. It so torments my mind, That my heart fail-eth; She wav-ers with the wind, As a ship sail-eth;
2. I woo'd her for to dine, But could not get her; Dick had her to the vine, He might en-treat her;
3. But if she frowns on me, She shall not wear it, I'll give it my maid Joan, And she shall tear it;

1. Please her the best I may, She loves but to gain-say, A-lack and well-a-day! Phil-lid-a flouts me.
2. With Daniel she did dance, On me she would not glance, Oh, thrice un-happy chance, Phil-lid-a flouts me.
3. Since 'twill no bet-ter be, I'll bear it patient-ly, Yet all the world may see Phil-lid-a flouts me.

A quaint 16th century conceit. The air is singular in structure, and undoubtedly very old, but it does not seem to have got into print before 1728-29, when it was used as a vehicle for new words in the ballad operas of that day. It is in the *Quaker's Opera*, 1728; *Love in a Riddle*, 1729, and *Damon and Phillida*, 1734. With the song the air is printed by Watts in *The Musical Miscellany*, vol. ii, 1729, and afterwards it is found in *The Convivial Songster*, 1782. In these old copies the tune is in three-two time. The song is mentioned in Walton's *Compleat Angler*, 1653, and the words are in full on a broadside of the 17th century in the *Roxburgh Collection*. Ritson in his *Ancient Songs*, 1792, gives a copy from the *Theatre of Compliments*, 1688, but there is another and better one in *Wit Restor'd in several Select Poems never before publish'd*, 1658 (p. 208 reprint). During the 17th century the song seems to have been a favourite, for there are frequent references to it in books of the period, besides which there were many parodies of it and songs set to the air. One of these in the *Crown Garland of Golden Roses*, 1612, is a lamentation for the death of Queen Elizabeth, composed by one of her maids of honour, and worked on a sampler! There are more verses to "Phillida Flouts Me" than we have been able to give above.

Cease your Funning.

Cease your funning, Forcc or cunning,

Nev - er shall my heart tre-pan; All these sallies Are but ma-lice To se-duce my

con - stant man. 'Tis most certain, By their flirting, Wo - men oft have en - vy shown,

Pleas'd to ru - in oth-ers' wooing, Nev - er hap - py in their own.

From the *Beggar's Opera*, written by John Gay, and acted at the end of the year 1727. The air, unlike the rest, is given without an old title in the early editions of the opera, and it has been absurdly claimed as a Welsh melody. About the period of the *Beggar's Opera*, another song was popular, set to the same tune, "When the hills and lofty mountains"; this is frequently headed, "Charming Billy" or "Lofty Mountains." A version under this latter title appears in Daniel Wright's *Complete tutor for ye flute*, circa 1735. As "Constant Billy" the tune is in the third volume of the *Dancing Master*, which there is every reason to believe was published late in the year 1726. This proves that the song "Constant" or "Charming Billy" was prior to Gay's lyric. The air, "Constant Billy," also occurs in one of Walsh's early dance books.

I am the Jolly Prince of Drinkers.

A drinking song, from R. Horsfield's *Vocal Music*, 1775; with some alterations in the words, it is also inserted in Ritson's *English Songs*, 1783. The air is a fine and marked specimen of English melody; probably of the same period as that of "Down among the Dead Men."

The British Grenadiers.

For note to this song see Appendix.

Sally in our Alley.

For note to this song see Appendix.

Come, Live with Me and be My Love.

Andante espressione.

1. Come, live with me and
2. Where we will sit on
3. A gown made of the
4. A belt of straw and

1. be my love, And we will all thy plea - sures prove, That grove or
2. ris - ing rocks, And see the shep - herds feed their flocks, By shal - low
3. fin - est wool, Which from our pret - ty lambs we pull, And shoes lined
4. i - vy buds, With co - ral clasps and am - ber studs. If, then, these

1. val - ley, hill, or field, Or wood or steep - y moun - tain yield.
2. riv - ers, to whose falls Me - lo - di - ous birds sing mad - ri - gals.
3. choice - ly for the cold, With buck - les of the pur - est gold.
4. plea - sures can thee move, Come, live with me and be my love.

These beautiful words rank with the best of our English pastoral poems. The question of authorship is not very easily settled. It seems certain, however, that some early poem on the same lines had suggested to several authors at the close of the 16th century the same ideas; hence the confusion. Shakespeare makes Sir Hugh Evans sing a snatch of the song, and Christopher Marlow, in his tragedy *The Jew of Malta*, written about ten years earlier than *The Merry Wives of Windsor*, uses the refrain, "Shall live with me and be my love." In *England's Helicon*, 1600, the song is printed as by "Chr. Marlow," and Izaak Walton, quoting it in *The Compleat Angler*, 1653, also mentions Marlow as the author. In *The Passionate Pilgrime and Sonnets to Sundry Notes of Musicke by Mr. William Shakespere*, London, printed for W. Jaggard, 1599, a portion of it is printed. Dr. Donne also, at a later period, wrote another version. In *England's Helicon*, 1600, there is "The Nymph's Reply," which is signed "Ignoto," generally considered to be Sir Walter Raleigh, as Walton puts it, "in his younger days." There are many allusions to the song in 17th century books. Regarding the tune, it was printed in Steevens's edition of Shakespeare from a transcript of a MS. "as old as Shakespeare's time," which was made by Sir John Hawkins; it is also contained in Corkine's *Second Book of Ayres*, 1612, among his "Lessons for Violls," under the first line title, but with no more of the words.

Drink to Me only with Thine Eyes.

For note to this song see Appendix.

Love is a Bauble.

RICHARD LEVERIDGE.

1. Love is a bauble,
2. Love is a fellow

1. No man is a-ble To say it is this, or 'tis that; An i-dle pas-sion, Of such a fashion, 'Tis
2. Clad all in yel-low, The can-ker-worm of the mind; A pri-vy mischief, And such a sly thief No

1. like I cannot tell what; Fair in the cra-dle, Bold in the sad-dle, Al-ways too cold or too
2. man knows where to find; Love is a wonder, 'Tis here and yonder. 'Tis common to all man-

1. hot; An er-rant li-ar, Al-ways a-fire It is, and yet it is not.
2. kind; A ver-y cheater, Ev'ry one's better. Then hang him, let him go.

The beautiful air to this song is by Richard Leveridge, to whom English national melody owes so much. The song with the air is printed in the sixth and last volume of *Pills*, 1720, with Leveridge's name attached.

The Honest Yorkshireman.

The words and music were written by Henry Carey for his little opera, *The Wonder; or, the Honest Yorkshireman*, acted 1735, printed in 1736. The title *rôle* was played by a Mr. Salway, and, with his name indicated as the singer, the song was included in Carey's *Musical Century*, 1740, etc. It may be noted that in several modern works, such as Ingledew's *Ballads and Songs of Yorkshire*, 1860, the song is dressed in a vulgarised dialect, for which there is no authority.

The Vicar of Bray.

In Nichol's *Select Poems* the statement is made that the song is the composition of a "soldier in Colonel Fuller's troop of dragoons, in the reign of George I." The present writer was able, some time ago in the *Musical Times*, to refute this popular error and to show that a version of "The Vicar of Bray" was written by Edward Ward, and inserted among his *Miscellanies* printed in the third edition of 1712, before George the First came to the throne; indeed, Ward's song may even have been published long before the above named date. For a selection from Ward's verses see the Appendix to the present volume. The original Vicar, of Bray (a little village on the Thames above Windsor), was supposed to have been Simon Aleyn; he was Vicar of Bray from 1540 to 1588. It is, however, uncertain as to which vicar gave rise to the proverb—"The Vicar of Bray will be Vicar of Bray still." The tune is an old one named "The Country Garden." In Daniel Wright's *Compleat Tutor for ye Flute, circa*, 1735, it is named "The Country Garden the New Way." Under the first title the air is used in the *Quakers' Opera*, 1728, and other ballad operas of the period. The first air (printed on half sheets) to ' The Vicar of Bray " is the old Scotch tune "Bessy Bell and Mary Gray," and it was not until quite late in the 18th century that the song became united to the tune we now know, i.e. "The Country Garden." The song is given in *Calliope; or, The Musical Miscellany*, Edinburgh, 1788, to a version of the present known tune, and this air was also used for a song, "The Neglected Tar," popular at this time.

poco cres.   *f*

1. teach my flock I nev - er missed, Kings were by God ap - point - ed, And
2. Church of Rome I found would fit Full well my con - sti - tu - tion; And
3. prin - ci - ples I did re - voke, Set con - science at a dis - tance; I'as -
4. cas - ion - al con - form - ists base, I damn'd their mod - er a - tion, And
5. in my faith and loy - al - ty I nev - er more will fal - ter, And

poco cres.

1. damn'd are those that do re - sist, Or touch the Lord's an - oint - ed.
2. had be - come a Je - su - it But for the Rev - ol - u - tion.
3. sive o - be - dience was a joke, A jest was non - re - sis - tance. ⟩ And
4. thought the Church in dan - ger was By such pre - var - i - ca - tion.
5. George my law - ful King shall be Un - til the times do al - ter.

f

colla voce.

poco cres.

this is law, I will main - tain Un - til my dy - ing day, sir, That

poco cres.

rit.

what - so - ev - er king may reign, Still, I'll be the vic - ar of Bray, sir.

rit.

The Bailiff's Daughter of Islington.

1. There was a youth, and a well-lov-ed youth, And
2. And as she went a - long the high road, The
3. "Be - fore I give you a pen - ny, sweet - heart, Pray
4. "If she be dead, then take my horse, My

1. he was a squire's son; He lov'd the bail - iff's
2. wea-ther be-ing hot and dry, She sat her down on a
3. tell me where you were born?" "At Is - ling - ton, kind
4. sad - dle and bri - dle, too; For I will to some

The best known tune to this ever popular ballad was picked up traditionally in the north of England, and printed by Dr. Rimbault in his *Musical Illustrations of Bishop Percy's Reliques*, 1850. The oldest printed air to the ballad is in *The Jovial Crew*, a ballad opera acted in 1731. The tune is there set to another song, and the old title given as "The Baily's Daughter of Islington;" it will be found in the Appendix to the present work. Another old and very pretty air to the lyric was obtained traditionally by the late Rev. John Broadwood, and printed in his *Sussex Songs*.

The ballad itself is long, and in the Roxburghe collection of 17th century broadsides it bears the title, "True Love Requited, or the Bailiff's Daughter of Islington, to a North-country tune, or 'I Have a Good Old Mother at Home.'" It is therefore evident that it was sung to at least two tunes, but whether to the printed or any of the traditional versions must remain an open question. Dr. Rimbault is said to have had a copy of the ballad opera air in an early late manuscript, under the name, "The Jolly Pinder." Bishop Percy suggests that the Islington of the song is more likely to have been the village in Norfolk with that name rather than the London suburb.

1. daugh - ter fair, That liv'd in Is - ling - ton. But
2. moss - y bank, And her true love came rid - ing by. She
3. sir," she said, "Where I have had many a scorn." "I
4. far coun-trie, Where no man shall me know." "O

1. when his friends did un - der - stand His fond and fool - ish mind, They
2. start - ed up, with co-lour so red, Catching hold of his bri - dle rein, "One
3. pri - thee, sweetheart, tell to me, O tell me if you know, The
4. stay, O stay, thou good - ly youth, She stand-eth by thy side! She is

rit.

1. sent him up to fair Lon-don, An ap - pren - tice for to bind.
2. pen - ny, one pen - ny, kind sir," she said, "Will ease me of much pain."
3. bai - liff's daugh-ter of Is - ling-ton?" She is dead, sir, long a - go."
4. here a live, she is not dead, And read - y to be thy bride!"

Sling the Flowing Bowl.

Thomas Linley.

1. Come, come, my jol-ly lads, The
2. Tho' to the Spanish coast We're

1. wind's a - baft, Brisk gales our sails shall crowd; Come, bustle, bustle, bustle, boys, Haul the boat, the
2. bound to steer, We'll still our rights main-tain, Then bear a hand, be steady, boys, Soon we'll see old

1. boat - swain pipes a - loud; The ship's un - moor'd, All hands on
2. En - gland once a - gain; From shore to shore While can - nons

1. board; The ris - ing gale fills ev -'ry sail; The ship's well mann'd and stor'd. Then
2. roar, Our tars shall show the haughty foe Bri - tan - nia rules the main. Then

This was first sung by a Mr. Gaudry in a pantomime named *Robinson Crusoe; or, Harlequin Everywhere*, acted in 1781. The music of the piece was by Thomas Linley, the father-in-law of Richard Brinsley Sheridan. The air is a fine and spirited one, and from its first appearance has always commanded popularity. A copy of the song is in *The General Evening Post*, February 10th, 1781, and with the music it was engraved as a half-sheet song. It is in most collections after 1781, in *Fielding's Vocal Enchantress*, 1783, *Edinburgh Musical Miscellany*, 1792, etc. It also appeared in *The Nightingale*, an American song book printed in 1804.

1. sling the flowing bowl, Fond hopes a - rise, The girls we prize Shall bless each jov - ial
2. sling the flowing bowl, Fond hopes a - rise, The girls we prize Shall bless each jov - ial

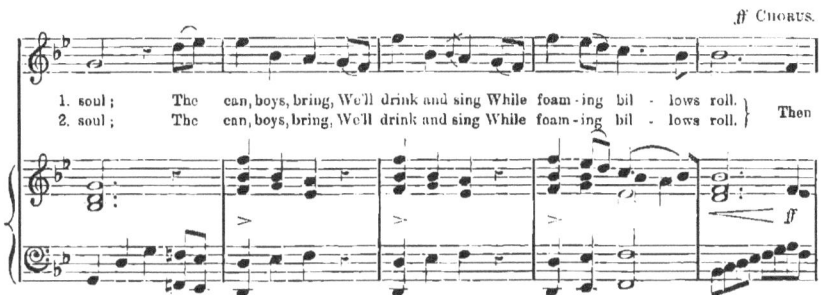

ff CHORUS.

1. soul; The can, boys, bring, We'll drink and sing While foam-ing bil - lows roll. } Then
2. soul; The can, boys, bring, We'll drink and sing While foam-ing bil - lows roll. }

ff

sling the flowing bowl, Fond hopes a - rise, The girls we prize Shall bless each jov - ial

rit.

soul; The can, boys, bring, We'll drink and sing While foam-ing bil - lows roll.

rit.

P

Sweet Nelly, my Heart's Delight.

1. Sweet Nel - ly, my heart's de light, ... Be
2. No; I am a la dy gay; . . . . . 'Tis
3. A fig for your kind and corn, ... Your
4. Be not in such haste, quoth she, ... Por -

1. lov - ing, and do not slight . . The prof - fer I make for
2. ve - ry well known I may . . Have men of re - nown in
3. prof - fer - ed love I scorn . . . . . 'Tis known ve - ry well my
4. haps we may still a - gree; . . . For, man, I pro - test, I

A pretty song, sometimes entitled "The Farmer's Son." Under this title it is in the second volume of Walsh's *Merry Musician, or a Cure for the Spleen,* circa 1728. It is next found, in 1729, in John Watt's *Musical Miscellany,* vol. i., p. 130, from whence copies were taken for the ballad operas, *The Beau in the Suds,* 1729, and *The Lover's Opera,* 1730. It is also in the first volume of Walsh's *British Musical Miscellany,* 1734. With the heading, "Sweet Nelly," the tune alone is in Daniel Wright's *Compleat Tutor for the Flute,* circa 1735. The song in the present work has had to be abbreviated.

1. mod · es · ty's sake, I hon · our your beau · ty bright. . . . . . For
2. coun · try or town. Go, Rog · er, with · out de · lay, ... Court
3. name it is Nell, And you're but a bump · kin born. . . . . . . Well,
4. was but in jest; Come, pri · thee, sit down by me. . . . . . . For

1. love, I pro · fess, I can do no less, For thou hast my fa · vour
2. Brid · get or Sue, Kate, Nan · cy, or Prue, Their loves will soon be
3. since it is so, a · way I will go; I hope no harm is
4. thou art the man that ve · ri · ly can Win me if e'er I'm

1. won, ... And since I see your mod · es · ty, I
2. won, ... But don't you dare to speak me fair, As
3. done. . . . . . Fare · well, a · dieu, I hope to woo As
4. won. . . . . . Both straight and tall, gen · teel with · al, There-

1. pray you a · gree, and fan · cy me, Tho' I'm but a farm · er's son. . . . .
2. if I were at my last pray'r To mar · ry a farm · er's son. . . . . .
3. good as you, and win her, too, Tho' I'm but a farm · er's son. . . . . .
4. fore I shall be at your call, To mar · ry a farm · er's son. . . . . .

Amyntor's Well-a-day!

JOHN ECCLES.

Andante con espressione.

1.
2. His
3. The
4. Up-

1. Chlo·ris, now thou'rt fled a · way, A · myn · tor's sheep are gone astray, And
2. oat · en pipe, that in thy praise Was wont to play such round · o · lays, Is
3. May·pole, where thy lit — tle feet So round·ly did in meas · ures meet, Is
4. on those banks you us'd to tread, He ev · er since hath laid his head, And

1. all the joy he took to see His pret · ty lambs run af · ter thee Is
2. thrown a · way, and not a swain Dares pipe or sing with · in his plain; 'Tis
3. bro · ken down, and no con · tent Comes near A · myn · tor since you went; All
4. whisper'd there such pin · ing woe As not a blade of grass will grow; O,

p espress e rit.

1. gone, is gone, and he a · lone Sings noth · ing now but "Well · a · day!"
2. death for an · y · one to say One word to him, but "Well · a · day!"
3. that I ev · er heard him say Was "Chlo · ris, Chlo · ris, Well · a · day!"
4. Chlo · ris! Chlo · ris! come a · way And hear A · myn · tor's "Well · a · day!"

The words of the song are given as by Dr. Henry Hughes in H. Lawes' third book of *Select Ayres and Dialogues*, 1653, and in the later edition of 1669. As the air is by no means so good as those by Lawes generally are, another tune by John Eccles, from *The Loves of Mars and Venus*, 1696, is adapted to it.

The May Pole.

The song is from a 17th century interlude by Robert Cox, named *Actæon and Diana*, the second edition of which was published in 1656. The tune is an old local Morris dance, called "Staines' Morris," and under this title it is in the first and several other editions of Playford's *Dancing Master*.

Oh! the Charming Month of May.

The song is a burlesque production, written by Joseph Addison, and published in his *Guardian* in August, 1713. It is there inserted as from a correspondent, who is supposed to write:—" I humbly beg leave to drop a song in your lion's mouth, which will very truly make him roar like any nightingale. It is fallen into my hands by chance, and is a very fair imitation of the works of many of our English lyrics. It cannot but be acceptable to all who admire the translations of Italian operas." With the above tune the song was reprinted in *The Merry Musician; or, a Cure for the Spleen*, 1716, and in *Pills*, vi., 1720, and probably also in the preceding edition. There are more verses than our space permits us to give.

Cupid's Trick.

Allegretto quasi andantino.

1. As I was a-walking one morning in May, Enjoying the sunshine, all careless and gay, My spirit was lightsome for whole was my heart, Nor yet was it pierc'd by Love's fatal dart.

2. And just as I enter'd a deeply-ing glade, I spied thro' the bushes a golden-hair'd maid; Oh, blue was her eye and her lips so rose-red, But scarce had I noticed them e'er she had fled.

3. I quickly did follow in tumult of mind, But never a trace of the maid could I find, While there, on the branch of a blossoming tree, The little god Cupid sat laughing at me.

An old and pretty folk melody taken from Daniel Wright's *Compleat Tutor for ye Flute, circa* 1735. The tune is without words and is there named "Once I had a Sweetheart." As a diligent search through song and music books of the period has failed to disclose any other copy, the words given above have been written for the melody by a contributor.

Sir Eglamore.

1. Sir Eg - la - more, that
2. There leaped a dra - gon
3. But as in chol - er
4. Then, like a cow - ard,

1. val - iant knight, Fa, la, lank - y down dil-ly, He took his sword and he went to fight,
2. from her den, Fa, la, lank - y down dil-ly, Who'd slain God knows how man - y men,
3. he did burn, Fa, la, lank - y down dil-ly, He fetch'd the dragon a great good turn,
4. she did fly, Fa, la, lank - y down dil-ly, Un - to her den which was hard by,

1. Fa, la, lank - y down dil-ly, And as he rode o'er hill and dale, All armoured with a
2. Fa, la, lank - y down dil-ly, And when she saw Sir Eg - lamore, Oh, that you had but
3. Fa, la, lank - y down dil-ly, For as a yawn-ing she did fall, He thrust his sword up,
4. Fa, la, lank - y down dil-ly, And there she lay all night and roar'd, The knight was sor - ry

1. coat of mail, Fa, la, la, fa, la, la, Fa, la, lanky down dilly.
2. heard her roar, Fa, la, la, fa, la, la, Fa, la, lanky down dilly.
3. hilt and all, Fa, la, la, fa, la, la, Fa, la, lanky down dilly.
4. for his sword, Fa, la, la, fa, la, la, Fa, la, lanky down dilly.

The song and air are given in the second part of *The Pleasant Musical Companion*, 1686-7, published by Playford, and, at a later date, in *Pills to purge Melancholy*, 1707-1719, etc. The song is a humorous satire upon the ballads and romances then popular, which related to the slaying of dragons by valiant knights, after the manner of the Seven Champions of Christendom. The words also appear on black-letter broadsides and in 17th and 18th century printed books, in *The Antidote to Melancholy*, 1661, *Sibbald's Poetical Magazine*, Edinburgh, 1797, etc. There are more verses than are here given.

The Roast Beef of Old England.

RICHARD LEVERIDGE.

1. When might-y roast beef was the English-man's food, It en-no-bled our hearts and en-
2. Our fa-thers of old were ro-bust, stout and strong, And kept o-pen house with good
3. When good Queen E-liz-a-beth sat on the throne, Ere cof-fee, or tea, or such

1. rich-ed our blood, Our sol-diers were brave and our cour-tiers were good.
2. cheer all day long, Which made their plump ten-ants re-joice in this song.
3. slip-slops were known, The world was in ter-ror if e'er she did frown.

CHORUS.

O! the roast beef of old Eng-land! And O! for old Eng-land's roast beef.

The air is of sterling merit, and is by that clever musician, Richard Leveridge, a singer and actor at Lincoln's Inn Fields Theatre in the early years of the 18th century. The song is supposed to be by Henry Fielding, who intended it for the air "The Queen's Old Courtier." In Fielding's play, Don Quixote in England, 1733, where it first appeared in print, the song is so directed to be sung. Leveridge's tune, printed in The British Musical Miscellany, vol. iii. (Walsh, 1734), soon quashed any other or earlier air to which it had been sung. Fielding's song consisted of only two verses, but the seven verses given in The British Musical Miscellany are headed, "A Song in Praise of Old English Roast Beef, the words and musick by Mr. Leveridge" and the two verses which are claimed for Fielding are there included. Late in the 18th century, a Scotch parody, entitled "The Kail Brose o' Auld Scotland," is to be found in print. The old tune was largely employed in the very early ballad operas, and, coming down to modern times, the air has been generally played at public banquets as the signal for dinner. At a vegetarian banquet in the north of England, when vegetarianism was of recent introduction, a hitch in the programme occurred, and it was gently hinted to a local singer that he might pleasantly fill in the hiatus with a song. Conscious by his own experience of the failure of vegetarianism, he appropriately and feelingly struck up "The Roast Beef of Old England!"

Broom, Green Broom.

Con spirito.

1. There was an old man and he lived in a wood, And his trade it was making of
2. The fath-er was vext and sore-ly per-plext, With pas-sion he enterd the
3. This wakened him straight be-fore it was late, As fear-ing the ter-ri-ble
4. Jack followed his trade and read-i-ly made His goods up for coun-try
5. The maid-en did call the steward of the hall, Who came in his silks and per-

1. broom, of broom; And he had a naughty boy, Jack, to his son, And he lay in
2. room, the room; Come, sir-rah, he cried, I'll li-quor your hide If you will not go
3. doom, the doom; Dear mother, quoth he, have pit-y on me, I'll fetch home a
4. grooms, for grooms; This done, hon-est Jack took them up on his back, And cried, Who will
5. fumes, per-fumes, He gave Jack his price, And thus in a trice He sold all his

1. bed till 'twas noon, 'twas noon, And he lay in bed till 'twas noon.
2. gath-er green broom, green broom, If you will not go gath-er green booom.
3. bun-dle of broom, green broom, I'll fetch home a bun-dle of broom.
4. buy an-y brooms, green brooms? And cried, Who will buy an-y brooms?
5. bun-dle of brooms, green brooms, He sold all his bun-dle of brooms.

This song, set to several different airs, has been picked up traditionally in Devonshire, Yorkshire, Northumberland, and Norfolk; these traditional versions are to be seen in the several recently published collections of folk melodies. The present version is taken from the sixth volume of *Pills*, 1720. Copies of the words are also to be found on old ballad sheets and in song garlands.

Phillis, I can ne'er forgive it.

Lente.

HENRY PURCELL.

1. Phil - lis, I can ne'er for - give it, Nor, I think, shall e'er out - live it;
2. Da - mon you so fond - ly cher - ish, Whilst poor I, — - las! may per - ish;

1. Thus to treat me so se - vere - ly, Who have al - ways lov'd sin - cere - ly,
2. I that love, which he did nev - er, Me you slight and him you fa - vour,

1. Thus to treat me so se - vere - ly, Who have al - ways lov'd sin - cere - ly.
2. I that love, which he did nev - er, Me you slight and him you fa - vour.

The song, with the air stated to be by Henry Purcell, is given in *Pills*, vol. vi., 1720. In Walsh's *British Musical Miscellany*, vol. iv.,
1734, the same words are given with a different air, as a "song set by Mr. Sams."

The Barley Mow.

A traditional south and west country ditty, the tune of which was first published by Chappell in his *Popular Music.* J. H. Dixon prints two versions of the song in his *Songs and Ballads of the Peasantry of England*, and gives an account of its being sung on the completion of the carrying home of the barley crop.

Begone, dull Care!

The original of this well-known favourite is a dance tune named "The Queen's Jigg," printed in Playford's *Dancing Master*, 11th edition, 1701, and in later ones, 1703-1716, etc. This old form is reproduced in the Appendix to the present volume. A single verse of the song appears in Playford's *Musical Companion*, part ii, 1687, commencing, "Begone, old care, I prithee begone from me." A similar version appears in *The Aviary*, circa 1745, and in several other collections of the same period. Towards the end of the 18th century the song was revived, and, with its present tune, began to be printed as "Begone, dull Care!" This was sung at Harrison and Knyvett's concerts. The air alone was printed in Aird's *Fourth Selection of Scotch English, Irish, and Foreign Airs* (circa 1794) in *Harford's Collection* printed at Cambridge (circa 1798) and in other works. The song and air were published on sheet music, and in Sibbald's *Vocal Magazine*, vol. ii., Edinburgh, 1798.

J. H. Dixon says of the above that the popular old ditty cannot be traced beyond the reign of James II., but it is believed to be older. "The origin is to be found in an early French chanson." No proof of this or further comment, however, is vouchsafed.

Down Among the Dead Men.

For note to this song see Appendix.

Come, all you Jolly Watermen.

Con spirito.

1. Come, all you jol - ly wa - ter - men That on the Thames do
2. The no - ble prince we've land - ed Has tipp'd us store of
3. Here's half is for our land - la - dies, And half is for our
4. So here's health to our no - ble King And our gra - cious Queen bo -
5. Al - so trade may flou - rish And pride may have a

1. ply, Haul up your boats and wet your throats, For
2. gold, Ne'er spare of wealth to drink his health So
3. wives, In wet or dry, wher - e'er we ply, We
4. side, Al - so the Prince of Or - ange, And we'll
5. fall, And dear old Eng - land hold her head As

1. row - ing makes us dry, For row - ing makes us dry.
2. long as our tiz - zies¹ hold, So long as our tiz - zies hold.
3. all lead jo - vial lives, We all lead jo - vial lives.
4. not for - get his bride, We'll not for - get his bride.
5. high as the best of all, As high as the best of all.

¹ Tizzie=sixpence.

For note to this song see Appendix.

Decrepit Winter Limps Away.

Ode to Spring.

Thomas Augustine Arne

1. De - crep - it win - ter limps a - way, Now
2. Hail! smil - ing sea - son, woo'd by thee, Town
3. Thrice hap - py man whose friendly fate Af-

1. youth - ful Spring, all trim and gay, ... Comes
2. has no long - er charms for me, ... Sa -
3. fords a pleas - ant coun - try seat, ... Se -

A charming melody, the composition of tuneful Dr. Arne. It probably appeared sometime about 1750 or 1760. The copy here used is from an engraved half-sheet with the heading, "Spring, an Ode." The words are in *The Masque*, 1767, and other song books of the period.

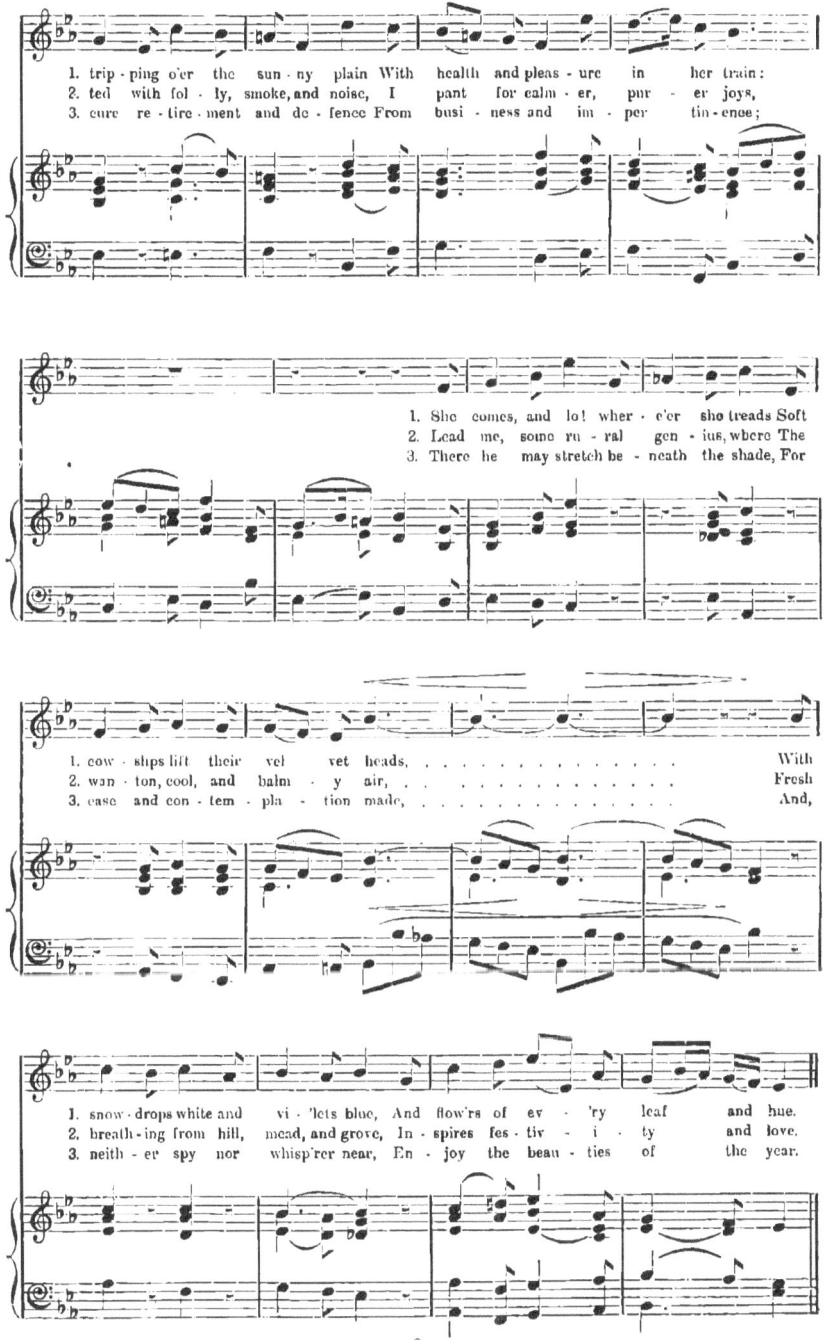

1. trip - ping o'er the sun - ny plain With health and pleas - ure in her train:
2. ted with fol - ly, smoke, and noise, I pant for calm - er, pur - er joys,
3. cure re - tire - ment and de - fence From busi - ness and im - per - tin - ence;

1. She comes, and lo! wher - e'er she treads Soft
2. Lead me, some ru - ral gen - ius, where The
3. There he may stretch be - neath the shade, For

1. cow - slips lift their vel - vet heads, ... With
2. wan - ton, cool, and balm - y air, ... Fresh
3. ease and con - tem - pla - tion made, ... And,

1. snow - drops white and vi - 'lets blue, And flow'rs of ev - 'ry leaf and hue.
2. breath - ing from hill, mead, and grove, In - spires fes - tiv - i - ty and love.
3. neith - er spy nor whisp'rer near, En - joy the beau - ties of the year.

Q

From the East Breaks the Morn.

The air is the composition of Joseph Baildon, and was printed in the second volume of *The Laurel*, a collection of Baildon's songs, published by John Walsh about 1750. From this time it attained great popularity as a hunting song, and is to be found in a great number of the 18th century song-books and on sheet music. Baildon was a noted glee writer, one of his most famous glees being, "Adieu to the Village Delights." He was born in 1727 and died 1774.

The Bonny Milkmaid.

Moderato.

1. Ye nymphs and syl-van gods That love green
2. The goddess of the morn With blushes
3. When cold bleak winds do roar, And flow'rs can
4. The country lad is free From fears and

1. fields and woods, When Spring, newly blows, Her-self doth a-dorn With flow'rs and bloom-ing buds; Come
2. they a-dorn, And take fresh air, Whilst lin-nets prepare A con-cert on each green thorn; The
3. spring no more; The fields that were seen So pleasant and green, By win-ter all can-died o'er; Oh,
4. jeal-ous-ie, When on the green He's of-ten seen With his lass, so fresh to see; With

1. sing the praise, Whilst flocks do graze In yon-der pleasant vale, Of those that choose Their
2. black-bird, thrush, On ev-'ry bush, The charm-ing night-in-gale, In mer-ry vein Their
3. how the town lass Looks with her white face And lips so dead-ly pale; But 'tis not so With
4. kiss-es most sweet He does her greet And swears she'll ne'er grow stale; Whilst the Lon-don lass, In

1. sleep to lose, And in cold dews, With clout-ed shoes, Do car-ry the milk-ing pail.
2. throats do strain To en-ter-tain The jol-ly train That car-ry the milk-ing pail.
3. those that go Thro' frost and snow With cheeks that glow To car-ry the milk-ing pail.
4. ev-'ry place, With her braz-en face, De-spis-es grace Of those with the milk-ing pail.

One of the many English songs in praise of the "Milking Pail." Some of the 17th century originals of these, having the general refrain, "To carry the milking pail," are among the Roxburgh ballads. The present song is by Thomas D'Urfey; it appears with a specially composed air in *Pills to purge Melancholy*, 1707 and 1719. It was sung in the "Second part of Don Quixote," written by D'Urfey and acted in 1694.

In Search of a Wife.

1. I have ram-bled, I own it, whole years up and down, And sigh'd o'er each
2. I will search the town ov-er the fair one to find, Nor fie-kle, nor
3. 'Tis time that the fol-lies of life had an end, And soon, may, this

1. beau-ti-ful nymph of the town, Such fan-cies have plagu'd me that oft in my
2. jeal-ous, nor vain, nor un-kind, Whose wit and good hum-our may hold it for
3. in-stant I'm read-y to mend; What won-der there'll be at so al-ter'd a

cres.

verses 1 and 2. *v. 3.*

1. life, I've been read-y to start at the name of a wife.
2. life, And then if she'll have me I'll make her my wife.
3. life, If you're wise, you like me will re-solve on a wife.

The song was sung by Thomas Lowe, a tenor singer, at Vauxhall about the year 1750. It appears in the *Universal Magazine* for August of that year, set to a rather florid melody. Shortly after this date the air, as given above, was published on a half-sheet. Lowe was a well-known singer at Vauxhall Gardens and on the stage from about 1745 to probably about 1775. He died in 1783.

Brave Grenadiers, Rejoice!

HENRY CAREY

Under the title "The Prince of Orange's March; sung by Mr. Hulett in *Britannia*," the words and music are given in Henry Carey's *Musical Century*, 1740. Carey may be author of the words as well as of the air. *Britannia; or, the Royal Lovers* was an entertainment produced to celebrate the marriage of the Prince of Orange with the then Princess Royal of England, in March, 1734. It was published with other works in 1736. Another piece named *Britannia and Batavia*, a masque by George Lillo upon the same theme, was printed in 1740. It is probable that Carey was the composer of the music of both these entertainments. The song was reprinted in Dr. Kitchiner's *Loyal and National Songs of England*, 1823.

1. pare; Let sil-ver trum-pets sound, ... Let braz-en drums re-
2. due. May all the gods a-bove ..... Re-ward their con-stant

1. bound, ... While shouts of joy fly round ... To hail the hap-py
2. love, ... And may they ev-er prove ... Still hap-py as they're

1. pair; Brave gren-a-diers, re-joice .... With gladsome heart and
2. true; For-got are war's a-larms .... And laid down are his

poco rit.

1. voice, ... For fair Bri-tan-nia's choice .... Your mar-tial sports pre-pare.
2. arms, ... For Ve-nus' pow'r-ful charms ... Can might-y Mars sub-due.

Spring.

A Pastoral.

HENRY CAREY.

The melody and (possibly) also the words are by Henry Carey, who heads the piece in his *Musical Century*, 1740, "'Pastoral,' made in the year 1715." The song and air are also inserted in Watt's *Musical Miscellany*, vol. iii., 1730; *Calliope; or, English Harmony*, vol. i., 1739; and the tune is also used in the ballad operas, *Silvia*, 1731, and *The Village Opera*, 1729.

1. sweet-ly sing. Joy, joy and plea - sure with-out mea - sure, Kind - ly hail the glo - rious Spring, Kind - ly hail the glo - rious Spring, Kind - ly hail the glo - rious Spring.

2. back the sound. Danc - - - ing, dancing, sing - ing, pi - ping, spring - ing, Nought but mirth and joy goes round, Nought but mirth and joy goes round, Nought but mirth and joy goes round.

The Lottery.

1. am a young dam-sel that flat-ters my-self, That I shall grow rich, have a
2. for-tune was told me that I should be rich, 'Twas by an old wo-man—I
3. Ro-ger he swears that he loves me as dear As tho' I was worth full three
4. if that a blank should be drawn up for me, If my mon-ey I lose still

1. bun-dance of wealth. I've got but one guin-ea, that's all I am worth, And a
2. think she's a witch. I have as good chance as the best in the town To
3. hun-dred a year; But if I a la-dy of for-tune should be, Why
4. cheer-ful I'll be; For I can have Ro-ger when at the last push, One

From an engraved half-sheet song, with the music, in date about 1700; it is headed, "'The Lottery,' sung at Sadler's Wells." The song has every appearance of having been sung in a play, probably in a revival of Fielding's ballad opera *The Lottery*, which was first acted in 1731. The song in the half-sheet does not occur in the opera as originally printed. The song with the air, "The Lottery," is also included in *Vocal Music; or, the Songster's Companion*, printed by Robert Horsfield, *circa* 1770-72. It is noticeable that the tune opens with the first strain of the "Keel Row."

1. for - tu - nate girl I have been from my birth, So I'll buy me a tick - et my
2. be a fine la - dy of fame and re - nown, For in buy - ing this tick - et I
3. should I ac - cept of such fel - lows as he? For in buy - ing this tick - et I
4. bird in the hand is worth two in the bush; And if in my tick - et no

1. hopes for to crown With a flat - ter - y in the lot - ter - y of ten thou - sand
2. hope to be crown'd With a flat - ter - y in the lot - ter - y of ten thou - sand
3. hope to be crown'd With a flat - ter - y in the lot - ter - y of ten thou - sand
4. hopes there are found, Fare-well, flat - ter - y in the lot - ter - y of ten thou - sand

1. pound, Ten thou - sand pound, ten thou - sand pound, With a
2. pound, Ten thou - sand pound, ten thou - sand pound, With a
3. pound, Ten thou - sand pound, ten thou - sand pound, With a
4. pound, Ten thou - sand pound, ten thou - sand pound, Farewell

1. flat - ter - y in the lot - ter - y of ten thou - sand pound.
2. flat - ter - y in the lot - ter - y of ten thou - sand pound.
3. flat - ter - y in the lot - ter - y of ten thou - sand pound.
4. flat - ter - y in the lot - ter - y of ten thou - sand pound.

Heart of Oak.

WILLIAM BOYCE.

Maestoso.

mf

1. Come, cheer up, my lads, 'tis to glo - ry we steer, To
2. We ne'er see our foes but we wish them to stay, They
3. They swear they'll in - vade us, these ter - ri - ble foes, They

1. add something new to this won - der - ful year; To hon - our we call you, not
2. nev - er see us but they wish us a - way, If they run, why, we fol - low, and
3. fright - en our wo - men, our chil - dren, and beaux; But should their flat bot - toms in

The music of this famous lyric is by Dr. Wm. Boyce, and the words are generally considered to be by David Garrick. It was first sung in a pantomime called *Harlequin Invasion*, a *Christmas Gambol*, acted in 1759. *Biographia Dramatica*, 1782, describes this piece as being on the plan of a supposed invasion made by Harlequin and his train on the domain of Shakespeare, and of the restoration of King Shakespeare; the dialogue was by Garrick. How far this is correct I am not aware, but certainly the different songs printed at the period as from *Harlequin Invasion* do not seem to bear upon such a plot. The song we are dealing with was printed with the music in the *Universal Magazine* for March, 1760, as "A new song, sung by Mr. Champness in *Harlequin Invasion*, also in the *Lady's Magazine* for August of that year. The expression used in the original version of the song, "Heart of Oak" has been carelessly corrupted into "Hearts of Oak"; the first correctly expresses the author's simile, the other makes more or less nonsense of it.

1. press you like slaves, For who are so free as the sons of the waves? Heart of
2. run them a-shore, For if they won't fight us, we can-not do more. Heart of
3. dark-ness get o'er, Still Bri-tons they'll find to re-ceive them on shore. Heart of

1. oak are our ships, Heart of oak are our men. We al-ways are read-y,
2. oak are our ships, Heart of oak are our men. We al-ways are read-y,
3. oak are our ships, Heart of oak are our men, We al-ways are read-y,

1. Steady, boys, steady! We'll fight and we'll con-quer a-gain and again.
2. Steady, boys, steady! We'll fight and we'll con-quer a-gain and again.
3. Steady, boys, steady! We'll fight and we'll con-quer a-gain and again.

When the King Enjoys his Own again.

Of the many ballads which have helped to "make history" few have had greater effect than this. To use a well-worn quotation from Ritson, "It is the most famous and popular air ever heard of in this country. Invented to support the declining interests of Charles I., it served afterwards with more success to keep up the spirits of the cavaliers and promote the restoration of his son. . . . At the Revolution [1688] it of course became an adherent of the exiled family whose cause it never deserted. It is believed to be a fact that nothing fed the enthusiasm of the Jacobites down to almost the present reign [George III.] in every corner of Great Britain more than 'The King shall enjoy his own again.'"

Perhaps the earliest known reference to the song is in a play named *The Gossips' Feast*, printed in 1647, and where, strangely enough, is a clue to the author of the words. One gossip says:—"By my faith, Martin Parker never got a fairer brat, no, not even when he penned 'When the King enjoyes his own again.'" The tune was printed in Playford's *Musick's Recreation on the Lyra Viola*, 1652,

1. he that gaz - eth on the skies. My skill goes be - yond the
2. right can there a shar - er be. For who bet - ter may our
3. home the branch I dear - ly love; And there will I wait till the

1. depths of a Pond, Or Riv - ers in the sor - est rain, Where-
2. high scep-tre sway Than he whose right it is to reign? Then
3. wat - ers a - bate Which now sur - round my swim - ming brain; For re-

1. by I can tell all things will be well When the king en - joys his own a - gain.
2. look for no peace, for the wars will nev-er cease Till the king en - joys his own a - gain.
3. joice will nev-er I till I hear the joy-ful cry That the king en - joys his own a - gain.

and in *Musick's Delight on the Cithren*, 1666, besides being in many later 17th century publications as well as in the Leyden MS. (*circa*, 1690-1700). There is very little difference in all these copies or even in ones printed at much later dates. The ballad by Martin Parker, the most famous of all ballad writers, is in the Roxburgh and other collections of black letter broadsides, and there are, of course, numerous parodies of all dates. The political allusions to Booker, Swallow, Rivers, etc., are fully explained in a small pamphlet, printed in 1711, entitled *The Ballad of the King shall enjoy his own again, with a learned comment there upon*. This was in part reprinted by Ritson in his *Ancient Songs*, 1791, and by other writers. The individuals referred to were professional astrologers and almanac makers who prophesied events according to the side they were on.

　　In the third volume of the *Dancing Master, circa* 1726, the air is called "The Restoration of King Charles," and in Wright's *Country Dances*, vol. i., *circa* 1730, it has the name, "Trusty Dick." There are many more verses than we have printed here.

The Sweet Rosy Morn.

Spiritoso.

RICHARD LEVERIDGE.

1. The sweet   ro · sy   morn · ing   peeps
2. The stag   rous'd be · fore us   a ·

1. o · ver the hills,   With blush · es a · dorn · ing   the   mea · dows and fields. The
2. way   seems to fly,   And pants   to the cho · rus   of   hounds in full cry. Then

mf CHORUS.

Melody by Richard Leveridge, whose music still pleases to-day, as it did a couple of centuries ago. In Bickham's *Musical Entertainer*, vol. i., 1737, the song is headed with a quaint engraved illustration, showing the huntsman carrying the large circular hunting horn which in those days seemed an essential, if cumbersome, item of the chase. With somewhat similar pictorial embellishment, the song is found in *Calliope*, vol. ii., 1739; *Universal Harmony*, 1745; *New Universal Magazine*, 1752; and, unadorned, in numerous other works. In *The Muse's Delight*, 1754, it is marked as sung in *Apollo and Daphne* (first acted 1734). A traditional survival of the words, united to another tune, were published by the Rev. John Broadwood, in his *Sussex Songs*, in 1843.

1. mer - ry, mer - ry, mer - ry   horn calls, Come, come, come   a   -   way!   A -
2. fol - low, fol - low, fol - low,   fol - low   The   mu - si - cal   chase,   Where

1. wake   from   your   slum   ber,   and   hail   the   new   day.   The
2. plea - sure   and   vig - or - ous   health   you   em - brace.   Then

1. mer   ry, mer - ry, mer - ry   horn calls, Come, come, come   a   way!   A -
2. fol - low, fol - low, fol - low,   fol - low   The   mu - si   cal   chase,   Where

1. wake   from   your   slum - ber,   and   hail   the   new   day
2. plea - sure   and   vig - or - ous   health   you   em - brace.

St. George, our Protector.

The air is by Dr. Jeremiah Clarke (born about or before 1669, died by his own hand in 1707). We have taken the above copy from Dr. Kitchiner's *Loyal and National Songs*, 1823, where it has the following note appended :—

"A song for the annual feast of St. George. This noble composition is newly adapted to the words, and arranged by Dr. Kitchiner and Mr. Watson, who have endeavoured carefully to preserve all the character of the original melody."

But in-vo-ca-tion is a su-per-sti-tious jest; All the world can't

show the like saint! All the sacrifice that we expend Is to drink fair, and to deal square, and to

love . . . our friend; Then this greeting, grate-ful meeting, Let not Taffy, Teague, nor

Scot re-vile; Drink for Saint George, Fight for Saint George, for Saint George and his fav-'rite Isle.

Since first I saw your Face.

Andante con espressione. THOMAS FORD.

con Ped.

1. Since first I saw your
2. If I ad - mire or
3. The sun, whose beams most
4. If I have wrong'd you

1. face I re - solv'd To hon - our and re - nown you; If
2. praise you too much, That fault you may for - give me, Or
3. glo - ri - ous are, Re - ject - eth no be - hold - er, And
4. tell me where - in, And I will soon a - mend it; In

Probably at the present day the greatest favourite among airs belonging to the madrigal period. It is the composition of Thomas Ford, a Court musician in the train of Prince Henry (son of James I.), where his yearly stipend appears to have been £30. Ford was the author of several canons and rounds, printed in *Catch that Catch Can*, 1652. The song, "Since first I saw your Face," is in *Music of Sundrie Kindes*, set forth in two bookes. . . . Composed by Thomas Ford. London : Printed by J. Windet, 1607, folio. Ford is said to have been born about 1580, and to have died in 1648.

Now, O now, I needs must part!

This is the composition of John Dowland (1562-1626), who was a lute player of note as well as a composer of many excellent works. Dowland travelled in Germany, Italy, and France, and ultimately became lutenist to the King of Denmark as well as to our own Charles I. He published three or four books of "Ayres," commencing with *The First Booke of Songes or Ayres of Four Parts*, printed by Peter Short in 1597. From this work the song, "Now, O now, I needs must part," is taken, where it is arranged for four voices. Dowland seems to have also arranged the air as a dance tune, under the title, "The Frog's Galliard." The melody in the Skene manuscript under the same name appears to have but little in common with Dowland's tune.

sempre con Ped.

rit.

It was a Lover and his Lass.

This dainty little song, sung by the two Pages in *As you like it*, act iv., is probably by Shakespeare himself, and the air is possibly the composition of Thomas Morley. The first record we have of the song and air is in a work issued in 1600: *The First Book of Aires; or, Little Short Songs to sing and play to the Lute with the Bass Viol; by Thomas Morley*, 1600. The first edition of the play, *As you like it*, was printed in 1623. Both words and music are to be found in a small manuscript volume bearing the date 1639, in the Advocates' Library, Edinburgh.

These early copies, like other Shakespearean music, do not appear to have been generally known until more recent times, and for the stage fresh tunes were composed by R. J. Stevens, the glee writer, William Linley, H. R. Bishop, and others. Bishop's setting was introduced by Miss M. Tree in the *Comedy of Errors*.

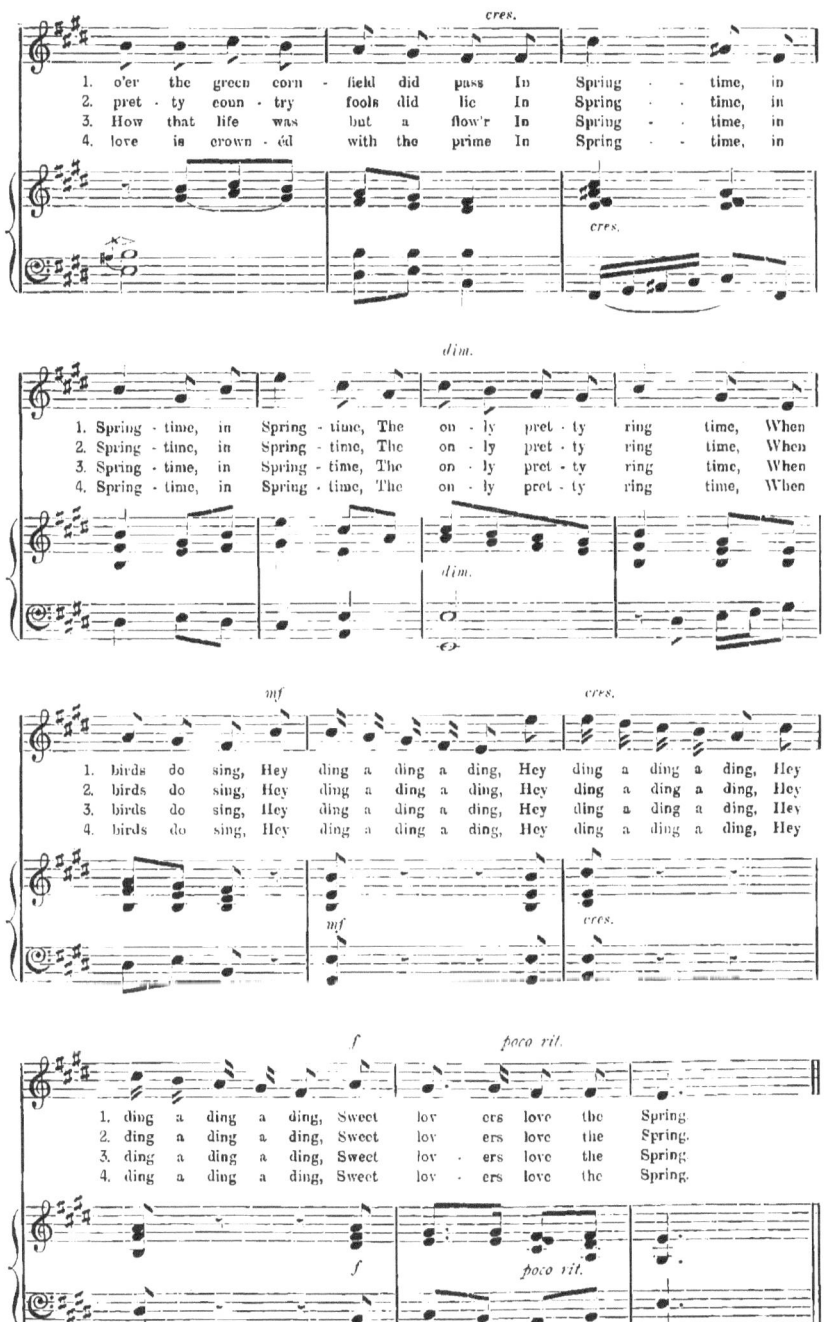

The Topsails Shiver in the Wind.

MICHAEL ARNE.

1. The top-sails shiver in the wind, The ship she casts to sea, ... But
2. Should land-men flatter when we've sail'd, Oh! doubt their art-ful tales; ... No
3. Sirens in every port we meet, More fell than rocks or waves; ... But
4. These are our cares, but if you're kind We'll scorn the dashing main, ... The

In the *Goldfinch*, a song-book published in Edinburgh with the date 1777, the song is entitled "The Sailor's Farewell, written by Capt. Thomson and set by Mr. Fisher." This is again repeated in the Glasgow and other editions of *The Goldfinch*. The song became immensely popular, and if a tune by Mr. Fisher is extant it certainly was soon superseded by the present one, composed by Michael Arne, and published in sheet form about 1780. Arne's air to the song was printed in *The Musical Miscellany*, Perth, 1786. *Calliope; or, the Vocal Enchantress*, 1788, *Dale's English Songs*, etc. It was sung at Vauxhall by Mr. Arrowsmith.

Come, each Gallant Lad.

1. Come, each gal - lant lad, who'll for plea - sure quit care, To the
2. Each night gai - ly, lads, thus we mer - ri - ly waste, Till the
3. Now ov - er the bot - tle our val - our we boast, While the

1. drum,   to the drum,   to the drum - head with spi - rit re-
2. drum,   till the drum,   till the drum tells us it is
3. drum.   while the drum,   while the drum beats a roll ev - 'ry

It is noticeable that among English national melody there are remarkably few military songs, while our naval wars during the 17th and 18th centuries produced countless numbers of sea songs. The present 18th century lyric was printed from an old copy in Dr. Kitchiner's *Sea Songs of England*, 1823. The name of the composer and author are alike forgotten.

1, pair,   Each   re   cruit   here   takes   his   glass,

2, past.   Pi - quet   arms   at   dawn   now   shine,

3, toast.   For   old   Eng - land   now   huz - zah,

1. Each young sol dier   with   his lass, When the   drum beats ta-too, When the

2. Each drum ruffs   it   down   the line, Hark, the   drum beats reveille, Hark, the

3. There we'll sing, love,   dance.   and play, And the   drum we'll unbrace, And the

1. drum beats ta-too,   Re   tires, the la - zy hours   to   pass.

2. drum beats reveille,   Sa   lut - ing the day   di - vine.

3. drum we'll unbrace   Till   a   war a - gain   calls   us   a - way.

Shall I, Wasting in Despair?

This celebrated poem by George Wither is from his *Mistresse of Philarte*, 1622. There are other versions of this type of poem, one beginning, "Shall I like a Hermit Dwell?" attributed to Sir Walter Raleigh. The song, or poem, has had several musical settings, the one we have selected being taken from *Pills*, vol. iv., p. 120, 1719, where, as "Love for Love," it is "set by Mr. King." Another and much later melody to the words is in *The Edinburgh Musical Miscellany*, 1792; the late Henry Phillips, the singer, rediscovered the song and made it a great success. The "Mr. King," who is the composer of the air we print, was probably Robert King, who died in 1711.

1. ro   sy   are?   Be she fair - er than the day,
2. come - ly   fea - ture? Or be she with good - ness blest,
3. she shall grieve: If she slight me when i woo,

1. Or the flow - 'ry   mead in May,   If she think not
2. As may de-serve of   men the best,   If she be not
3. I will scorn and slight her, too;   For if she be not

rit.

1. well of me,   What care I,   what care I how fair she be?
2. so to me,   What care I,   what care I how good she be?
3. fit for me,   What care I,   what care I for whom she be?

Wine and Glory.

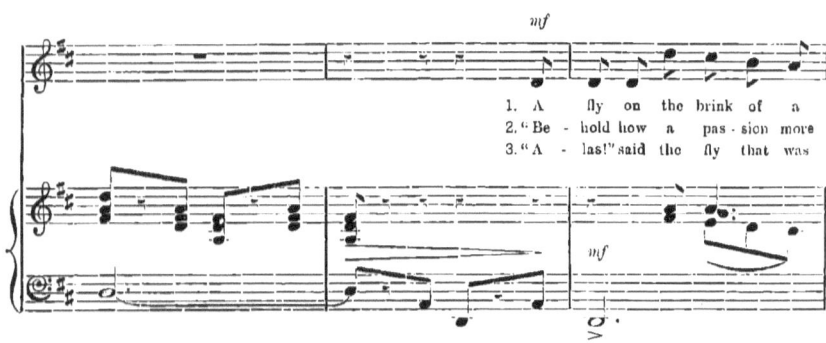

1. A fly on the brink of a
2. "Be - hold how a pas - sion more
3. "A - las!" said the fly that was

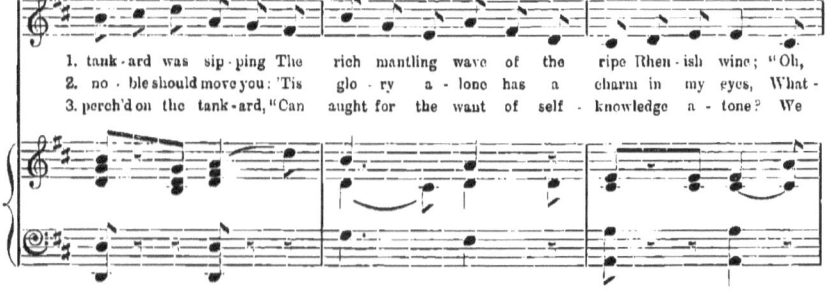

1. tank - ard was sip - ping The rich mantling wave of the ripe Rhen - ish wine; "Oh,
2. no - ble should move you: 'Tis glo - ry a - lone has a charm in my eyes, What -
3. perch'd on the tank - ard, "Can aught for the want of self - knowledge a - tone? We

The old name of this tune is "The Bath Medley," from a song commencing :—"The Spring's a-coming, all Nature is blooming," written by Tony Aston, and included in Watt's *Musical Miscellany*, vol i., 1729. It is a clever but rather rambling description of fashionable life in the city of Bath at the period of the lyric. Another song set to the tune was "Young Virgins Love Pleasure," from the ballad opera, *The Beggar's Wedding;* it was also employed in numerous other ballad operas of the day. In the third volume of *The Dancing Master, circa* 1726, the air is named "Humours of the Bath." In place of the rather unvocal "Bath Medley," a fine song which the late Dr. Charles Mackay wrote to the melody and published nearly half a century ago is taken.

1. what are you do - ing? you rush to your ru - in; Be wise, fool - ish fly, and to
2. ev - er be - tide me, its radiance shall guide me; Good - bye, sil - ly top - er, and
3. rail a - gainst oth - ers, see faults in our brothers, And blame ev - 'ry fol - ly and

1. rea - son in - cline." Thus ar - gued an - oth - er, car - eer - ing in glad - ness A -
2. learn to be wise." Thus say - ing, he sport - ed his wings for a min - ute, Then
3. vice but our own!" But whe - ther this fly was con - vert - ed from top - ing, Or

f

1. round the bright flame of a ta - per a - far, "All drinking's a fol - ly, and
2. flew to the light that so tempted his gaze: But burning his pin - ions in
3. led a new life, is not ea - sy to say; If flies are like drinkers 'mong

1. brings mel - an - chol - y, Take warn - ing and shun it, lest fly that you are!
2. glo - ry's do - min - ions He fell in the can - dle and died in the blaze.
3. two leg - ged thinkers, 'Tis like - ly he sips the red wine to this day.

Strike the Viol.

A fine and but little known specimen of Henry Purcell's music. The song and air were printed for the first time in the *Orpheus Britannicus*, vol. i., 1698. The fine work under this title is a collection of Henry Purcell's compositions, issued three years after the composer's death by Henry Playford, a second volume being printed in 1702. It is adorned with a portrait, and later editions were published in 1706-11 and 1721. John Walsh, at a subsequent date, published an *Orpheus Britannicus*, made up of single half-sheet songs, the composition of Purcell, which he had issued from time to time. It contains, however, only a small selection compared with the original Playford edition.

You Gentlemen of England.

1. You gen - tle - men of Eng - land, That
2. If en - e - mies op - pose us, And
3. Some - times in Nep - tune's bo - som Our
4. But when the dan - ger's ov - er, And

1. live at home at ease, How lit - tle do you
2. Eng land is at war With an - y for - eign
3. ship is toss'd by waves, And ev - 'ry man ex -
4. safe we come on shore, The hor - rors of the

Dr. Callcott's well-known glee, under the title "The New Mariners," was written to the above words in the early part of the 19th century, and has, as far as popularity goes, superseded the fine old original air, a version of which is printed in two editions of *150 Loyal Songs*, 1686 and 1694. Another copy is given in Ritson's *English Songs*, 1783, and is the one employed above. The ballad itself is very long and varies a good deal in the several copies. One by Martin Parker, the 17th century ballad writer, is entitled, "Saylers for my Money," and the tune is frequently named from the refrain, "When the stormy winds do blow." This refrain is also used for a number of other sailor ballads.

As in the case of Dr. Callcott's composition superseding the original air, so has Thomas Campbell's fine lyric, "To Mariners of England" now supplanted the old words.

1. think up-on The dan-gers of the seas; Give
2. na - - tion, We fear not wound or scar; To
3. pect - - ing The sea to be our graves; Then
4. tem - - pest, We think of them no more; The

1. ear un-to the mar-in-ers, And they will plain-ly show All the
2. hum - ble them, come on, my lads, Their flags we'll soon lay low; Clear the
3. up a-loft she's mount - ed, And down a-gain so low, In the
4. flow - ing bowl in - vites us, And joy-ful-ly we go, All the

cres.   CHORUS.

1. cares and the fears, When the storm-y winds do blow, All the
2. way for the fray, Tho' the storm-y winds do blow, Clear the
3. waves on the seas, When the storm-y winds do blow, In the
4. day drink a - way Tho' the storm-y winds do blow,

1. cares and the fears, When the storm - y winds do blow.
2. way for the fray, Tho' the storm - y winds do blow.
3. waves on the seas, When the storm - y winds do blow.
4. day drink a - way, Tho' the storm - y winds do blow.

Woman, Love, and Wine.

Con spirito.

1. The murm - 'ring brooks, the fan - ning breeze, Gay
2. The rest - less wretch who doats on gold, And
3. May youth and age of all de - grees Ou
4. Ye sons of joy, for true de - light, In

1. myr - tles, flow - 'ry banks, and trees, To doat on some in -
2. would in flames the world be - hold To see his trea - sure
3. such in spir ing com - forts seize, 'Twill ev - 'ry sense re -
4. wo - men, love, and wine u - nite, This great re - solve is

A clever little song taken from *Vocal Music; or, the Songster's Companion*, printed by Robert Horsfield, *circa* 1770-2. No composer's or author's name is there indicated.

The Bonny Grey-Ey'd Morn.

Andantino tranquillo.

1. The bonny grey-ey'd morn be-
2. Up - on his bosom Jen - ny

1. gan to peep, When Colin, rous'd with love, came blithe - ly on, And
2. laid her head, And, blushing, heard his pret - ty tale of love; Her

This has been claimed as a Scottish melody, but Hawkins asserts that it was composed by Jeremiah Clark, and was introduced in D'Urfey's comedy, *The Fond Husband, or, The Plotting Sisters*, acted in 1676. The air, under its own title, is in the additional sheet to the second part of the *Dancing Master*, 1686 and 1698, while it also appears in the 1703, 1716, and later editions of the *Dancing Master*. With the words it is contained in *Pills to Purge Melancholy*, 1698, 1707, vol. i. and in vol. iii. of the 1719 edition. Allan Ramsay used the tune with fresh words in *The Gentle Shepherd*, 1725, as did Gay in *The Beggars' Opera*, 1727-8.

From its introduction in Allan Ramsay's work it was considered by Scottish collectors as belonging to Scottish national melody and was printed as such in Oswald's *Caledonian Pocket Companion* and many other works, Stenhouse, in his notes to *Johnson's Museum*, doubts the statement that Jeremiah Clark was the composer of "The Bonny Grey-Ey'd Morn." He had sufficient reason for this if Clark was born in 1669 (Brown and Stratton say "or earlier"), and if the tune came out with the first performance of *The Fond Husband* in 1676. There does not appear to be a copy of the first edition of the play in the British Museum Library, and the song is not printed in either the 1685 or the 1711 editions. It may be that it was introduced by some singer at a subsequent period, and Hawkins perhaps has found it stated on a music sheet to be sung by such singer. Personally, I am unable to trace the air in print prior to 1696, but both words and tune indicate it to be an Anglo-Scotch song of that period. As the old words are scarcely fitted for the modern drawing-room the above adaptation of them is used instead.

1. he, who long had lain de - priv'd of sleep, Ab - horred the la - zy hours that
2. yielding heart, at ev 'ry word he said Did flut - ter up and down and

1. slow did run; But ma - ny were his joys, when, in his view, He
2. strange - ly move; She sigh'd, he kiss'd her hand, and vow'd and swore That

1. at a window spied his on - ly dear, And on the wings of love he
2. she a - lone did hold his heart in thrall, And now he begg'd that ere a

rit.

1. to her flew: For he had fancied all his heav'n was there.
2. month was o'er That Jen - ny he might then his fair bride call.

rit.

Russell's Triumph.

An early sea song, which for over a hundred years enjoyed great popularity. It relates to the victory of the English (under Admiral Russell), combined with the Dutch, over a large French fleet, off Cape la Hogue, on May 19th, 1692. The victory was celebrated by Queen Mary by the giving up of her palace at Greenwich for the use of disabled seamen, and by the foundation of the present Greenwich Hospital. The song and the tune, under the title, "'The Sea Fight in Ninety-two,' set by Mr. Akeroyde,'" appear in *Pills*, iv., 1719, and later on half-sheets and in many song books. Copies of the air vary considerably, especially in the first four bars of the second strain; the earliest and best is here used. In regard to the words, early versions begin, "Thursday in the morn the *Ides* of May." Samuel Akeroyde, the composer of the melody, was a Yorkshireman, whose compositions figure largely in the later publications of Henry Playford and D'Urfey.

1. lof-ty sails of France ad-vanc-ing to. "All hands a-loft," they cry, "let
2. sink the Eng-lish ad-mir-al at his feet. Now ev-'ry val-iant mind to
3. see their lof-ty stream-ers now no more. At six o'clock tho red, the

1. Bri-tish val-our shine, Let fly a cul-ver-in, tho sig-nal of the line, Let
2. vic-t'ry doth as-pire, The blood-y fight's be-gun, tho sea is all on fire; And
3. smil-ing vic-tors led To give a sec-ond blow, the fa-tal o-ver-throw. Now

1. ev-'ry man sup-ply his gun. Fol-low me, you shall see That the bat-tle it will
2. might-y Fate stood look-ing on, Whilst a flood, all of blood, Fill'd the scup-pers of the
3. death and hor-ror e-qual reign: Now they cry, run and die, Bri-tish col-ours ride the

1. soon be won, Fol-low me, you shall see, That the bat-tle it will soon be won.
2. Ris-ing Sun, Whilst a flood, all of blood, Fill'd the scup-pers of the Ris-ing Sun.
3. vanquish'd main, Now they cry, run and die, Bri-tish col-ours ride the vanquish'd main.

Queen Besses' Dame of Honour.

Air—"I am a lusty, lively lad."

1. Since now the world's turn'd up-side down, And all things chang'd in na - ture. As if a doubt were new-ly grown We had the same Cre - a - tor; Of ancient modes and former ways I'll teach you, sirs, tho man - ner, In good Queen Bess-es' gold-en days, When I was a Dame of Hon - our.

2. I had an an - cient no - ble seat, Tho' now 'tis come to ru - in, Where mut - ton, beef and such good meat In th' cel - lar full I was the year - ly don - or; Where top - ing knaves had ma - ny a pull, When I was a Dame of Hon - our.

3. My men of home-spun hon - est greys Had coats and come - ly bad - ges, They wore no dir - ty ruffled lace, Nor e'er complained for wa - ges; For gaud - y fringe and silks o'th'town I feared no threat'ning dun - ner, But wore a de - cent grogram gown, When I was a Dame of Hon - our.

4. My neighbours still I treat - ed round And strangers that came near me; The poor, too, al - ways welcome found, Whose pray'rs did still en - dear me; Let, therefore, who at court would be No churl, nor yet no fawn - er; Match in old hos - pi - tal - i - ty Queen Bess-es' Dame of Hon - our.

For note to this song see Appendix.

Bright was the Morning.

1. Bright was the morn-ing, cool was the air, Se-rene was all the sky, When on the waves I left my dear, The cen-tre of my joy; Heaven and na-ture smil-ing were, And noth-ing sad but I.

2. Each ros-ic field did o - - dours spread, All fra-grant was the shore; Each riv-er god rose from his bed And sigh'd, and own'd her pow'r; Curling their waves they deck'd their heads, As proud of what they bore.

3. Glide on, ye wat-ers, bear these lines, And tell her how dis-tress'd; Bear all my sighs, ye gen-tle winds, And waft them to her breast; Tell her, if e'er she prove un-kind, I nev-er shall have rest.

A song in the first volume of *Pills*, 1719. The same words, set to an air by William Turner, appear in Henry Playford's *Theater of Music*, 1685. The melody used above is the one from *Pills*, and differs from that by Turner.

Sweet Nan of the Vale.

1. In a small plea-sant vil-lage by na - ture com-plete, Of a
2. Till young Ro - ger, the smartest of all the gay green, Who

1. few hon-est shep-herds the qui - et re-treat, There liv'd a young lass of so
2. late - ly to Lon-don on fro - lic had been, Came home much im-prov'd in his

Another of Dr. Arne's tuneful pastoral melodies. The song was sung at the public gardens about the year 1751. One engraved half-sheet states: "Sung at the New Spring Gardens, Greenwich." As "A New Song" it appears in The Universal Magazine for November, 1751. It is also in The Muse's Delight, Liverpool, 1754; Clio and Euterpe, vol. i., 1758; Fielding's Vocal Enchantress, 1783, etc. The words may be possibly by John Cunningham, although they are not included in the small edition of his works published in 1765.

1. love - ly a mien That sel - dom at balls or at courts can be seen.
2. air and ad - dress, And bold - ly at - tack'd her, not fear - ing suc - cess.

p

1. The sweet dam - ask rose was full
2. He said hea - ven form'd such ripe

con espress.

1. blown on her cheek, The li - ly dis-play'd all its white on her neck; The
2. lips to be kiss'd, And press'd her so close - ly she could not re - sist; And

1. lads of the vil-lage all strove to pre-vail, And call'd her in raptures sweet Nan of the Vale.
2. show'd the dull clowns the way to as - sail, And brought to the al - tar sweet Nan of the Vale.

Just as the Tide was Flowing.

Con spirito.

1. One morn - ing, in the
2. Her dress it was as
3. I made a bow, and
4. No more was said, but

1. month of May, Down by a roll - ing riv - - er, A
2. white as milk, And jew - - els did a - - dorn her skin, It
3. said, Fair maid, How came you here so ear - ly? My
4. on her way We both did go to - - geth - er; The

Taken, by permission, from *Traditional Tunes: a Collection of Ballad Airs chiefly obtained in Yorkshire and the South of Scotland*. . . . *Collected and edited by Frank Kidson*, 1891.

The tune was taken down in the East Riding of Yorkshire from traditional singing and has been heard to the same words in the North Riding. The words were frequently printed on broadsides. The air has a distinct similarity to a dance air named "The Peacock."

1. jol - ly sail - or he did stray, And there be - held a
2. was as soft as an - y silk, Just like a la - dy of
3. heart by you it was be - tray'd, And I could love you
4. small birds sang, the lambs did play, And pleas - - ant was the

1. lov - - er; She care - less - ly a long did stray, A -
2. hon - - our; Her cheeks were red, her eyes were brown, Her
3. dear - - ly; I am a sail - - or come from sea, If
4. wea - - ther; We both being wea - ry sat us down Be -

1. view - ing of the dais - ies gay, She sweet - ly sang a
2. hair, in ring - lets hang - ing down, Her love - ly brow with
3. you'll ac - cept my com - pan - y To walk and see the
4. neath a tree with bran - ches round; Then to the church we

1. roun - de - lay, Just as the tide was flow - ing.
2. out a frown, Just as the tide was flow - ing.
3. fish - es play, Just as the tide was flow - ing.
4. soon were bound, Just as the tide was flow - ing.

T

The Poacher's Song.

1. In thorn - y woods in Buck-ing-ham-shire, Right fol lol de
2. I and my dogs went out one night, Right fol lol do
3. When I had rang - éd all that night, Right fol lol de
4. Then I went home and went to bed, Right fol lol de
5. Now ses - sions are o - ver, 'sizes are near, Right fol lol de

1. li de O, Three keep - ers' hous - es stood three square, Fol de rol lol de re
2. li de O, The moon and stars they shone so bright, Fol de rol lol de re
3. li de O, Un - til the morn - ing 'twas day - light, Fol de rol lol de re
4. li de O, And limp - ing Jack went in my stead, Fol de rol lol de re
5. li de O, Now Jack and I we must ap - pear, Fol de rol lol de re

Taken from *Old English Songs, as now Sung by the Peasantry of the Weald of Surrey and Sussex*, folio, collected by the late Rev. John Broadwood, and published anonymously in 1843. The words are on ballad sheets and in Dixon's *Songs of the Peasantry*, where the locality is probably more properly named "In Thornehagh-Moor woods in Nottinghamshire." This is near Newark. As the whole of the verses, with the "Fol de rol" chorus, is more than our space permits, we only use a selection from them.

1. da, . . . Three keep - ers' hous - es stood three square, A -
2. da, . . . O'er hedg - es ditch - es, gates, and stiles, With
3. da, . . . When I had rang - éd all that night, Un -
4. da, . . . In Park - more fields O there he found A
5. da, . . . Your bucks and does may range so free, But

molto cres.

1. bout a mile from each oth - er they were, In or - der to look
2. my two dogs close at my heels, To look for a buck in
3. til the morn - ing was day - light, I thought it high time to
4. brave fat buck run - ning o - ver the ground, And my two dogs soon
5. hares and rab - bits they are for me, A poach - er's life's the

molto cres.

1. af - ter the deer. Fol de rol lol de rol li do.
2. Park moor fields. Fol de rol lol de rol li do.
3. take my flight Fol de rol lol de rol li do.
4. pull'd him down. Fol de rol lol de rol li do.
5. life for me ! Fol de rol lol de rol li do.

f

The Northumberland Bagpiper.

The ballad is on black-letter broadsides in the Roxburghe and the Bagford Collections, and it is also printed in *Pills to purge Melancholy*, vol. iv., 1719, united to the tune we give. Chappell says that the air alone is also contained in the 1693 edition of *Apollo's Banquet*, where it is named, "A New Dance in the Play *The Marriage Hater Matched*," which, by the way, is a play written by D'Urfey and acted in 1692. The tune of "The Northumberland Bagpiper" bears a strong similarity to one in the Leyden Ms. (in date about 1690-2) named "The Watter of Boyne," which is the same as "The Boyne," in Daniel Wright's first volume of *Country Dances*, circa 1735. These last named tunes are probably the original ones to which a version of the political ballad "Boyne Water" was sung, although this song is now associated with a totally different air. We have found it necessary to make some slight alterations in the song given above.

1. hon - our of that ho - ly day, A dit - ty he did
2. gath - 'ring rush - es on the down; Her bon - grace was of
3. find I can keep time and rule; Right well she danced and

1. chant a - long, That goes to the tune of Cat - er - Bor - dee; And
2. wend - ed straw, From the sun's hot beams her face is free; And
3. grace - ful - ly She kept time to his har - mon - y; And

1. ma - ny were the songs he sung, And piped he there most
2. thus she be - gan when she him saw, Thy chant - er tune, I'll
3. look - ing on him smil - ing said, Take thou a kiss for

1. fam ous - ly.
2. dance to thee.
3. pi per's fee.

Tobacco's but an Indian Weed.

Andantino.

1. To -
2. The
3. The

1. bac - co's but an In - dian weed, Grows green at morn, cut down at eve; It
2. pipe that is so li - ly white, Where-in so ma - ny take de - light, Is
3. pipe that is so foul with - in, Shows how man's soul is stain'd with sin; And

1. shows our de - cay, We are but clay: Think of this when you smoke to - bac - co.
2. broke with a touch, Man's life is such: Think of this when you smoke to - bac - co.
3. then the fire it doth re - quire: Think of this when you smoke to - bac - co.

The song is at an early date (period of James I.) found in a manuscript volume which at one time belonged to Mr. Payne Collier. It is there signed "G. W.," and this is considered by some to stand for the initials of George Wither. The song has not been traced in print earlier than 1670, at which date with slight variation, it was included in *Merry Drollery Complete*, and also began to be printed on broadsides. It is included, with the tune, in all editions of *Pills* from 1698-99 to 1719. The versions of the song are innumerable, and to a German translation, the composer J. S. Bach wrote a melody with figured bass. During the early part of the eighteenth century, the Rev. Ralph Erskine included the poem, with an added second part in his *Gospel Sonnets*, which sequel is, after its pithy predecessor, a perfect failure. The old forms of the song have the expression "drink tobacco," an early and characteristic expression, alluding to the method of inhaling the smoke and passing it back through the nostrils. Readers of *Handy Andy* will remember fragments of the song there introduced.

Early one Morning.

This traditional English melody was first published by Thomas Moore in the sixth number of his *Selection of Popular National Airs*, quarto, *circa* 1828. He called the melody "Old English," and wrote words for it commencing "Hope comes again." It was next noted down from tradition by Mr. William Chappell, and printed in his *National English Airs*, 1838, and in his *Popular Music*, from which it has fallen into many collections of English songs. The words are extant on penny garlands of songs published early in the 19th century.

Every Man take his Glass in his Hand.

A fine tune, associated with good sturdy verses. The air alone, under its proper title, is in the second volume of the *Dancing Master*, 1718, 1719, and 1726, p. 317; next, with the song, in Watt's *Musical Miscellany*, vol. iii., 1730, and in many later song books; in *Convivial Songster*, 1782; *Musical Miscellany*, Perth, 1786; Ritson's *English Songs*, 1783; *Calliope; or, the Vocal Enchantress*, 1788, etc. The tune was also employed for a song in the *Jovial Crew*, 1731. The air bears much resemblance to a once popular melody (with words by Dr. Parnell), "My Days have been so Wondrous Free," to be seen in Watt's *Musical Miscellany*, vol. iv.

What shall I do to show how much I love her?

HENRY PURCELL.

1. What shall I do to show how much I love her?
2. Thus I am rack'd by my love's cruel re - pul - ses,

1. Or to make known the con - stan - cy I feel?
2. Which, while re - pell - ing, still at - tract me more;

1. That which wins oth - er hearts can nev - er move her,
2. So that the ten - our of my heart's im - pul - ses

The melody of this fine song is by Henry Purcell and forms part of the vocal music in *The Prophetess; or, The History of Dioclesian*, printed in 1691, but produced in the previous year. The song and air are in vol. iv. of *Pills*, 1719.

John Gay used the air for the sixth song in *The Beggar's Opera*. Henry Purcell was born in 1658; the world of music was made poorer by his early death in 1695.

The Golden Vanity.

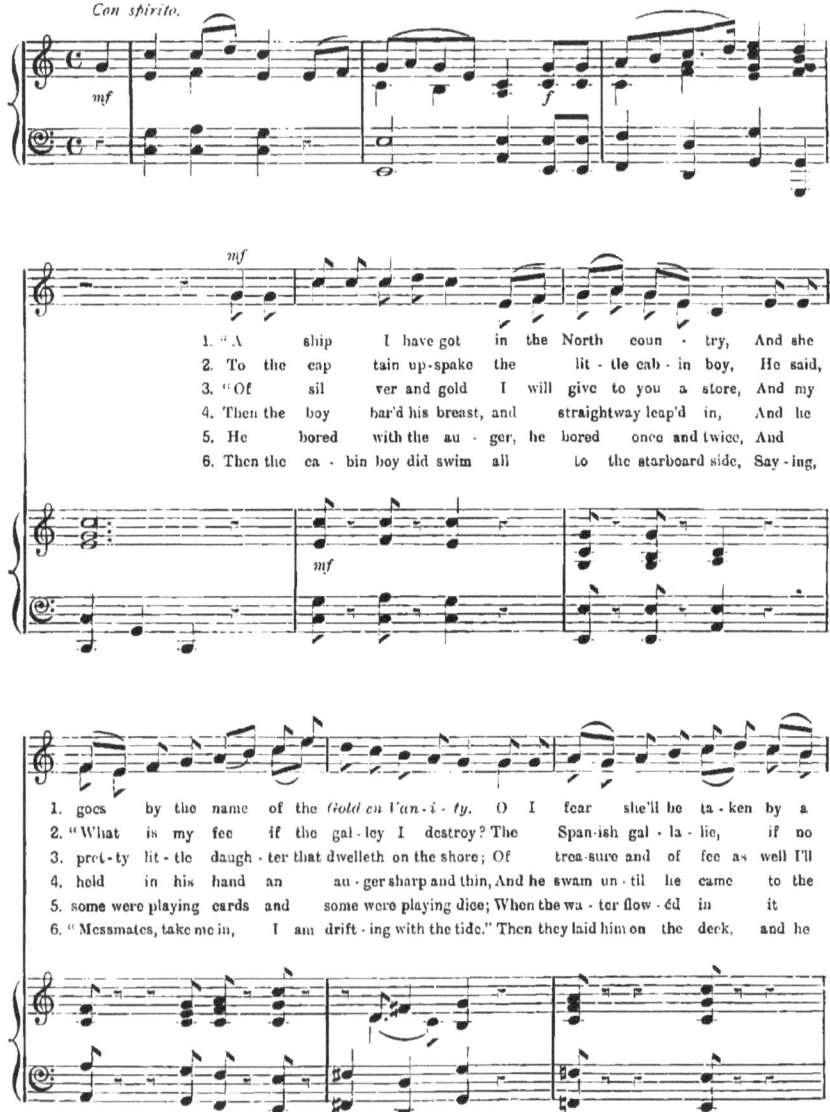

Con spirito.

1. " A ship I have got in the North coun - try, And she
2. To the cap tain up-spake the lit - tle cab - in boy, He said,
3. " Of sil ver and gold I will give to you a store, And my
4. Then the boy bar'd his breast, and straightway leap'd in, And he
5. He bored with the au - ger, he bored once and twice, And
6. Then the ca - bin boy did swim all to the starboard side, Say - ing,

1. goes by the name of the *Gold en Van - i - ty*. O I fear she'll be ta - ken by a
2. "What is my fee if the gal - ley I destroy? The Span-ish gal - la - lie, if no
3. pret-ty lit - tle daugh - ter that dwelleth on the shore; Of trea-sure and of fee as well I'll
4. hold in his hand an au - ger sharp and thin, And he swam un - til he came to the
5. some were playing cards and some were playing dice; When the wa - ter flow - éd in it
6. "Messmates, take me in, I am drift - ing with the tide." Then they laid him on the deck, and he

1. Span·ish gal · la · lie, As she sails by the Low · lands low, As she
2. more it shall an · noy, As you sail by the Low · lands low, As you
3. give to thee ga · lore, As we sail by the Low · lands low, As we
4. Span·ish gal · le · on, As she lay by the Low · lands low, As she
5. daz · zled their eyes, And she sank by the Low · lands low, And she
6. clos'd his eyes and died, As they sail'd by the Low · lands low, As they

ff Chorus.

1. sails by the Low · lands low."
2. sail by the Low · lands low."
3. sail by the Low · lands low."
4. lay by the Low · lands low.
5. sank by the Low · lands low.
6. sail'd by the Low · lands low.

By the Low - lands

poco rit.

low, As she sails by the Low · lands low.

poco rit.

This famous old sea song dates from Queen Elizabeth's days, and there is an early broadside version extant, entitled "Sir Walter Raleigh Sailing in the Lowlands, shewing how the famous ship, called the *Sweet Trinity*, was taken by a false galley, and how it was again restored by the craft of a little sea boy, who sunk the galley, as the following song will declare. To the tune of 'Sailing in the Lowlands.'" There are many variants of the tune current; the one given above is from *Songs of the West*, by permission of Messrs. Methuen & Co. and of the Rev. S. Baring-Gould and H. F. Shepard.

302

Cupid's Garden.

A quaint old-fashioned love song which, even so late as the forties and fifties, was a great favourite traditionally in most country places. Chappell suggests that "Cupid's Garden" should be "Cupar's Garden," a pleasure resort on the Surrey side of the Thames, but I feel disposed to question this, and imagine that it is simply an allegorical fancy on the part of the writer of the song. The present tune has not appeared in print much more than forty or fifty years, but it is certainly an early air. In the *Dancing Master*, 1690, and in later editions there is an air which fits the words and may be their original tune. I give this in the Appendix.

1. view the fair - est flow - - - ers That in that gar - den
2. there I saw two pret - ty maids Sitting 'neath a sha - dy
3. you en - gaged to any young man, Do tell to me, I
4. solv éd was the sail - or boy To know her full in -

1. grow; The first it was the jes - samine, The
2. bow'r; The first was love - ly Nan - cy, So
3. pray? I'm not en - gaged to any young man, I
4. tent; To know if he would slight - ed be, When to

1. lil - y, pink, and rose, And sure - ly that's the fair - est flow'r That
2. beau - ti - ful and fair, The oth - er was a maid - en Who
3. sol - emn - ly do swear, I mean to live a maid - en And
4. her the truth he told, Oh no, oh no, oh no, she cried, I

rit.

1. in that gar - den grows, That in that gar - den grows.
2. did the laur - el wear, Who did the laur - el wear.
3. still the laur - el wear, And still the laur - el wear.
4. love a sail - or bold, I love a sail - or bold.

The Ploughboy.

1. Come, all you jolly plough - boys, Come, list - en to my lays, ... And join with me in
2. So early in the morning The plough - boy he is seen; . . . . . . He hast - ens to the
3. So early in the morning To har - row, plough, and sow, ... And with a gen - tle
4. The corn is now a - grow - ing And seed - time it is o'er, . . . Our mas - ter he does
5. The corn is now a - grow - ing The fields look fresh and gay, The cheer - ful lads come

One of the numerous songs in praise of a ploughman's life over any other worldly occupation. It is from the Rev. John Broadwood's *Collection of Sussex Songs*, issued in 1843. It is to be noticed that while in the south country the folk song is frequently one having for its theme the pleasures of a rural life, yet as we advance northward this kind of ditty is gradually left behind, and probably the more barren land and the greater hardness of winning crops make the farmer and his labourer less inclined to sing of the joys of farming.

1. cho - rus, I'll sing the plough - boy's praise. . . . . . My
2. sta - ble, His hor - ses for to clean. . . Their
3. cast, my boys, We'll give the corn a throw. . . . . This
4. wel - come us, And opes the cel - lar door. . . . . . With
5. in to mow, Whilst dam - sels make the hay. . . . . The

1. song is of the plough-boy's fame, And un - to you I'll re - late the same, He
2. manes and tails he will comb straight, With chaff and corn he does them bait, Then
3. makes the val - leys thick to stand With corn to fill the reap - er's hand, All
4. cake and ale we have our fill, Be - cause we've done our work so well, There's
5. ears of corn they now ap - pear, And peace and plen - ty crown the year, So

1. whis - tles, sings, and drives his team, The brave plough - ing boy. . . .
2. he'll en - dea - vour to plough straight, The brave plough - ing boy. . . .
3. this, you may well un - derstand, Does the brave plough - ing boy. . . .
4. none can here ex - cel the skill Of the brave plough - ing boy. . . .
5. we'll be mer - ry and drink whilst here To the brave plough - ing boy. . . .

Rule, Britannia!

THOMAS AUGUSTINE ARNE.

Molto maestoso.

1. When Bri - tain first, ... at heav'n's com - mand, A -
2. The na - tions, not . . . . so bless'd as thee, Must
3. Still more ma - jes - - tic shalt thou rise, More

1. rose . . . . . . from out the a - - zure main, A - rose, a - rose, a - rose from out the
2. in . . . . . . their turns to ty - - rants fall, Must in, must in, must in their turns to
3. dread - - - ful from each for - - eign stroke, More dreadful, dreadful, dreadful from each

"Rule, Britannia!" first occurred in a masque, written by command of Frederick, Prince of Wales, for an entertainment produced in the gardens of his house at Clicfden, on the Thames, on August 1st, 1740. It was in honour of the birthday of his daughter (then three years old) and in commemoration of the Hanoverian succession which commenced on August 1st. The masque was repeated the following day. The title of the masque was *Alfred*, and it was jointly written by David Mallet and James Thomson, the author of *The Seasons*, the music being by Dr. Arne. On the same occasion was performed *The Judgement of Paris*, another of Dr. Arne's works. In 1745 the masque, *Alfred*, was performed at Covent Garden and Drury Lane, and rewritten by Mallet, again at Drury Lane in 1751. In the early printed versions the song, "Rule, Britannia!" is headed "An Ode." It has been much in dispute as to whether Thomson or Mallet wrote the words of this, and it is now most frequently assigned to Thomson. For this, however, there has never been the slightest particle of evidence put forth; indeed, while the matter is still likely to remain an unclearable mystery, a careful examination will show that the honour may with greater likelihood rest on Mallet.

In 1751, Mallet, in a note prefixed to his altered version of *Alfred*, tells us he "was obliged to reject a good deal of what I had written, neither could I retain of my friend's part more than three or four single speeches and part of one song." Here he distinctly states that the only lyrical part of Thomson's work left in the piece is one song, of which there are four so named, one headed "Stanzas," and the remaining one titled "An Ode," this latter being, of course, "Rule, Britannia!" Unless Mallet wished to wilfully deceive, had the ode been by Thomson he would have explicitly so named it. In 1751 some verses were added to the "Ode" by Lord Bolingbroke, but they form no part of the version now sung.

Arne's music to the "Ode" was published by Henry Waylett in folio at the end of the music in *The Judgement of Paris*. "Rule, Britannia!" did not spring into very great fame until well on in the 19th century. The song with its music was, of course, well known and frequently reprinted, but it by no means quickly became the national song of England, the position it now so worthily holds. It may be worth while mentioning that "*rules* the waves" is a modern change, the old and original form being "*rule*."

1. a - zure main,   This was the charter,   the char-ter   of the land,   And
2. ty - rants fall;   While thou shalt flourish,   shalt flour-ish   great and free,   The
3. for - eign stroke;   As   the loud blast,   the   blast that tears the skies   Serves

cres.   *f*

1. guar - dian   an - gels sang this strain,—   Rule,   Bri - tan - nia!   Bri -
2. dread   and   en - vy of them all.   Rule,   Bri - tan - nia!   Bri -
3. but   to   root   thy na - tive oak.   Rule,   Bri - tan - nia!   Bri -

cres.   *f*

1. tan - nia, rule the waves,   Bri   tons   nev - er   shall be slaves!
2. tan - nia, rule the waves,   Bri   tons   nev - er   shall be slaves!
3. tan - nia, rule the waves,   Bri   tons   nev - er   shall be slaves!

CHORUS.   *poco rit.*

Rule, Bri-tan-nia! Bri - tan-nia, rule the waves,   Bri - tons nev - er shall be slaves.

ff   *poco rit.*

NOTE.

THE verses of the songs entitled :—

    COMELY SWAIN, WHY SITT'ST THOU SO? (except first four lines).

    COME YOU NOT FROM NEWCASTLE?   THE PERILS OF THE ISLE.

    GO FROM MY WINDOW, GO.   TOM TINKER'S MY TRUE LOVE.

    THE COUNTRY PARSON.   WHILE O'ERHEAD THE STORM.

have been written by FRANK KIDSON to replace unsuitable lyrics, or to supply the deficiency where no words of any kind were available.

Miss KATE MOFFAT has contributed the song entitled :—CUPID'S TRICK.

The undermentioned are Copyright, and are used by Permission :—

    COME, HERE'S TO ROBIN HOOD. (Words.) Chappell & Co.

    THE GOLDEN VANITY. (Words and Tune.) Messrs. Methuen & Co.

    CUPID'S TRICK. (Words.) Miss Moffat.

    SPOTTED COW.   Words and Tune from Frank Kidson's *Traditional Tunes.*

    BUCKS A-HUNTING GO.   Do.   do.   do.

    PRETTY PLOUGHBOY.   Do.   do.   do.

    JUST AS THE TIDE WAS FLOWING.   Do.   do.   do.

APPENDIX.

Note.—Where Playford's *Dancing Master*, 1650, is mentioned, it must be understood that the reference is to the first edition, which is dated 1651, though really published in the latter part of the previous year.

HOW SHOULD I YOUR TRUE LOVE KNOW? (See page 9).

The ballad air may be compared with a tune used to the words, "My simple heart is fled away," in *Love in a Riddle*, 1729, and with the following from the opera, *The Wonders in the Sun; or, the Kingdom of the Birds*, 1706:—

IN THE FIELDS IN FROST AND SNOWS.

See *Pills*, vol. ii., 1719, and *Dancing Master*, 1719.

MY SIMPLE HEART IS FLED AWAY.

From *Love in a Riddle*, 1729.

THE SPANISH LADY (See page 10).

From Dauney's *Ancient Scotish Melodies*, 1838.

ADMIRAL BENBOW (See page 25).

A famous forecastle ditty apparently dating from the death of Benbow, who was fatally wounded in action in 1702. The tune is a fine and sturdy English melody, and we take as the best version the one from Dale's *English Songs*, folio, *circa* 1800. Before this date it had appeared in Fielding's *Vocal Enchantress*, 1783. The words there commence, "O we sail'd to Virginia and thence to New York," and the song has two more verses than usual. The tune alone is in Aird's *Selection of Scotch, English, Irish, and Foreign Airs*, book 5, and for his collection, printed in 1805, the Rev. James Plumptre wrote another ballad to the melody, commencing "When in war on the ocean." The original song was sung on the stage by Charles Incledon. Readers of *Jacob Faithful* will remember old Tom singing the ditty. Another "Death of Admiral Benbow," begins "Come, all ye sailors bold, lend an ear," but this is entirely different in verse and structure, and is fitted to a fine tune of its own.

THE THREE RAVENS (See page 32).

There can be but little doubt that the ballad of "The Three Ravens" is among our very early existing fragments of traditional ballad poetry. Its equivalents are found among Scottish and Danish folk ballads, and the present writer has rescued from tradition a version of the ballad and air once current in Derbyshire (see Kidson's *Traditional Tunes*), and there may still be lingering remembrances of the ballad and air in other parts of rural England. The air and ballad were first printed in a collection of part songs, entitled *Melismata*, published in 1611. The Scottish form of the ballad is "The Twa Corbies," copies being in Scott's *Minstrelsy of the Scottish Borders*, Motherwell's *Minstrelsy*, 1827, and other collections. Motherwell also gives a traditional air. James Sibbald, of Edinburgh, first unearthed the *Melismata* version for his new series of *The Vocal Magazine*, 1800, and after this followed Chappell's reprint.

TOM TINKER'S MY TRUE LOVE (See page 37).

The original song commencing "Tom Tinker's my true love, and I am his dear," is an early 17th century one, but is probably not that intolerably coarse production which is printed in the sixth volume of *Pills*, 1720. As no other version of "Tom Tinker," except this has been discovered, a fresh song has been written for the purpose of enabling the very pretty melody, which is the one employed by D'Urfey in *Pills*, and by Gay in *The Beggars' Opera*, to be sung. Previous to those copies is an air given in the first [1650] and later editions of Playford's *Dancing Master*, but this, though possibly once fitted to an original version of the song, is quite different from the more musical one we use. The *Dancing Master* set will be found below. Doubtless Purcell, when he composed the last movement of his *Golden Sonata*, had the melody of "Tom Tinker" in his memory.

TOM TINKER.

From the *Dancing Master*, 1665.

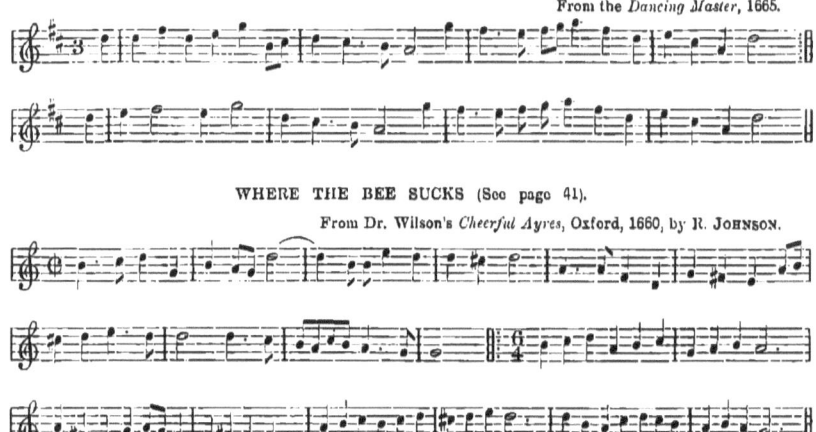

WHERE THE BEE SUCKS (See page 41).

From Dr. Wilson's *Cheerful Ayres*, Oxford, 1660, by R. JOHNSON.

COME YOU NOT FROM NEWCASTLE? (See page 48.)

A song sung to the "Northern tune, 'Cam'st thou not from Newcastle?'" is quoted in a black letter volume printed in the time of Elizabeth, called *The famous Historic of Fryer Bacon*, and a fragment of the original song is in the Percy folio as follows:—

> "Come you not from Newcastle,
> Come you not thereaway?
> O met you not my true love
> Riding on a bonny bay?
> *   *   *
> Why should I not love my love,
> Why should not my love love me?"

The tune itself under the name "Newcastle" is in *The Dancing Master* from 1650 to the 8th edition of 1690. An entirely new song has been written for the present work, in which is included the above fragment of the original words.

AS I WALKED FORTH ONE SUMMER'S DAY (See page 51).

A rather unusual song to be seen in printed collections of its period. It is to be found with the air by "Mr. Robert Johnson," in *The Treasury of Musick*, 1669, entitled "A Forsaken Lover's Complaint." Robert Johnson, of whom there seems but little known, was a lutenist and composer, whose name occasionally crops up in the Playford publications and in other places. The song itself appears to be part of a version of the lengthy ballad, "Near Woodstock town," for several of the verses of each are practically the same. As before suggested, it is rather remarkable to find what is evidently a folk ballad included among the classic compositions of the 17th century.

BRANGILL OF POICTU (See page 60).

From the *Skene MS.*

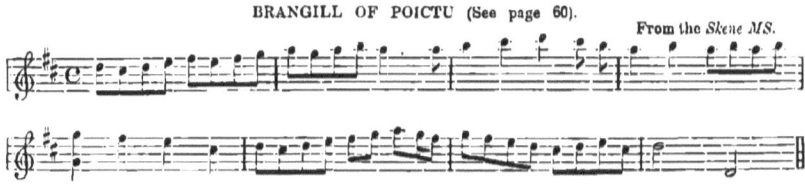

JOG ON, MY HONEY (See page 70).

From the *Dancing Master*, 1670 and 1690.

HALF HANNYKIN (See page 72).

Dancing Master, 1670.

HARVEST HOME (See page 74).

Sung in Purcell and Dryden's opera, *King Arthur; or, the British Worthy*, acted in 1691. The stage directions run - "Enter Comus with three peasants, who sing the following song in parts." Comus sings the first verse, and the peasants follow with a verse each. As the original manuscripts of Purcell's music to *King Arthur* were in part lost, it is uncertain whether the above tune first found in *Pills* and there set to the song, is the original one composed by Purcell. Be this as it may, it became the one always associated with the song, and this frequently commenced with the first line of the second verse, "We're cheated the parson." Under this title it is given as the old name for the tune in *Achilles*, 1733, *Lover's Opera*, 1729, and a number of other ballad operas. The song was printed on ballad sheets with the first line changed to "Our oats they are howed, and our barley's reaped.' It provoked a ballad "Answer," in which the long sermons of the parson are defended (see Chappell, p. 583). A portion of the tune was used in the second part of "Boys and girls, come out to play," printed in the third volume of the *Dancing Master, circa* 1724-7.

BOYS AND GIRLS, COME OUT TO PLAY

The new way, From the third volume of the *Dancing Master, circa* 1726.

LOVE WILL FIND OUT THE WAY (See page 87).

The tune is in *Musick's Delight on the Cittern*, 1666, and with the song attached, in *Forbes' Cantus*, 1661-1683, 1682. Chappell refers to a copy in *Musick's Recreation on the Lyra Viol*, 1652; he also states that it is quoted in Broome's play, *The Spanish Garden*, 1635. The song with the air is in *Pills to purge Melancholy*, vol. vi., 1720, and in Ritson's *English Songs*, 1783. It seems to have been very popular, for it is on black letter ballad sheets, and there are several parodies of it. In Scotland the song was united to a different melody and began "Quite over the mountains" (see Johnson's *Museum*, vol. ii., 1788). This is the setting printed in M'Fadyen's *Repository of Scots and Irish Airs*, as in M'Goun's work of the same title, both Glasgow publications printed near the junction of the 18th and 19th centuries.

GIPSY SONG (See page 106).

A folk ballad taken from the Rev. John Broadwood's book of Sussex songs, published in 1843. The words frequently occur on ballad sheets under the title, "The Lost Lady found," and another setting of the song is printed in the late Dr. Barrett's *English Folk Songs*. This latter copy was obtained in Cheshire; the melody, however, is wrongly placed with the words, for it is the tune to the folk ballad, "The Summer Morning" (see Dixon's *Songs of the Peasantry*, Kidson's *Traditional Tunes*, etc.), which is always united to its own particular tune throughout Yorkshire, Lancashire, and the other northern counties. We have only used a selection of the verses, and have to thank Miss L. E. Broadwood for the loan of the rare volume in which they and the tune originally occur.

ROBIN HOOD AND LITTLE JOHN (See page 133).

The Helston Furry Dance is one of the most singular customs still retained in England. The dance is a survival of a "morris," and is performed to the tune given above, every old May day, *i.e.*, 8th of May, at Helston, in Cornwall. Parties of ladies and gentlemen dressed in bright attire with a profusion of flowers, trip in couples, to the number of thirty or forty, through the streets, and even through the houses of the little town. While a band plays the historical old tune given above, the couples sing the verses here given under the music. The festival is supposed to be a survival of a very ancient rite dating from an early British period. The air is distinctly an old "morris" dance tune; it seems to have first seen the light of print in Jones' *Bardic Museum*, 1802, from whence it was taken into Geo. Thomson's *Welsh Melodies*, vol. fi., 1811, and another version is given in Davies Gilbert's *Ancient Christmas Carols*, 1823. It also found a place in Wm. Chappell's *National English Airs*, 1838.

THE LEATHER BOTTLE (See page 148).

From *Pills to purge Melancholy*, 1707.

GATHERING PEASCODS (See page 152).

From the *Dancing Master.*

BLACK-EY'D SUSAN (See page 164.)

The words of this sweetest of English lyrics were written by John Gay before 1723. The tune now popular is by Richard Leveridge, a composer and a bass singer, born 1670, died 1758. His tune was by no means the first or only one set to the song, the earliest traceable being an air headed, "Black-Ey'd Susan," in a small manuscript volume of airs for the violin, in the library of the writer, dated on the front page, "Patrick Cummings, his book, Edinburgh, 1723," and on the last page the same name with the date 1724. The tune from this manuscript is printed below. Next in date to this comes an air for it by Henry Carey engraved with the words on half-sheet music, *circa* 1725-30. Carey's tune was not much of a success, and it soon gave place to a version of the present well known one by Richard Leveridge, who was composer of so many of our best English airs. Part of Carey's air is used in *The Beggars' Opera*, and for a song, "In Praise of Annie," in the first volume of Watts' *Musical Miscellany*, 1729. It is also found on the early half sheets; one by Carey, another by Leveridge, and a third "by Sigur. Sendoni." Leveridge's tune is used in the *Village Opera*, 1729, and with the song (as in most early copies), entitled "Sweet William's Farewell to Black Ey'd Susan," is also in Watts' *Musical Miscellany*, vol. iv., 1730. Besides Sigur. Sendoni, J. F. Lampe wrote an air for the song, and this is printed in *The Music's Delight*, Liverpool, 1754. Attention must be drawn to the fact that the version of the tune as now sung was first printed in its present form by Chappell, and he seems to have had no early authority for the change in the first two or three bars, which are precisely like Dr. Greene's "Fair Sally loved a bonny seaman."

BLACK-EY'D SUSAN.

From a Manuscript dated 1723-4.

QUODLING'S DELIGHT (See page 180).

Fitzwilliam Virginal Book.

From *Musick's Delight on the Cithren*, 1666.

THE BRITISH GRENADIERS (See page 214).

This the most noteworthy of British military tunes, as it now stands, is probably of the reign of Queen Anne. Since that period it has evidently passed down traditionally in the regiment to which it refers, until about 1750, when it appeared on half-sheet music. The present copy is taken from one of those sheets. The air has much affinity to certain other melodies, as, for instance, "Sir Edward Nowell's Delight," "All you that Love Good Fellows," "The London Prentice," etc. There is also an air in the Fitzwilliam Virginal Manuscript called "Nancie" which bears considerable resemblance to this tune. "The London Prentice," or "Blow the Candle Out," has its melody printed in *Pills*, vol. vi., p. 312, 1720, and is evidently the same air as "All you that Love Good Fellows," and this air thus printed is a version of "The British Grenadiers."

Irish musicians have laid claim to the tune of "The British Grenadiers" as the composition of Carolan. Carolan's tune is named "Grace (or Grey) Nugent," and is included in the edition of his works published by John Lee of Dublin, about 1780; in *Bunting's First Collection*, 1790; Miss Owenson's volume, etc. With words by Robert Burns, commencing "Louis, what reck I by thee?" the first part of the air is printed in Johnson's *Museum*, vol. v., 1797, Burns himself having obtained the air. A much earlier edition of Carolan's "Grace Nugent" occurs in a very rare book, printed about 1727-8, by Daniel Wright, London, entitled *Aria di Camera, being a choice Collection of Scotch, Irish, and Welsh Airs*, 12mo. As this work is excessively rare the air in question is reprinted below as the earliest printed copy of Carolan's tune known. Those interested may decide how much or how little "Grace Nugent" resembles the sturdy tune "British Grenadiers"; the writer is free to confess his inability to reconcile the two. It must also be remembered that "Sir Edward Nowell's Delight," a melody far more like the "British Grenadiers," was printed in a Dutch book in 1634, thirty-six years before Carolan was born; also, that other tunes with a great resemblance to the one just named are to be found in manuscript and in print at even earlier dates.

GRACE NUGENT BY CARRALLAN [CAROLAN].

From *Aria di Camera, circa* 1727.

THE LONDON PRENTICE

From *Pills to purge Melancholy*, 1720.

SALLY IN OUR ALLEY (See page 215).

The story of the writing of this our best-known English song is to the effect that Henry Carey, then a young man, accidentally observing the simple courtship of a shoemaker's apprentice and his sweetheart during a holiday, followed them unobserved through all the delights of Moorfields, the Farthing Pye House, Bedlam, and the Flying Chairs, and composed the song which relates the guileless love of the 'prentice for his dear. This must have been some time about 1713, or a couple of years later. Carey, who was then supplying the town with hosts of ballads and tunes, composed an air to the song he had written, which, under the title, "Sally in our Alley," is printed in Walsh's *Compleat Country Dancing Master*, vol. ii., 1719. As "London Sally" the melody occurs in later dance books published by Walsh and by Daniel Wright, and as "Charming Sally" and "Pretty Sally" Carey's tune is used in the different ballad operas, including *The Beggars Opera*, *The Fashionable Lady*, etc. It must, however, be noted that Carey's tune, though an excellent one in itself, is not the air now known to the words, which was originally fitted to a ballad named "The Country Lass." The ballad itself probably dates before the middle of the 17th century; it begins—

"Although I am a country lass
A lofty mind I bear—a," etc.,

and although this was sung to several airs, the present tune for it did not get into print much before 1731—in that year as "What though I am a Country Lass!" A version is printed in *The Devil to Pay*, and as "The Virtuous Country Maid" in Daniel Wright's *Compleat Tutor for ye Flute, circa* 1735. A copy of this air as well as Henry Carey's original one is given on following page. Carey's air was displaced probably not much before 1790-8. It was about this period that Charles Incledon and Dignum sang the song to a version of the tune now known; but to the various copies printed from about 1790 to 1810 the tune has much variation in its versions and is by no means so satisfactory a melody as either the "Virtuous Country Maid" of circa 1735, or Carey's own air.

VIRTUOUS COUNTRY MAID.

From Wright's *Compleat Tutor for ye flute, circa* 1735.

SALLY IN OUR ALLEY.

Henry Carey's original Air, from his *Musical Century*, 1740.

Of all the girls that are so smart There's none like pret - ty Sal - ly, She is the dar - ling of my heart, And she lives in our . . . . al - ley. There s no era la - dy in the land . . That s half so sweet . . as Sal - ly, She is the dar - ling of my heart, And she lives in our . . . . al - ley.

DRINK TO ME ONLY WITH THINE EYES (See page 217).

The words of this beautiful and ever-popular song are by Ben Jonson. They are among his earlier poems, and are addressed "To Celia." The first musical setting of the lyric is uncertain, the present tune probably not dating much prior to 1750 or 1760. The composition of the melody has been ascribed to a Colonel Mellish, and in an American work even to Mozart! but while it is impossible to satisfactorily identify the writer of it we may rest well assured that the melody is purely English. The air appeared as a glee for three voices in sheet music published by S. Babb (1770-1780), Dale, A. Bland, and others of later date, and thus arranged for three voices it was printed in many books of catches and glees. Among song books the tune and words are given in *The Vocal Magazine*, Edinburgh, 1798, *Corri's Collection*, Edinburgh, folio, Dale's *English Songs*, Crosby's *English Musical Repository*, etc., etc.

Before the present well-known tune came into notice the song had other musical settings; one entitled "The Thirsty Lover" was printed by James Oswald on a half sheet about 1750. Another air to the words is to be found in a folio manuscript collection of airs dated 1752 in the writer's library. There is also a fresh setting in Linley's *Posthumous Works (circa* 1812) probably by T. Linley.

COUNTRY GARDEN (See page 220).

The new way, From Wright's *Compleat Tutor for ye flute, circa* 1735.

Da Capo.

Early version of "THE VICAR OF BRAY," from Edward Ward's *Miscellaneous Writings in Verse and Prose,* vol. iii., 1712.

THE RELIGIOUS TURNCOAT; OR, THE TRIMMING PARSON.

I lov'd no king in forty-one
  When Prelacy went down;
A cloak and band I then put on,
  And preached against the Crown.

Chorus—A turncoat is a cunning man,
  That wants to admiration,
And prays for any side, to gain
  The people's approbation.

    *   *   *

When brewer Noll with copper nose
  The stinking Rump dismounted,
I wisely still adher'd to those
  Who strongest were accounted.

I preached and prayed for Oliver,
  And all his vile abettors,
But curs'd the King and Cavalier,
  And cried 'em down for traitors.

When Charles returned unto the land,
  The English Crown's supporter,
I shifted off my cloak and band
  And then became a Courtier

The King's religion I profest,
  And found there was no harm in't;
I coged and flattered like the rest,
  Till I had got preferment.

When Royal James began his reign,
　And Mass was used in common,
I shifted off my Faith again,
　And so became a Roman.

When William had possess'd the throne,
　And cur'd our country's grievance,
New principles I then put on,
　And swore to him allegiance.

I then preached up King William's right
　Pray'd for his foes' confusion,
And so remained a Willianite,
　Till another Revolution.

But when Queen Anne the throne posses't,
　I then, to save my bacon,
Turn'd High Church, thinking that was best,
　But found myself mistaken

For soon discerning very plain,
　The Whigs had got the better,
I turn'd Low Churchman, so remain
　A Trimming Moderator.

Therefore all you, both high and low,
　Let me for once direct you,—
Serve no cause longer than you know
　The party can protect you.

The writer is in possession of a version of the above (having considerable variation), engraved as a half-sheet song, with music. The air employed is one popular at this time, named "London is a Fine Town," and the last monarch named in the song is the first George. The sheet was probably engraved about 1720-30.

THE BAILY'S DAUGHTER OF ISLINGTON (See page 222).

From *The Jovial Crew*, 1731.

THE QUEEN'S JIGG (See page 237).

From the *Dancing Master*, 1703.

DOWN AMONG THE DEAD MEN (See page 238).

A Tory song of the reign of Queen Anne and of George I. Although originally merely expressive of loyalty to the sovereign and the fair sex, many political songs became associated with the tune. Hogg, in his *Jacobite Relics*, first series, gives one version with the remark that he is "unacquainted with the song and air;" nevertheless, this fine melody has been deservedly a great favourite in England, and is probably as good an example of a characteristic English tune as could well be chosen. On a half-sheet, engraved about 1790, it is headed :—"A Song, sung by Mr. Dyer at Mr. Bullock's Booth, at Southwark Fair." In singing the song at Lincoln's Inn Theatre at a later date, the singer above named introduced an additional verse. The tune, without the words, is given in the third volume of the *Dancing Master*, circa 1726, and is also to be found in several early dance collections issued by John Walsh, senior. It is hardly necessary to mention that the "Dead Men" of the song are the drained bottles, which were usually thrown under the table.

COME, ALL YOU JOLLY WATERMEN (See page 239).

From a half-sheet song in the British Museum, circa 1734-40. The song bears upon the marriage of the then Princess Royal of England with the Prince of Orange in March, 1734. The event made a profound sensation in England, and there are numerous songs, musical odes, dance tunes, etc., extant which it called forth. (See *Theatrical Musces*, p. 65, for one of these.) The title on the musical half-sheet which is here used runs :—"The Jolly Waterman, sung by Mr. Bardin in the Entertainment at the Theatre in Goodman's Fields " and Mr. Barclay Squire, who kindly forwards a copy, makes the likely suggestion that the tune is probably by Henry Carey, who wrote a musical entertainment named *The Happy Nuptials*, which was inserted in *Britannia : or, the Royal Lovers*, performed at Goodman's Fields on the occasion of the wedding.

QUEEN BESSES' DAME OF HONOUR (See page 284)

This song was sung by Mrs. Willis in D'Urfey's opera, *The Kingdom of the Birds* (1706), and was printed in *Pills*, vol. i., 1719, to an air of its own. This air is in the present volume replaced by a spirited English tune of a rather earlier date, known as "The Prodigal's Resolution," originally given to a song beginning "I am a lusty, lively lad." It is found with the words in all editions of *Pills to purge Melancholy*. The verses formed one of the songs in a city pageant, and were published in 1672. Earlier than this, the tune, under the title, "Jamaica," was printed in the 4th (1670) edition of the *Dancing Master*, as well as in many later ones. Chappell suggests that the name "Jamaica" refers to taking of that island from the Spaniards in 1655.

CUPID'S GARDEN (See page 302).

From the *Dancing Master*, 1690.

RULE, BRITANNIA (See page 306).

Since the note to this song was penned, Mr. John Churton Collins has advocated the claim in favour of Thomson, as author of the words of the famous lyric, in his *Ephemera Critica*, 1901. It does not appear, however, that Mr. Collins has advanced any absolutely fresh facts bearing on the matter. He certainly holds a very poor opinion of Mallet as a man, but the statement, even if true, that David Mallet "was notoriously a man who could not be believed on oath, and was an adept in all those bad arts by which little men filch honours which do not belong to them" is scarcely argument, inasmuch that Mr. Collins admits that he was "a respectable poet" and had already written songs, poems, and ballads, with marked success. "The Dirks of Invernay," and "William and Margaret" are now thoroughly incorporated into Scottish song. The initials which are appended to the verses in *The Charmer* of 1752, and the full name, "Jas. Thomson," in the edition of 1782, really afford the strongest claim that may be adduced in favour of Thomson; but as this ascription appears to be otherwise unsupported, it is quite within the bounds of possibility, that the editor appended Thomson's name, rather at haphazard, knowing that Thomson was joint author of *Alfred*.

The authorship of "Rule, Britannia," is unlikely to be ever satisfactorily settled, and we cannot at this length of time definitely say whether the writing is that of one man or the result of collaboration. The glorious tune has had a far greater influence than the words on the adoption of the lyric as our National Song. For a very thorough *resumé* of facts relating to "Rule, Britannia," and for an advocacy of claims on behalf of Mallet, see Dr. Dinsdale's *Ballads and Songs of David Mallet*, 1857.

INDEX OF TITLES AND FIRST LINES.

To facilitate reference, titles and first lines commencing with "A" and "The" are indexed according to the next succeeding word.

INDEX OF SONGS AND AIRS REFERRED TO
IN THE NOTES.

INDEX OF COMPOSERS.